A BEAUTIFUL SONG

A Musical Soul Story

MICHAEL CANTWELL

KSM Publishing

www.michaelcantwellbooks.com

ISBN-10: 0615545211
ISBN-13: 978-0615545219

Dedicated To:

My wife Anne,
my children, Kristen, Samantha and Matthew
for being a wonderful family.

To all who have made us smile with their
music.

To all who have served in the United States
armed services. I thank-you for your service.

TAKE CARE OF YOUR
MEMORIES. FOR YOU
CANNOT RELIVE THEM.

BOB DYLAN

CHAPTER ONE

Years ago, I had an English teacher, who told me I had the ability to become a great storyteller. From that day forward, I began to keep journals of my life. Good thing, since my brain is pretty scrambled. My stories in the past were songs. I figured, maybe I should tell my life story while I still can.

It all started the day I eye balled my personal holy grail, which sat in the window of heaven on earth, or known to the local pickers as Gordy's Guitars. I would stroll home from school every day in 1969 passed a shopping center where Gordy and that miniature, but majestic store made my world a better place.

I caught others drooling in the same semi-moldy storefront window, which possessed a 1968 CF Martin D45 acoustic guitar made with Brazilian rosewood, an ebony fret board, and some of the finest pearl inlay known to man. When the sun sat at the perfect time of day, the guitar would glisten like the sunset on the Atlantic Ocean. However, back then, I was a thirteen year-old school kid with maybe a dollar in nickels and dimes in my pocket.

Most days I would stop in and ask Gordy if I could clean floors or dump trash. He wasn't convinced he could use my help. I wore him down after asking three different times. The place stunk like our school library when they didn't open the window for a long time. After entering the store, the guitars hung on the left wall, a glass counter rested on the right. The middle of the store overflowed with unopened boxes stacked three high along with rows of guitar straps, speakers and music stands. In the back, were two rooms where people gave lessons and piles of printed sheet music rested on an old wooden shelf.

Cleaning around the store offered me an opportunity to listen to real guitar players who could strum a G chord. The better musicians would bang out a Beatles riff, while some of the more daring would break into a few bars from Led Zeppelin. I knew Gordy caught me doing more listening than cleaning, but he only paid with me a couple of bucks each day along with a half-hearted smile and occasional advice.

"Stu, never forget one thing, a real player finds their own voice; not a bad rendition of John Lennon's," Gordy would grumble at me. I had no clue what he meant. I only understood that when I heard tones floating from guitars inside the store and through my brain, I discovered peace.

Gordy Davis was the most famous person any pimple faced teen could ever hope to meet. A week before he entered my life, he had returned from vacation. He told tales of heading to an upstate New York music festival called Woodstock.

"I've seen many things in my life, Stu," Gordy said, "but that place was a new experience. Joan Baez sang about stopping the war and Sly Stone pranced around the stage like a wild man playing a style of music I have never heard. I missed some of the music because I didn't want my boots getting caked in mud and my clothes becoming soaked from all the rain. All I heard were the raindrops pelting my canvas tent for hours."

"How did everyone else stay dry and clean?" I asked. "Did everyone have a tent? I saw on the news it took place on a farm with not much around. They didn't even have a burger joint within miles."

Gordy smiled. "Most of them didn't mind the rain and jumped naked in the lake. I thought about it myself, but I think I've outgrown those things. I decided to get closer to the music once the rains slowed. I wanted to hear The Who and see Pete Townsend play. However, it was Jimi Hendrix, who blew me away. Most missed him because the festival ran late. Jimi didn't hit the stage till early Monday morning. Trust me, he was worth the wait."

I enjoyed hearing the stories and hoped they would have another music festival one day so I could go too. I was surprised at Gordy's reaction when I told him my thoughts.

"Don't you worry about places like that for now, kid. Oh, it was all about peace and love, but I witnessed several carted off in ambulances because of drug overdoses. You keep your nose in your study books and I'll let you keep hanging out around here. If you get off track, don't come back. That's our deal. Got it?"

What could I say? Hanging around Gordy's shop made me smile. "Ok, Gordy, we've got a deal."

Gordy stared at me. I studied the creases in his leather like face as he spoke. "I don't mean to be hard on ya, kid. But' I've seen the light. My life turned out far different than I ever expected. With the help of a great man and the Lord above, this shop saved me."

I pressed Gordy for more information about his past. The only thing I got was a quick smile and a gesture to go back to pushing a broom across the faded black linoleum floor. I did my best to stay in his good graces. I wiped down the counter, took out the trash and even cleaned the bathroom with the leaky pipe hidden in the back of the store.

One at closing time, Gordy locked the front door and flipped over the sign letting the public know the store had closed. I wiped my brow and leaned the push broom against the wall. Gordy removed the rubber bands from his ponytail and asked me to come to the wall where the beat up guitars he used as rentals hung.

"You did an extra good job today, kid. Let me give you a quick lesson before your ride shows up," Gordy said.

I jumped at the chance. I don't think my feet hit the floor as I made my way to the seat where Gordy asked me to sit. He showed me a few chords and one major scale. I could feel my heart pound as my fingers wandered around the neck of a Fender Stratocaster for the first time. It didn't matter that my fingertips were sore after a few moments. I would never forget that moment.

"Now git home and do your chores and homework. If you do a good job again next week, maybe I'll teach ya something else. And one last thing, kid. Always follow His Word. If you listen close, you'll hear it, instead of tones from a stressed out Strat."

"Well, maybe if you tuned this thing better," I said, "I could hear whatever word your talking about, plus it might make this guitar sound better." I thought my teenage humor hit the mark. It didn't. Gordy escorted me out the front door. Lesson learned.

Then again not too many understood this thirteen year old boy's humor. In particular, my heavy handed father, John, who was a staff sergeant at a nearby training base. My mother, Margaret was a court stenographer, who worked part time and tried to keep my younger brother and sister from running wild after school. It was just another reason for hanging out with Gordy and the cast of misfit musicians, who really looked up to Gordy. Sure, I had a few friends away from the music shop, as most boys my age did, but most were into things I knew would only lead to trouble with my strict father.

I grew up in your typical suburban area just outside of Princeton, New Jersey. Dad pushed me into little league and boy scouts. Unfortunately, from the first day I wandered past Gordy's, I really lost interest in playing centerfield for Aaron's Electric. Besides, how many times can a boy strike out with the bases loaded, before you realize that watching fastballs over the outside corner of the plate wasn't the best use of your time? As far as the boy scouts went, how many knots can you learn to make, before wanting to run screaming into the night? How many Princeton versus Rutgers football games can you attend singing one hundred bottles of beer on the wall on the bus ride home, before you want to jump out of the back of the rented school bus?

No, even at an early age, I learned life was all about choices. Speaking of which, it seemed it was the choice of Sister Mary Joseph to pull the tiny hairs next to my right ear lobe every time I peeked at Linda Jacobs' paper seated in the desk next to me.

I was an average student all through school. Like most, I did my homework and studied enough to keep my parents from grounding me, but I never worked hard enough at my studies to be class valedictorian. Being the next Albert Einstein was never my gig.

The summer after eighth grade freaked me out. It meant graduating from the local small catholic elementary school to a much larger and intimidating high school. There were unknown students from different parts of the area, who I only somewhat knew from playing sports. I got an even better view while watching from the bench. Someone has to keep the bench warm you know.

I think Gordy liked the idea I played sports after school. I could only run the broom across the linoleum floor so often before even he would feel guilty. If I complained I had a hard life as a youngster, I'd be lying to you. I didn't always like having to cut the grass and wash the dishes after dinner, but what rational kid does?

I tried to fit in with the neighborhood kids. There was a vast array of characters. The three Kerns brothers terrorized kids for lunch money, but sure were your best friends when they wanted to shoot hoops in your back yard. There were the two Farley brothers, who I think beat on each other, more they did anyone else.

Who could forget Beets McHenry? That kid could mess up the lyrics of every song ever written. He still thinks Brown Sugar was written about what his mom put in his birthday cake every year. Sly Kearney was one of my best friends. His mom served a wicked chicken roll sandwich, and being able eye his cute sister was only a bonus when we hung out at his house.

There was Chris and Jeff Homes and another close friend Danny Sutcliff. Up until that summer, they would get me to play ball at the schoolyard on Saturdays. On Sundays, we all spent time in church as Alter boys. I volunteered for the Saturday night masses for a few weeks. That was until Kerry Kerns took apart the bells when I wasn't looking. When I rang them, they didn't work. Kerry blamed it on me. Father Daniel banished me back to the earliest Sunday mass when only my grandmother and a few stray nuns would worship.

Some would later call it the, 'Summer of Love.' I called it the summer of trepidation and despair. The summer started out like most summers. I was awake to do my chores in the morning as my brother and sister watched, 'I Love Lucy' reruns. They didn't understand why I wanted to get my chores done long before lunch. My siblings didn't have the same responsibilities as I did. I was a few years older and had more chores. So unfair.

My grandmother lived a few blocks away. One of my chores was to walk her dog every morning. He was a mean old German shepherd, who only let a few people approach him. Baron was supposed to be trained, but I think even he had gotten too old and cranky to want to obey anyone, including me. He did however appreciate the fresh air from time to time. After all, my grandmother's house had an odor that smelled like a dirty sneaker doused with perfume.

After the walk and chores, I would meet up with the neighborhood boys for game of basketball or maybe a game of pool over at my friend Chris's house. Sometimes, we would play poker, but most wanted to play pool or stay outside. I think the poker game became far less popular when one day we were all talked into playing a game of strip poker and Chris's mom came home early and caught most of us down to our tighty-whities. Not our finest moment that summer.

The local grocery store was at the opposite end of the shopping center where Gordy owned his shop. Every once in a while, I would go with Mom food shopping pretending to help. I was really attempting to get her to walk by Gordy's for a peek at my future prized guitar. She somehow managed to park nowhere near the music shop. To rub salt in my wound, she would turn the car in the opposite direction on the return trip home. All of my best efforts failed to get her into Gordy's shop.

My parents never knew how much time I spent at Gordy's over the years. As long as your grades were ok, the police weren't at our door, and my clothes didn't smell like smoke, they didn't ask many questions. My father could smell French fries on my breath from ninety feet.

I guess by now you might think I was a nerd. Maybe you would be correct. However, I was a shy kid who knew his place. I was never one to bust up Mr. Johnsons new mailbox or egging the cars of people who didn't give out good Halloween candy. It wasn't in me to hurt others. Maybe, it was all the bible studies during nine years of Catholic school. Better still, possibly it was Dad's icy stare when rumors swirled of the neighbor's cars being egged.

The summer came to a rapid close one Saturday morning when Mom reminded Dad that I would need a lock, along with school supplies for the start of school later in the week. His stare never worked on mom, only us kids. Her stare worked on him, though we rarely saw it. As fate would have it, the school supply store was next to Gordy's shop. I jumped into the station wagon once Mom gave Dad the icy stare. He grumbled a few words about getting home in time for the game of the week and joined me in the car.

"You had better not take long picking your supplies", he moaned. I didn't care about the color of my notebooks. I ran up and down the aisles getting all my supplies.

As we were leaving the store, I begged Dad to visit the music shop for a minute to meet Gordy. He refused to meet Gordy after looking at him through the store window.

"Please, Dad? I want you to meet Gordy and see the store. Please?"

Gordy was standing in the window with his torn jeans, long hair and tie-dyed tee shirt. Gordy waved us in, but Dad refused to budge.

"There is nothing that hippie can tell me that I want to hear, Stu. All I see in there are punks. I have no desire to go in there, now or later. Forget it," Dad said.

I was stunned at the comment. For the first time in my life, I wasn't proud of my own father. Somehow, those words, that I was not proud, dribbled off my tongue and out of my mouth. I am not sure who was more stunned.

He looked at me in a way I had never witnessed. I stood confused. After what seemed like hours, he walked slowly into the music shop for the first time. Gordy opened the door for my father with the same hospitality he had always showed me in the past.

"It's my pleasure to meet you Mr. Edrich," Gordy said. "You must be so proud of Stu. He's a great kid."

My father took a step back grumbled something under his breath that sounded like, "thanks."

Gordy didn't stop there. "I know he's very proud of you. He tells me all the time how hard you work and how he appreciates the fact that you keep him straight."

Dad stood frozen until he finally pulled his hand from his rigid waistline, to offer a shake with Gordy. Gordy later winked my way when Dad wasn't looking. Gordy knew how to sell.

I proudly proceeded to tell Dad how the Martin D45 guitar in the window would soon be mine. Dad glanced at the price tag and before following with his familiar stare.

"Stu has some ability with the guitar, Mr. Edrick," Gordy said.

"Not with the one in the window, I can assure of that," Dad said.

"Your son isn't ready for a fine guitar," Gordy said. "Don't worry. I wouldn't let you buy it for him, even if you offered me cash right now. Stu needs to learn how to respect an instrument before he can touch something like a new Martin guitar."

I think Dad became unsure of Gordy. How could someone like Gordy, who Dad went out of his way to avoid, actually be someone he could respect? Maybe it was not that dramatic, but I knew Gordy didn't care. Gordy Davis was happy with the person he had become in life. He reminded me every chance he got.

"I'll tell you what Mr. Edrich," Gordy said, "Stu's been busting his butt cleaning up the place for weeks round here and I know he wants some guitar lessons. I'll be happy to offer them at half the normal costs. However, only if he promises to keep his grades up, and work here four hours a week. How does that sound to you?"

My father, ever the non-believer asked to see a price sheet. After Gordy objected, claiming he was an honest person, and his offer was legitimate, Dad backed down from his request. It would be eight dollars a week for two lessons, and another two dollars a week for the use of a beat up Fender Stratocaster.

Dad peeked at his watch and informed us that the game of the week was about to start. Nothing came between my father and the baseball game of the week on Saturday afternoon television. Gordy informed him the offer was good for a week. Dad smirked and thanked him for his time.

Over the next few days, you would have thought our house was made of eggshells. I wasn't about to get under Dad's skin. Not once did I bring up the subject of lessons, but it was apparent on my father's gruff face, he knew what was on my mind. High school was starting on Thursday. On Tuesday night, my grandmother fell while trying to walk the dog before bed. Grandma knew she should have stopped walking the dog at nights, but she was a stubborn old bird.

Dad announced at the dinner table on Wednesday evening that I was now in charge of walking my grandmother's old dog, Baron all the time. It would occur before school every morning and before bedtime. You never refused my father's commands. Truth be told, I didn't want my grandmother having to do it any longer, and I would have happily done it, had she had asked.

"I stopped by and met with Gordy," Dad said. "I paid for one month's worth of lessons. However, the first time you miss taking that dog out, or don't get your homework done, the lessons stop. Is that understood?"

"Yes sir, and thank you," I said wearing a large smile.

Finally, my pursuit of becoming a real guitar player was only a few days away. Everyone chuckled after I announced how by the end of the first semester of school, not only would I be on the honor roll, I would be ready to hit the recording studio with my first band.

CHAPTER TWO

The first day of high school grabbed my attention, but never rocked my world. The new school matched my last one in some ways, but with fewer nuns and longer walks between classrooms. The first attempt to open my locker led to confusion. A big bulky dude wearing a letter jacket, who hadn't shaved, yet still smelled like Dad's cologne, brushed me aside. My locker number was 312, not 302.

I ventured off to my first class where the teacher had the nerve to hand out assignments not due until Christmas. That freaked me out. However, I wrote it down in my trusty notebook that now had my locker number plastered in big letters on the front cover.

The following day was another new experience. Gym class. Ugh. Mr. Woody, our teacher actually made us shower in one large group. It's not as if I broke a sweat playing volleyball. Who needed a shower anyway? However, I did as instructed so not to get into any trouble before my first real guitar lesson, which would be the following morning. My brain reminded me of the lesson all week, like a songbird announcing spring.

Saturday morning started with an early dog walk and listening to Dad, tell me how the porch had to be swept, before I could go to my lesson. No sweat. Mission accomplished as I stood in the shadow of Gordy's Guitars ten minutes before that shop was to open at ten.

To my surprise, Gordy wasn't already inside preparing for my lesson. Didn't he realize what a momentous day this was for me? He arrived two minutes short of ten. When I questioned if he showed up right before opening every day, he snickered and said, "Be lucky the coffee kicked in and I'm here on time, kid."

Gordy flipped on a few lights and opened up the cash register. "Turn around the sign that says we're open, will ya, kid?" Gordy asked.

Everything creeped along in slow motion. My ten o'clock lesson was already three minutes late in starting. I glanced again at the clock. I became more ticked off with every movement of the second hand. "My parents are paying good money for this you know," I said with a sour tone. Gordy acted unfazed with my impatient comment.

Gordy continued to march around the store moving boxes, adjusting inventory and wiping down the glass counters. I felt the heat build in my head with his every step. At seventeen past the hour, he pulled the old Stratocaster off the rack putting on new strings and tuning the tired out instrument. All I knew, my lesson was almost over, before it had begun. He asked me to sit in the swivel seat next to him.

At twenty-four past the hour, Gordy leaned and said, "Stu let me tell you how we're going to begin each lesson."

I remember thinking he meant the latest riff from The Rolling Stones or Cream. He slowly put the guitar in my lap and said, "You will never appreciate your talents until you give thanks to the one who gave you those talents."

"John Lennon," I said with a wry smile.

Gordy's face turned crimson red and remarked, "I've told you before and I will tell you once again, you have been given a gift from your maker and I refuse to teach you anything until you give thanks."

"Come on Gordy" I barked, "I get enough of that crap in school. I didn't come here for life lessons. I came for a guitar lesson."

The middle aged Gordy swiped the guitar from my grasp and placed it back on the lap of his faded Levis. "Today's lesson is now over," he said.

Shocked would have been an understatement. My next thought was to run home and tell Dad how he got ripped off. However, I had to work off the last two hours left of my four hours for that week. Gordy told me that if I didn't do my two hours, there would be no lesson on Tuesday. I did my two hours of penance and sulked home. My vision of learning how to play, "Born to be Wild" was over in a flash.

I hid in my room the rest of the day, until dinnertime. "How was the lesson?" Mom asked at the dinner table. "And why didn't you bring home the guitar to practice?"

In an angry tone, I let the family know about my sorry day. "Gordy refused to give me a lesson because he showed up late. If I were you, Dad, I'd go see Gordy and get my money back. Maybe you're right, you can't trust those hippies."

I'll never know if Gordy had contacted Dad in advance of my blow up at dinner or not, but Dad said, "Before I ask for my money back, my only question to you is, did you follow his orders?"

"Whaddya mean, Dad?"

Dad smiled gently. "In my line of work, people follow orders.

14

It's that way in life, Stu. I'll ask you again, did you do as Gordy asked, or did you pop off and assume you knew better?"

"I thought I had," I said with my head tilting towards my dinner plate.

"I'll leave it up to you, Stu," Dad said. "If you want me to go over on Monday and ask for my money back and stop your lessons, I will. Or, we can wait until after your lesson on Tuesday and see if you have a change of heart."

I sighed. "Let's wait till after my lesson on Tuesday." Dinner finished with a quiet hush.

Monday was my first full day of high school. The day was endless. Homework piled on from one class to the next. With all the homework to be done and still being a bit steamed at Gordy, I skipped heading over to the shop after school.

When I arrived for my lesson on Tuesday Gordy smiled and asked why I didn't stop by on Monday. "Too much homework," I mumbled.

We again sat down on the swivel stools in the back of the shop and he again asked if I had given thanks to my maker. Not wanting to make the same mistake, I closed my eyes and thanked My God for allowing me the opportunity to do something I loved so much. Relived. My lesson could begin.

Gordy reached around to an old rusty metal rack with reams of sheet music on it and set up one sheet on the stand in front of me. "This is a major scale," He said. "Let me show you where to place your fingers on the fret board. After that, you are to play the same scale until your fingers bleed."

Once again, I sat motionless and more than a little shocked. I wanted to learn, 'Stairway to Heaven', not a dopey scale on a sheet of slightly faded yellow paper.

"By Saturday, I want perfection," Gordy said. "I expect you to play the scale forwards and backwards. If you get really ambitious, attempt to find the scale farther down the neck and learn it there too."

"Fine," I said. "Now can we learn, 'Honkey Tonk Woman' with the remaining twenty-eight minutes and thirty seconds of the lesson?"

"Not today, my friend," Gordy said as he fixed the green band in his ponytail. "Learn the basics and one day you'll be a better player. Do that and one day, I'll show you want to play, but not today."

I started to rethink the entire instrument thing. Dad was paying for lessons not for some hippie to hand me a sheet of paper and tell me to play that until my fingers bled. Who plays scales on a guitar neck I thought.

I could hear someone giggle from the front of the store. He sat with a fella named Skunk, who hung out banging on any new guitar Gordy brought into the store. It annoyed me every time Skunk laid his grimy fingers on my Martin. I never saw him buy a thing in the store. Skunk never once pushed a broom around the store, yet he acted as if he owned the joint.

I practiced for twenty-eight endless minutes before putting the guitar down, thinking I had mastered my first scale. Gordy had the nerve to have me play it one time in front of Skunk. "Keep at it, kid, you'll will get it one day," Skunk said.

The freeloader must have been tone deaf. I played every note in the scale exactly as printed. My fingers were so sore at that point, I refused to show off my talents any longer. Gordy asked

Skunk to play the same scale for me, borrowing my rented Strat. I'm not sure he played the same notes. It sounded the same, but it sounded somehow different. Skunk's version offered a sound of passion in the same notes I had played moments earlier. His fingers touched the fret board like trained ballet dancers prancing across a stage. I played my first major scale. He played an instrument with passion and desire. I hated him even more.

Weeks flew by in a blur. The first semester was almost over, but I had to work extra hard to get my algebra grade up from a C to a B to remain eligible for the honor roll. Final grades were three A's and four B's which kept me in lessons for another semester.

A week before Christmas Day, I wandered into the shop and noticed something was very wrong with the world. A Gibson guitar sat in the shop window, not my Martin D45. I asked Gordy what was up and he informed me that someone bought the guitar for his kid for Christmas.

"You can't sell my guitar," I screamed at Gordy.

Gordy smiled and said, "Kid, this is a music shop. I sell instruments here." Reality had never hit so hard.

By the holidays, I learned scale after scale up and down the neck of the guitar. I felt Gordy was taking advantage of my parent's generosity in paying for lessons. I felt cheated in not learning any songs, only scales. However, I had learned a few times to keep my mouth shut when Gordy threatened to call off the whole thing if I didn't do exactly as he commanded. He would tell me constantly how I would understand one day his methods of teaching. He became emphatic that I do as he demanded and only as he demanded.

My last lesson before Christmas, Gordy asked me if I knew

the true meaning of the holiday. "Of course, every kid knows what Christmas is Gordy, don't be silly," I said.

He of course had a different meaning and informed me that was the Lord's birthday. "I want you to play happy birthday for Jesus on your guitar," Gordy said.

"Sure," I said. "Hand me the sheet music."

"Stu," Gordy said staring at me with his blue eyes, "you don't need sheet music. You know every scale you need to know, in every octave you need to know, to play just about any song you want to play. Close your eyes, and play happy birthday. Visualize the sound in your fingers. Feel the sound, Stu. Hear it in your fingers."

I took a moment, heard the sound in my brain, and found the first note without looking at the neck of my guitar. After a couple of mistakes, I played the song in full. I finished playing it with my chest all puffed out when Gordy said, "Great, once again you can play the notes, now play the song. I have taught you how to bend strings, hammer on strings, play the song like it's your birthday, Stu."

He made me play happy birthday the entire thirty-minute lesson. My next assignment was to play, 'Silent Night' by our next lesson with no sheet music. I worked it out within thirty minutes at home. Not only did I know that song by the next lesson, I learned the opening riff to many of my favorite songs.

Throughout the remainder of the school year, Gordy taught me how chords were built along with music theory. By summer, I could hear a song on the radio and within a short time work out the chords as well as learn many of the lead parts without anyone's help. I had learned to be a player without knowing I was learning all along. I would still get yelled at all the time by Gordy, who would tell me his shop is full of kids who can play scales, but not who could play a song with meaning. It started to make sense to me.

Gordy kept telling me how I was given a gift that few were ever given, and that if I ever stopped seeing that or appreciating it, he would refuse to give me any more lessons.

Sophomore year had begun and my playing had come a long way in a few short months. I would go home on weekends and not leave my room for hours feeling like that tired black Stratocaster had become an extension of my hand. I would occasionally play a song or two for my mom and dad just so they could hear their money wasn't going down the drain. I learned, 'Somewhere over the Rainbow' for Mom since that was one of her favorites. She smiled every time I played it for her. Dad told me once I learned, 'Tchaikovsky's 1812 Overture' he would be impressed.

By my third year in high school, my lessons were only once a week. Gordy would allow me sit in and jam with some of the musicians, who would come in after the shop had closed. Skunk would show me a few odd chords that he claimed he invented. He hadn't been around much because he was the guitarist and off recording with a band out of New York, who had released albums.

It wasn't until that point that Gordy told me that he too had recorded on many singles and albums. He sat in on many songs recorded in the late 1950's. I realized he could play quite well, but he rarely would show off his skills for me or anyone else in the shop. Only during those sessions did he let loose now and again when Skunk tried to show off his chops too much.

I was learning how to work with others and fill in where they left off with a song or go off on an occasional lead for myself. I became a fan of The Beatles and loved playing their songs. Gordy jammed Elvis Presley for some reason and Skunk really tried to add a jazz element to his playing. Between us three and a couple others, who wandered in and out of the group, we varied in our styles.

Late in that school year, a friend from school introduced me to a kid, who played keyboards and wanted to write songs. I ventured over to his house and took the Gibson acoustic that Mom and Dad had bought me for Christmas. It was used, but Gordy assured me he had kept his eye out for a nice second hand acoustic guitar for me. It had a big sound and was more to my liking than the beat up Stratocaster.

The keyboardist had played for about as long as I had, but I quickly realized I was the better musician. However, it was cool to play with someone other than another guitarist and with someone closer to my age. His name was Kevin Carpenter and his best friend happened to be a beautiful red head I peeked at in a few of my classes. I wasn't sure if they were a couple or Debby Fletcher just liked being around Kevin and his music. She was unlike most females I had encountered. She knew all the awesome rock and roll stations up and down the dial and knew sports better than I did. She looked hot in a pair of jeans too.

We hung out mostly on weekends. My time grew short for socializing, because I had a part time job washing dishes at the local restaurant. Between doing chores at home, working and keeping my grades up, it was a struggle to do much more. I had to play my guitar for a minimum of two to three hours a day or I felt lost.

One day Kevin invited me over to his neighbor's house. His

neighbor had recently started to play the drums. We tried to play a few songs. Randy, or as he liked to be called Sticks, could barely hold a beat. He would start us off and Kevin and I would go into some kind of a personal trance. I'm sure to the passing ear it sounded horrible.

I didn't really notice much since by then I was doing my best Eric Clapton imitations and wasn't paying any attention to the rhythm section. One time, I remember closing my eyes and playing a killer version of 'While My Guitar Gently Weeps.' The only problem as the two in the band were playing an old Monkees tune.

Kevin, who inched just over six feet with long dark hair wasn't amused, but Debby started to sit closer to me than Kevin at each passing session. Eventually, we did work at it enough so we could eek out about five or six songs. Randy tried hard, but he wasn't accomplished enough to keep a solid backbeat for more than a few songs. Kevin's temper held us back at times too. Debby was our biggest fan and groupie, but other than Randy's dog, she was also the only living creature who would listen to us play for more than ten minutes at a time.

It was such a difference from playing with Gordy and the group on Tuesday nights versus our rag tag group on Saturdays. On Tuesdays, I was just another player, where on Saturdays it was obvious I was by far the best musician of the group.

However even on Tuesdays, I could keep up with the others. Gordy would still put me in my place now and again to keep me level headed, but it was obvious I was catching up to even his abilities rather quickly. I knew he noticed when he gave me an old guitar strap he said was given to him from none other than Elvis Presley himself. I asked him if he knew Elvis well and he would only say that he knew how to get to Graceland and had met Elvis more than once. He would never really tell me stories about his past, only things from his recent years in owning the store.

CHAPTER THREE

Word floated around school that I could play the guitar. A friend of a friend asked if I would play at his sweet sixteen birthday party, but without my two playing partners. He only wanted me to play a few songs solo. I told him I could, but not sing. When my band partners found out, they were pissed.

I had some serious fence mending to do. I convinced the person who asked me to play to allow the band to play one set and I would do one solo. That was my first venture into having others offended because of music. I never enjoyed the politics of a band.

During my negotiations, Debby proudly announced that she had been learning to sing a few Beatles tunes along with some other songs. She wanted to know if she could sing while I played the guitar. I told her that I didn't want to go back to ask a third time, but if I was to ever play like that again, I would gladly accept her offer. I had yet to hear her sing, so I really didn't want to set myself up for an even larger disaster at that point. I knew the first set with the other two would be enough of a struggle.

The night of the party came and somehow I ended up having to split the fifteen bucks equally, despite pulling double duty and doing them a favor. I had originally planned to play for free, but I think after all the hassles and lugging the drums and keyboards, the host felt guilty.

Debby wasn't invited to the party, but she wasn't going to miss the event. I told the host that she was my assistant. She sat quietly off to the side. There were about twenty-five of our classmates at the party. We knocked out two old Monkees tunes, two Beatles and a very bad rendition of Proud Mary.

After a quick break, I ended up sitting in a chair in the back yard with every one sitting on the ground and playing for over an hour. I knew maybe twenty songs by heart, so it was easy to play for an hour. No one seemed to mind too much that I wasn't singing, though I did hear Debby humming them off to my left.

When I got to school on Monday, I was surprised when a few classmates, who had never bothered to say hello before, came and told me they heard I did well at the party over the weekend. I did however get a cold shoulder from my now constant lunch partner Debby. She shared the same icy stare with my father. Kevin bounced around the cafeteria as if we were the second coming of the Rolling Stones. I grew to become very critical about my sound and didn't enjoy playing with what I considered inferior bandmates.

I felt good about myself when I wandered over to the shop for my Tuesday night jam session with Gordy and the locals. When I walked in, I noticed the group was a bit larger than the usual four or five. Skunk was back after a couple month hiatus. He had brought with him the band he had been recording with and they had just got back from an east coast tour promoting their recent release.

Gordy had played their record for me in the shop, so even though I hadn't met the band before, I felt like I knew them on some level. The song writing was impressive and Skunks lead licks made me envious. I knew I was in for a treat to hang with touring musicians.

What I was not ready for was the humbling experience I endured. These men were pros. They were a tight bunch. Even though I had played there for about a year with Gordy, I was way out of my league. They would play chords and keys I was not even close to being familiar with at all. None of which was on their two albums.

Skunk told me that they were transforming into more of a jazz fusion band and leaving all the three chords and rock and roll life behind. A few times, I was supposed to take over, but I became so embarrassed I didn't want to play anymore. I only wanted to listen and not screw up any longer. I'm not sure if I was upset more because I could not keep up or because I had arrived thinking I would rock the place that night. I was sadly mistaken. I now knew how far I still had to go to be a professional musician.

The next time I saw Gordy he asked me what I thought of the band. "I guess you set me up to show me playing a birthday party in a backyard isn't the same as a concert hall," I said.

"Ah, don't be so hard on yourself, kid. It wasn't a set up at all. They happened to be in the area and dropped by unannounced. Those guys have been perfecting their craft since before you were born. You should be proud at how far you've come, but you're right, you're not quite at their level yet. Give it another ten years and give thanks to the Lord for all the talents you have been given."

The following week, our local church decided to add another Sunday service, but it would not be in the main hall, but in the basement. It would be a worship service with live music and not a traditional mass. Father Daniel, who knew I played guitar, asked me to bring my instrument and join in on Sunday. He sold me out by calling Mom and asking her to make sure I showed up. He even mailed her sheet music to four songs I was to learn in two days.

I didn't want to do it. I mean despite my humbling experience the previous week or so I was still a rock and roll player. A Christian band wasn't for me. However, if I wanted to eat the following week, Mom insisted I show up a quick rehearsal before the ten am service.

Once again, I suffered a humbling experience. The surrounding adults could really play, and play all styles of music. My task was to play rhythm and strum a few chords while the older musicians took the lead. I had seen and worked out the songs, but with the entire band, the songs rocked.

I didn't know until that morning they had been practicing as a band for a few weeks at night. I accepted my role as an additional side player in the band. It was however, the first time I felt as though I was playing for others and not for me. Up until that point, it was all about me, and my selfish kid's trappings. I wasn't playing for a higher purpose. I was now starting to understand what Gordy had been trying to get through to me. We played two songs before the service started and two more near the end.

Possibly, Gordy had been there in the beginning, but I noticed during the second set of songs he was sitting in the last row of chairs with a smile on his face I had never seen in all the years of knowing him. After the service, I was asked to join the weekly group and come to practice on Tuesday night. I declined. After telling Gordy the story, he informed me that he no longer had time to play on Tuesday nights.

"Stay in the church group, kid. The Tuesday thing was never meant to be a permanent gig," he said.

I called Father Daniel and accepted later that night. For some reason he really didn't seem surprised by my call.

The more I played with the church band, the more I part of a group that had meaning. The service grew from about forty people to almost two hundred over a few short weeks during the summer. I even convinced Gordy to sit in with the band one week. I told him the Lord came to me in a dream and told me to ask him to play. He didn't like my sixteen year old humor any more than he did my thirteen year old humor.

My old neighborhood friends started to come to that service as well. I rarely saw them anymore. I was working thirty hours a week at the restaurant for the summer. After band practice and my own lessons, I had little time left to hang around the neighborhood with friends.

The Saturday group bumped along until Debby finally convinced us to let her sing one song. Kevin sang lead, but he really wasn't any better than me.

"I'll tell you what, Debby," I said. "If you can sing, 'Here, There and Everywhere' better than Kevin, that's your song in our set. If you sing it really well, maybe you can do another."

Kevin shot me a frown showing is disapproval, but without me, that band would disband.

Debby sucked in a deep breath and when she hit the first note, I thought she was a gift from heaven. Her voice was incredible. Who knew? I asked why she never wanted to sing with us before and I quickly learned how quickly women can turn on you. I thought her cold shoulder from a couple of months back was bad, I had no idea.

She instantly became our new lead singer. Even Kevin knew

he was going to be limited to one or two songs and back up after one song from Debby. We started to learn songs that Debby could sing in her vocal range. At first, mostly slow ballads, but I didn't care. I was willing to allow her to be the main reason for our band to exist. Assuming of course anyone ever would again. Being with the church group had taught me that being a part of a competent band was fun. I also had to admit that I liked that adults would come up to me after Sunday service and tell me that I made them smile. I realized my playing was appreciated.

When we came back for our senior year of high school, we discovered that one of our classmates died in a drunken driving accident down at the Jersey shore during the Labor Day weekend. The school wanted to do an awareness campaign and fund raiser to help pay for her funeral costs. It would be an outside event. Bands were asked play thirty-minute sets. I would play once with the church band and once with the Saturday group. The Saturday group could now play ten songs with Debby singing lead. We picked our best six and gave it a shot.

I borrowed the old Stratocaster from Gordy to plug in jack up my sound across the parking lot. Approximately three hundred people attended our set. Debby sang like a songbird. She made all the difference with our band. I really enjoyed accompanying her voice with the guitar. It the largest group I had ever played in front of live. By now, Sticks had become competent enough to play the songs that we knew. Kevin could play a solo or two on the keyboards and I took over many leads on guitar. However, we still needed a bass player to round out our sound. No one we knew played bass guitar.

During our set, someone from another school was heard us play and asked if he could sit in as our bass guitarist in the future. His name was Brian Jones. He had a heart tattoo on his left arm.

He informed us that he went to a school across town and drove a rusted out 1969 Chevy Camaro that was in need of a new muffler. He needed some cash and wanted to join a band.

We quickly found out that really he was far more interested in Debby and her cute jeans than in being a member of our band. Kevin was still ticked off that Debby invited me as a lunch partner with her and Kevin. Now with Brian hanging around and flirting, band politics were a mess.

"Yo, Brian, being in a band is hard enough without you trying to pinch Debby in the ass," I said. "Ya gotta back down or you can't come back." He agreed to tone it down, but the drool running down his chin told a different story.

He needed less than thirty minutes of practice time with us before the problem became obvious. We needed Brian as much or more than he needed us. The kid could play bass guitar. He told us he was in a band once before, but would not say why he was no longer with that group. Our trio had grown by two members in less than a week.

After practice, Debby asked to speak with me. "Stu, you would be doing me a huge favor if you would play an open mic night with me this weekend. It's over at the Wayside Inn and first prize is fifty bucks. Please, please, play on stage with me."

I gazed into her jade green eyes and soft smile. She made it hard to resist. "I'll only do it if you tell the guys this was your idea and not mine. I don't want them all in my grill again about me trying to play without them."

She batted her long lashes and blew me a kiss. "Thank you, thank you. I'll tell em. We can split the prize money. I'm sure we'll win. I've been there before during open mic, we can blow them away."

I went over to her house the next afternoon and we worked out, 'Heart of Gold' by Neil Young and 'You've Got a Friend' by Carol King and James Taylor.

After our performance, the place went nuts. We had the loudest ovation by far. I was already counting the money in my head when the winner's name blared across the microphone.

"The winner is…. Kendra Robinson for her set of Motown classics."

Lesson learned. Oh, Kendra was a fine singer. She was also the girlfriend of Kenny Jackson, the restaurant owner's son. Mom and Dad came for dinner and support. I'm sure the disappointment in my face after the results. Dad came up to me later and said, "It wasn't the 1812 Overture, but that was some fine playing, son." It took some sting out of losing my half of the first prize.

CHAPTER FOUR

Kevin grew into quite the young entrepreneur. He managed to get our band booked at the local CYO (Catholic Youth Organization) dance hall for the Friday night dances for four straight weeks. We were obligated to play two, forty-five minute sets. We decided the band would play one set as a full band then the other set would be a combination of the band, along with five songs with only Debby and myself on stage. At first, the others grumbled, but Debby and I won out.

Brian insisted we practice much harder as a band. Kevin and Sticks had become more than adequate. We could now comfortably play fifteen songs as a band. Debby and I learned ten more as a duo. We were all set to play the dances and not play the exact same set each week. We were still not as good as the church group, but that was for an entirely different purpose. However, we had come a very long way since the day we played at the fundraiser.

Even at a tender age, Debby knew how to bend and shape her seventeen-year old slender body to make people take notice of more than just her voice. Her stage presence hid many of our mistakes as a band. Our following grew beyond our local sphere of friends and classmates. New faces arrived each week.

Our collected fifty dollars a week as a band. However, the money was secondary to me. I developed as a musician. I needed an audience. Debby flourished as a local star among the high school crowd. I learned fast where to hitch my wagon. She recognized I would hide her vocal limitations in the song selection, but also understood her attraction. We trusted each other.

By the third week of the month, the CYO had booked us again for two months later. Kevin found a restaurant that wanted a band on Friday nights, so we played there for a couple of weeks. We started to feel better about playing outside of a garage. We learned a few newer songs hitting the radio. I could figure them out in my room and if I had trouble in spots, I would ask Gordy for help. He was an expert at playing by ear.

I wasn't hanging out at the shop as much. My brother had taken over many of my chores, including walking my grandmother's dog. I still had band practice with two bands, my schoolwork and playing with the bands on the weekends. My grades were starting to slip at the wrong time. Applications for colleges were beginning. I began to think about my future beyond the scope of my local area. Moving away seemed scary, yet exhilarating.

Kevin had been accepted to a college in Philadelphia and he made it very clear he would not be able to commit to playing every weekend or come home for practice during the week. Since the drive was well over an hour to where he was going to school, we all understood. Debby too planned to attend a small college outside of the Philly area. Sticks was a year younger than the rest of us and Brian wasn't sure he would make it out of high school. I told Brian a few times that if he actually showed up at school more than three days a week, maybe they would let him graduate.

Dad informed me that if I didn't attend college, I wasn't permitted to stay living at home. I'm not sure that was a good enough incentive to apply for college, but I got the point. The problem was, I had to cut back somewhere and somewhere was hanging down at Gordy's Guitars.

However, one day I did convince Gordy to open the shop for the old Tuesday gang. Debby tagged along and sang with us. Gordy was semi impressed and told me to make sure she stayed in her vocal range.

Debby did try to expand her vocal abilities. Her dad sprung for voice lessons after we did so well at the open mic night. She seemed to have the touch over her own dad as much as she did the local audience.

As the Christmas holidays approached, the church band decided to do a ninety minute performance. Once on Saturday night before Christmas and once on Christmas Eve. What it really meant was extra practice time and learning many new songs. I really didn't have the time for extra work, but I knew my time in that band was ending as well. I agreed to the extra practice for four weeks.

For the effort, I would play two solos during the performance. No longer did I sit in the back of the stage solely as rhythm player. I stood next to the lead guitarist and the lead singer on stage. The church built a slightly larger stage and the band added two horn players to the band. Our worship service had become the most attended of all the services offered at the church. Even the older generation of church attendees would occasionally come to our service in the basement.

I for the very first time had gotten down on my knees and asked the Lord for a path to get all my studies and band activities done, as well as my weekly visit with my grandmother. I didn't think I could make it through that month, but it was over so fast I barely noticed. The two performances were a huge success. The band was asked to do a New Years' Eve performance in the morning instead of our usual service, since it was on a Sunday. We agreed. The next day, I crashed and watched football with my dad and brother the entire day. I didn't pick up my guitar even once, which was so rare I couldn't even remember the last time that had happened.

The holidays were just what I needed to regroup and catch up on my college admissions. I had not yet been accepted anywhere, so I applied to a local college as a backup plan. My grades were good enough for some good colleges, but I had applied to only top schools. Father Daniel had made a few calls for me. I was getting some interest from a small Christian college in North Carolina for a music scholarship. I didn't think I wanted to go in that direction, but it was nice that he thought enough of me make the call. His old college roommate was the admissions director. I learned the lesson that it's always good to have connections.

Over the break, I stopped by to see Gordy. He offered me a job after school to give lessons to a few young kids who were starting out. I assumed he had lost patience with the young kids and he knew it would get me in the shop more. I quit my job at the restaurant and started to offer lessons twice a week after school and on Saturday mornings. I made more money than working at the restaurant and it gave me an excuse to be at the shop again. Overall, it was a good move.

As much as I loved playing, I discovered that teaching wasn't my strength. However, I persevered. Gordy knew it forced me to practice my scales again while assisting the beginners. I did however show them how to play a few classics that they could play without much skill. I think that helped to keep the parents paying for lessons and kept the younger ones somewhat interested.

At the end of the holiday break, Kevin gave me call and could barely contain his excitement. I don't think I had ever heard him that joyous, but after he calmed down, I think I was the one who couldn't breathe. There was going to be an outdoor concert at the end of March at the local racetrack and it was going to be an all-day show.

The list of bands were mostly local bands, but the headliner was a new band from the Jersey shore area called Bruce Springsteen and the E Street Band. We had been hearing reports they were about to break out big time and had released their first album. Kevin's father was a bigtime lawyer in town and were one of the main sponsors of the event.

Our turn would come early in the day and be for thirty minutes. We understood we had to learn a couple of new songs for the event. It would be imperative to be at our best. It was also yet another lesson for me in who you know as opposed to what you know that got our band on the bill. When I told a few friends of mine what had happened they didn't say congrats and good luck. They only wanted to know if I could get each of them free tickets and an autograph from Bruce. I sarcastically thanked them for their support.

The last semester of my high school life was about to begin. I looked back briefly and wondered where it had all gone. So many requests came for our band to play at parties on weekends that I began to feel used. Most of our classmates wouldn't give me the time of day, except for when they went to Kevin thinking we would play some party for free. I felt I was a generous person, but I really fought with Kevin about playing parties without pay. He was using it for his stature amongst our classmates, thinking he was going to win some kind of popularity award at the end of the year.

Brian didn't even go to our school and grumbled more than I did about playing for free. We refused to play any more parties unless money changed hands. Debby was caught in the middle since most of those who asked where her friends too, but I was now looking at this as a serious band. They just wanted to have fun.

For once, I played politics within the band and we won the vote 3-2 not to play for free any longer. I really only had to convince Sticks to vote my way, since I knew Brian's vote was in my back pocket. Sticks went along with us once his dad told him he had to pay for half of his lessons and he needed a way to make money. He was tired of babysitting and wanted the band to make more money too. The local CYO seemed to be rotating three local bands now. We only played once every three months there.

Sometimes when you live a good life, you're rewarded in ways you're not expecting. I had to admit the Good Lord must have been watching out for me in the spring of 1973. The band played a set in front of over a thousand people early in the day at the outdoor festival and we were paid two hundred bucks. We also sat back stage and watched the E Street Band play a three-hour show later that night in front of over five thousand adoring Bruce fans.

It was my first rock and roll concert and my band was a part of it. The following Monday, I got a call from a man at the Juilliard School in New York City, telling me he was told I might be a good candidate for their school. At that point, I was still thinking of majoring in business, but this was the second time I was approached about music.

I realized I had progressed nicely over the years, but with Gordy keeping me humbled, I never really thought much about a real career in music. I needed to rethink my position. When I told my parents I wanted to visit NYC for the interview, Mom was thrilled, but Dad became skeptical. I knew little to nothing about Julliard, but Gordy convinced me I would be crazy not to check into it.

Two weeks later, Debby, Kevin and I hopped a train and spent the day in the city. I went for my interview while they saw the sights.

My interview went well. I discovered during the course of the conversation that someone in the crowd at our outdoor gig spotted my talent. He was an alumnus of Julliard and recommended me for at least an interview.

Mr. Dobbs, who interviewed me also asked about Debby. I let him know that even though she loved performing, her father would be broken hearted if she didn't work towards her original career choice in medicine.

After a talk about my work with the two bands and my commitment to being a Christian, I performed three pieces of music with the guitar. Thankfully, I wasn't asked to sing.

As the interview wrapped up, Mr. Dobbs explained that Skunk had also graduated from the school and was a close friend of Mr. Dobbs. Knowing Skunk was from my area, Mr. Dobbs contacted Skunk and to my mild surprise, he offered a high recommendation for me to attend Julliard. I hadn't seen Skunk in months. His band had been touring Europe.

With the interview complete, I met up with Debby and Kevin

near the school and we toured around the city for a few more hours before returning home. The buzz of a big city had caught my attention.

A month later, a letter arrived letting me know of my acceptance into Julliard. It also outlined the tuition costs, along with a partial scholarship. Mom jumped for joy with the news, but Dad never saw music as a viable career.

"It's all I'm good at, Dad. I suck at math, forget science and history bores me. Think about it. Have you ever seen me work harder at anything than music?"

We compromised. Dad relented on my choice of schools as long as I promised to pick up some business courses at another school in the summers or at nights. I agreed. I called Mr. Dobbs and accepted.

My life had taken a turn not anticipated only a month earlier. Debby and Kevin were both set as well in going to college in Philly. I didn't think they would ever separate too much. I had learned over time that they weren't a couple, but were more like brother and sister.

Graduation couldn't come fast enough once I was set with my commitment to attend Julliard. I had made Dad a promise I would do my best to make the honor roll and finish high school strong. I made it again by a percentage point. I knew that meant a lot to Dad and it eased his pain with me not going to school for business. I did have to have someone from Julliard call him and assure him the school would assist me in finding business classes nearby.

I played with the church band through the Easter service, but decided it was time to leave the group. It had been fun playing with them. The band had grown to a nine-piece band over the years. The other band crumbled after the dust up about not wanting to play birthday parties for free. It put a distance between us and Randy withdrew hanging around with us. He was late for practice many times, which was unlike him. It became clear the outdoor show was our highlight and swan song.

High school graduation came and went. For the first time in years, I was no longer in a working band. Other than a few lessons at Gordy's I was free from all commitments for the summer. My grandmother stunned me when she gave me a Martin D-28 for graduation.

Gordy had found one that someone was returning since his spoiled rotten kid wouldn't practice. It had been dinged up a bit, but I didn't care. It had a wonderful sound to it. I played that guitar for hours each day.

I spent more time with some friends from the neighborhood, along with Debby over the summer. We ended up taking the train to the new Veterans Stadium to see a couple of Phillies games. One hot August evening, Gordy took me to see Elvis Presley and I met Elvis after the show. Now that was cool. Elvis acted happy to see Gordy. I kept asking Gordy all the way home how he knew Elvis and all he would say was that "It's in the past, kid, but I enjoyed seeing The King again." He mumbled that it had been, "too many years." Elvis looked tired to me, but it was extra special to see a legend perform.

CHAPTER FIVE

Julliard rocked my word as a musician. My roommate dazzled on the keyboards. Scott Karstens, a tall boney looking kid from Ohio, wrote songs and performed with a jazz band in his hometown. He wanted to return home after graduation to teach piano and help students appreciate music. Neither of his parents had an ounce of musical talent, but sacrificed in driving Scott to recitals and performances for years.

All of my instructors were amazing musicians. I really felt like I belonged there even though everyone here was every bit as good and better as I was as a performer. I knew instantly, Julliard was home.

Speaking of which, Mom threatened to stop paying my bills if I didn't visit her after being gone for over a month. I was having so much fun meeting students from around not only the United States, but also from as far away as China. I sent a letter to Debby hoping she would be home the same weekend. I missed her. I did manage to squeeze in one weekend to visit everyone, including my family, grandmother and Gordy. I also met up with Debby and Kevin. However, most weekend were filled with trips to see bands or hanging out with new friends from school.

The first semester went by as smoothly as listening to side two of The Beatles, 'Abbey Road.' Gordy instilled in me a solid foundation in music theory, but I became forced to stretch my talent. I reflected back on the time Skunk's band had come over and humbled me and showed me there was so much more to music than the major scales. Scott and I started to write very moody songs and used minor scales almost entirely. Gordy had taught me all those scales long ago, but since I was playing rock and roll, I didn't use them often. I was now playing different styles of music, partly because of Scott's influences and partly because of what I had to do for my schoolwork.

I spent the entire holiday break catching up with my family and hanging out at the shop with Gordy. I went to see my grandmother daily since I could tell she had grown frail since the last I had seen her. She told me I would soon be challenged to hold true to my core principals and who I was in life. She begged me to hold true to my values and never let anyone take them from me. I told her it was never an issue, but she kept insisting on thinking about what she was trying to tell me.

Grandma somehow knew everyone's future. Her shrinking body never stopped her mind from working overtime. Some thought she was an old woman suffering from dementia. I knew better. She came from Germany with her brother with nothing in her pocket but lint. When she retired, she owned a string of convenience stores she had started in the area with my grandfather. He had passed away when I was quite young, but my grandmother ran those stores well into her late sixties.

She finally sold them to a national chain who wanted market share in our area. She was a very shrewd businessperson. I remember one time when I was maybe eight, Mom and I had stopped in one of the stores to see Grandma. She was ripping into some poor salesman. He was late delivering a product already due in the store. I have no doubt he left knowing he had better not come back without what he had promised on his next visit.

The moment he left, Grandma imparted a giant smile and hug like an entirely different person. She was tough and one of the most disciplined people I knew. When she tried to offer a life lesson, I listened. I had a sinking feeling though, that she had given me her last lesson. She seemed so adamant about me paying attention to that one.

Father Daniel caught me after Christmas service and asked if I would play at a retirement home that he had been visiting. I asked Debby to come and sing for me. She obliged. I think she missed singing with me. We played about an hour, three times over the holidays. I noticed her range had gotten much better. When I asked her about it, she told me that she had found a chorus group near her college and was singing with them twice a week.

"There's someone in the group who has taken a liking to me," Debby said. "She thinks I have a special talent and she's encouraging me to keep improving."

At the end of break, while visiting with Gordy, Skunk wandered in. It had been well over a year since I had seen him. He had changed. He drove a new sports car. His long yellow locks were now styled. A new diamond earing hung on his earlobe. His band Dr. Wu had reached the top of the charts. They're latest release contained five top forty hits.

You couldn't turn on the new album oriented stations in New York and Philly and not hear Dr. Wu. "We just got back from playing seven sold out shows in Japan," Skunk said with a smirk. "Donnie Brecker got pissy when the sound wasn't right in Tokyo, but we managed. The man can be too much of a perfectionist. Shit. We've been out on the road for eighteen months. We all need a hiatus from each other."

Skunk talked about playing for a live audience and how it

gave him a high you couldn't understand unless you stood on stage at Madison Square Garden and experienced it for yourself. I hung on every word.

"By the way, Gordy," Skunk said, "that's the reason for my visit. The band has one more gig at the Garden before we're taking several months off the road. I got four back stage passes for ya, if you want em? Why don't you bring the kid with ya?"

"Thanks, Skunk, but the store keeps me busy," Gordy said. "Why not give Stu the tickets."

Skunk slanted his eye at me and nodded. "Don't git in any trouble backstage, kid," he said as he handed me an envelope that looked like gold to me.

Two nights later, we were off to witness Dr. Wu perform at Madison Square Garden. The four of us were led down a long hallway and onto a small platform back stage where we couldn't see the entire stage, but could see where Skunk would be standing. I took Scott and his girlfriend, who was a drama student. I called her his, 'Drama Queen' because everything always had to be about her. She never made my Christmas card list.

I had no clue what he saw in her, other than her near perfect model shape and complexion. I asked him he ever planned to look above her shoulders and see if she had eyes or not. I peeked many times. Ice. She later went on to be the villain on a long running soap opera based in New York. It was the perfect role for her. No acting needed.

My date was a violin player from school. Cute, but I think in the back of my mind I wanted to date her because she had actually performed the 1812 Overture. I wanted to tell Dad that even though I still hadn't played it, I dated someone who had.

None of the three believed I had sat in with the band in a small guitar shop, until we were firmly entrenched backstage, and the band members said hello to me as they walked onto the stage.

The house lights went up. Skunk soon played his first solo. I stood mesmerized. Skunk's long hair twisted across his shoulders as his fingers walked up and down the neck of his instrument. His bushy mustache reflected off the red and blue lights, but when the white spotlight hit him, there was no doubt Skunk controlled the garden party.

Skunk had always been the best musician I met, but all the work on the road had made him into an incredible live performer. His body barely moved as his fingers ran across that fret board while he appeared to be in a trance. The crowd roared after each song and each solo. I understood why he practiced those long tiresome hours. I also realized why Gordy pressed me so hard to learn the basics.

Skunk was the big time. I realized why Gordy let him hang around the store and show kids like me some lessons. The man grew into being a world class musician.

Back at school, I became immersed into song writing. I developed skills and learned the techniques of how to build a piece of music. I took a song writing class and learned a lot from it. My instructor had written songs for some singing groups in the mid-sixties. He had credibility when he spoke.

I was more and more convinced that music was now my life's work and passion. Middle management in some department store was never going to be career, despite my father's wishes. I think he recognized that fact over the break, but he pretended like he didn't notice. I received top grades and as promised, I found a night class teaching basic business. It made it hard on Dad to bitch at me.

Scott and I wrote about twenty-five songs together, ranging from very bad to almost decent. He joined me in the song writing class. We both managed an A for the class. We must have learned something.

The end of the first year was near. The thought of going back home and teaching ten-year old beginners scales all summer made me puke. I knew my parents were expecting me home, but I couldn't do it. Scott was heading back to Ohio for the summer, as were most of my new friends.

My girlfriend Elise was in an orchestra put together by the school to tour the country for a few weeks over the summer. She wasn't going to be around much either. After the tour, she was going back home to North Carolina for a few weeks. In the end, I held my breath and reluctantly did return home. The day I arrived home, my grandmother passed away. I didn't have time to see her and say good-bye. Something I still regret.

I had seen her over spring break and she looked a bit stronger, but her heart finally gave out. In her Will, she left me a ring that was my grandfathers. It was inscribed underneath, "Be True." I figured she meant wanted to reinforce her lesson one last time.

We talked very briefly about putting the band back together for the summer, but Brian said he had stopped playing and Kevin really didn't want to do it either. Brian had become distant, pale and lost weight. He was never a chubby person to begin with, so the loss made him look ill.

Debby and I picked up a Friday gig playing three, forty- five minute sets at a new coffee house in town for the summer. It didn't pay well, but I had to play a certain amount of hours in public to graduate. I called my school administrator and made sure I received proper credit. Besides, it gave me one night a week where I could be with Debby again and play some music.

We had added many new songs since her voice now had a wider range. We even played two songs that Scott and I had written and one I wrote myself. I wrote it with Debby in mind. She sang it beautifully. I never told her it was about her, but I suspect she knew since she delivered it with great passion. I worked part time at the guitar shop and even worked one full day to give Gordy some time off during the week. I think he had some health issues, but didn't want to tell me. He only said he could use one afternoon off to do some errands. He had another part time person working the store, but I think he got caught with drugs in the store. Gordy quickly banished him forever.

I wrote a few songs over the summer, but mostly I chilled. I did help clean out my grandmother's house. My parents sold it at the end of the summer. Her dog died a few weeks after my grandmother did. I don't think Baron enjoyed living at my parent's house any more than I did that summer.

CHAPTER SIX

During my second year at school, I had to perform in a band. My advisor suggested I play in an orchestra, but I begged for a jazz band. I wanted to learn to be more improvisational and not be restricted to printed notes on the sheet music. Scott and I also found a few musicians from school to join up on weekends, in the hope of landing a paying job later in the year. New York overflowed with talent. Finding a good paying gig came close to impossible.

My grades stayed up, which pleased Mom and Dad. Elise and I grew closer, even though it was tough to track her down during the week. Her residence was at the opposite end of the campus, but we managed to see each other a few minutes each night for dinner. Her orchestra practiced a lot in the evenings. My jazz band met in the late afternoons, so our times never matched. She was a wonderful person, who I enjoyed being around. Scott finally broke it off with the drama queen. Well, that's his side. Truth was she had found a GQ model who drove a corvette. Scott might have been heartbroken at first, but he was far better with her gone. He would do so much better than a future soap star with a sour attitude and bleached hair.

Elise Andrews on the other hand was a quiet unassuming southern belle. Her shyness enticed me as much as her smile. Her family never had the income to send her to college. They ran a small farm in the hills of North Carolina. Her entire family for generations played either the banjo or the fiddle. Elise was raised a devout Christian. While in high school, she was fortunate to have had a classically trained music teacher, who put Elise on the path to classical music.

Her father shared the same issues as mine. He never understood why anyone would pay to hear music. In the backcountry of Carolina, everyone played for the love of it. He didn't object however to Elise obtaining a full scholarship to play music.

Shorter than an your average teenager, her bright green eyes with blue speckles, made me crumble every time I peered too deep into them. Now and again, she used that to her advantage by getting me to attend church service with her, or go into the city and visit a museum. She loved history.

About once week, she would tell me, "Listen here, Stu my boy, if you don't know your history you are doomed to repeat it, now let's go learn something today."

Skunk called me at the school and invited me and my roomie over to a recording session for Dr. Wu. I had been in a recording studio for school, but not an actual working professional one. We heard them work on a track that later became one of their biggest hits during our visit. Skunk promised us dinner too, but Don Brecker was such a stickler, he refused anyone to leave until every note reached perfection.

At eight in the evening, we decided to head back to the cafeteria before it closed. Overall, it was a great experience. It was the first time I saw a band work out a song with a producer in a recording studio. The first time I heard that song on the radio, I smiled the rest of the day. It's funny, but what I remember most about that day was how Don Brecker was in the face of Walt

Farner and Skunk had to get in the middle to keep them from punching each other right inside the studio. Then not ten minutes later, they were all joking about it and acting like brothers. Skunk Baxter was not only a first rate musician, he was a great mediator as well.

My second year at Julliard ended. A classmate asked me to join a band, which had a full time job as a house band down the Jersey shore for the summer. The contract ran from the last weekend in May, until the first weekend of September, six nights a week, four hours a night. A grueling schedule indeed, however it more than fulfilled my requirement to play over the break.

We would all share one apartment a few blocks from the beach. Mom and Dad didn't like the idea, but I had to learn to live on my own. The band had been the house band for the previous year as well, but the lead guitarist from the year before moved to California to work in his dad's wine business.

Scott and Elise were both going home for the summer. If I heard Scott say, "Ohio is my home" one more time I might have punched him. Scott hated to be away from home and called his parents at least twice a week to check on the family and the farm animals. Having grown up in the suburbs, I didn't understand. Maybe that's why Scott and Elise got along so well. She understood him.

The first day in our Jersey shore apartment, I recognized trouble brewing. Well, giant bongs filled with pot to be more precise. All the members in the band were heavy pot smokers. I had never tried it. I had seen it around campus a few times, but had always excused myself when I knew what was going on. Billy Potts was the leader of the band and the first time they started to get high, I excused myself.

I heard him say as I left, "Anyone who won't share a smoke with his mates, can't be trusted." The place constantly smelled like someone had poured beer all over the furniture as well.

It took some adjusting to playing four hours each night. My bias aside, I was clearly the best musician in the group and I think the only one who took our responsibility seriously. We were close to being fired after two weeks because Billy showed up stoned most nights. The owner objected. He insisted the band not show up smelling like an overused bong every night. It took the bar owner actually firing us for one night before the others decided not to show up high.

Billy and I had no desire to be in each other's company. I spent most of my days laying on the beach, while the rest of the band would be sleeping or getting high. On our days off on Mondays, I would trek home to see my family.

Three good things occurred during that summer. First, I started to learn how to work an audience. I thought back to the night watching Skunk at the Garden. On a much smaller scale, I did my best to hypnotize college girls in the audience. We had our share of groupies, who would pack the club more than once a week. I tried hard to get the band to change the sets from night to night because of the repeat audience and to keep it fresh, but I think Billy fought the idea mostly because I suggested it. I also think they were too lazy or stoned to bother.

Second, Billy lost it just past midsummer when for one week Debby's parents rented a place nearby. I talked to the owner of the club Johnny G, into allowing Debby and I to do a twenty minute set each night before the band started. Billy acted like a child. He would intentionally try to get me to screw up at least once a night.

Debby and I killed it. The owner loved our set and chemistry on stage. It meant an extra set for me, but I didn't care. I loved playing with Debby. During the day, we would walk the boardwalk then lay on the beach until it was almost time to go on stage. One day at the end of boardwalk there was a billboard sign advertising Fats Domino and Little Richard playing at the Atlantic City Convention Center.

Debby said, "One day our names will be there." I smiled and thought to myself that wasn't the worst idea she ever had. Debby had developed into a beautiful, if not stunning woman. Her nearly six-foot frame, green eyes and soft red hair made others take notice. Her arms were littered with freckles, but the few on her face made her smile shine.

Rarely was she down or upset, Debby was the most positive person I had ever met. She had been missed more than I realized. That week, I felt guilty because for the first time we acted more like boyfriend and girlfriend, rather than classmates and band mates. All I could think about was Elise back in North Carolina playing in some barn for the pigs and cows, or so I pictured it in my mind.

Debby and I kissed on the beach after my last set under a full moon with the ocean water drifting across our feet and ankles. It was our very first kiss. I never knew how soft her lips were until that kiss. I hoped it would not be the last time I tasted her strawberry lipstick or smelled the scent of shampoo in her hair. I wished that week would never end, but it did, far too quickly.

After Debby left, the summer couldn't end quick enough for me. I would only be in that apartment long enough to sleep about five hours before heading to the beach for another two hour power nap. I would head back for a shower a quick change and meet the rest of the band on stage. I did get a kick out of the young girls in the audience, who would toss their phone numbers or occasional bra on stage at my feet. Billy was the lead singer and bass player and never once did that happen to him. I made sure he knew it every time it happened too.

I would pick up the phone number or clothing between songs and say, "Thank you to the cute girl in the pink top, you made my night" or whatever she was wearing at the time. I would then turn and look at Billy and strike my finger in a downwards manner like, there's yet another one for me, asshole. I signed my first autograph that summer. It was on the left breast of some hot looking woman, who looked to be about ten years older than I was. I later found out it was her bachelorette party.

The third good thing that happened that summer was my electric guitar. Gordy still used that old Stratocaster for lessons, so I traded in my Gibson acoustic and some of the cash he owed me from the lessons I gave for a Gibson Les Paul. I still had a balance I owed on credit, but I needed a good electric guitar. The only catch was in order to get the store credit for ninety days; I had to promise Gordy that one day I would do him a favor.

Gordy told me that was his, "Marlon Brando moment like in the Godfather." No chance I would have refused a request from Gordy, even before the credit. However, I never gave his request a second thought. I took the Les Paul and ran.

I paid off the balance every Monday when I visited home. By summer's end, I had a Martin guitar for my acoustic sets with Debby and a Les Paul for electric sets. I assumed I would never need or buy another guitar in my lifetime.

The morning after our last set, I packed up and went home as quickly as I could, armed with about twenty girl's phone numbers, a pink bra and a few addresses. I only kept them to prove to Scott, or 'Mr. Buckeye,' as I called him, my stories were legit.

CHAPTER SEVEN

Upon my arrival back at school, Elise was madder than hornet on a hot day in the Carolina Mountains. Granted, she had written me every week, and I had only written her maybe once a month, and only called her once all summer. However, I didn't think she would be that upset. Her cold shoulder remained unthawed for weeks. Rumors spread we were no longer a couple. I think she started them. I finally broke down and took her for a nice dinner and Broadway show to soothe hurt feelings. I also had to promise that it would never happen again as long as we were together.

I think Scott got a big kick at all my groveling to Elise. For a few weeks, he called me his, "drama queen roommate." I wasn't amused, but guess I had it coming.

Since I had promised Dad I would continue with some business classes, I found a couple classes at a nearby school, which took up even more of my valuable time. However, Dad paid for them.

I became more inquisitive about the business side of music since Johnny G taught me a few things about how he ran his club. I didn't like the fact that he sold T-shirts all summer with our bands name and his clubs name on it and we didn't get a penny for the use of our name. That was another example of why I didn't really care to see Billy Potts every again. He granted that right in our contract. I don't think Billy ever bothered to read the contract, other than our fee or have someone else read it on our behalf. I learned a lesson watching Johnny sell a few hundred shirts with my name on the back without my permission or royalties.

However, what really struck me the most was how much I missed being up on a stage, any stage. It had been over a month and I ached for an audience. Screaming girls at my feet had become my drug of choice. On weekends, I took my guitar to every open mic night I could find in the city. I didn't care if I won or not, I needed to play in front of a crowd.

One night, a young guy came up to me after the performance and asked me if I had a manager. I told him I really had no reason for one.

"Then go ahead and play open mic nights the rest of your life. See if I care," he said. Those words clung to me like Elmer's Glue to a piece of wood. He made his point.

Carl Peterson became my manager. That was of course after I called Dad and he ran it all by his attorney. I wasn't about to make the same mistake Billy Potts had made in entering into a bad agreement. Carl talked a big game. He stated how he knew all the big wigs at a national record label. He claimed he also knew all the local club owners and would get me in front of an audience on a regular basis.

Carl was a brash loud mouth twenty-five year old, who had recently graduated from Fordham Law School. He hadn't passed the bar exam yet, but seemed hungry and talked a good game. He had less money in his bank account than me. He owed the government a ton of money in school loans. He needed to work hard and fast.

A position at a local law office awaited Carl if he passed the bar exam by the following month. "My goal is be the beast damn agent for entertainers this town has ever seen," he boasted. I was his first client. I I soon learned he didn't know all the big wigs with the record labels. His father was a regional salesperson for Yale Records. That was his "inside connections." I didn't care really, he seemed like he could sell ice cubes to an Eskimo and I liked his charm. If he was that good with others as he was with me, I was going to be in front of an audience again very soon.

Scott began taking education classes. He still wanted to return to Ohio and teach kids music. He found an opportunity through Julliard to go into a poor section of the city and teach elementary school kids about music. He came back from that on cloud nine every time, telling me how he was sure he had made a difference in someone's life. I admired his ambitions, but at the time, assumed he could have done so much more with his life.

Scott convinced Elise and me to tag along. After five minutes in a classroom full of ten year olds, I knew I'd never have the patience to be trapped in a small room day in and day out. It made an impression on Elise. She went along several times with Scott.

Carl passed the bar exam with his first attempt. We went out for dinner to celebrate. He invited his dad, who was in town for the week. I met Carl's dad for the first time. I quickly found out where Carl learned his salesmanship. Carl kept bragging on and on about how I was going to be on the Yale label one day and that his dad would be out peddling albums with my name on them. I ignored it all and just kept asking Carl how he was going to get me a record deal if he couldn't even get me job in a local club. He assured me now that he had passed his exam and was about to move into his new office downtown, I would soon be working.

His dad did insist that no record label would ever offer a contract to anyone with my name. "Stu Edrich, no chance," he said.

We discussed it over dinner. He asked who my influences were at the time. He forced me to think about it, even though Gordy had always impressed on me to be myself. However, as the hour was getting late, I told him that I wanted to speak the words of Bob Dylan with the soul of James Brown. From that moment on, I morphed into Dylan James in my professional life. Of course, I had no job, no degree and no real future, but I did have a cool name.

Schoolwork piled up. Band practice, night classes, day classes, it all became a chore. However, I knew my priorities to keep Dad paying the bills. Good grades, happy Dad. He was still upset I didn't major in business, but was starting to come around to see how important music had become in my life. He acknowledged my talent, but in his world, real men didn't play music for a living. Dad was a huge Frank Sinatra fan, a man who made his fortune in music, but somehow that fact always seemed to escape Dad.

I took a voice class during my first semester. I started to become more comfortable with my singing voice. I knew if I was to play solo in clubs, no one wanted hear someone who only played guitar. I figured if Bob Dylan could get away with his voice, so could I.

The first week of December, Carl called and told me he had an offer for me to play solo in a small club starting the day after Christmas running through and New Year's Day. The regular act would be on vacation. I knew my mother would be very upset with me, but I took the job anyway.

I convinced Debby to perform with me. Singing and playing

alone for more than one set, terrified me. I gave her half of my cut, even though she only played half of the sets with me. The pay sucked and after Carl took his fifteen percent and the government took their cut and with Debby's split I had just enough for gas money, but I was working with an audience again. I played four hours a night with breaks, so I played about ninety minutes with Debby and just over an hour alone. The owner was so happy with our work that he wanted to extend it another week. However, I had promised my family I would be home for a week while on break from classes, as did Debby. Much to Carl's disapproval, we declined. We did offer our services over the summer if he wanted us back.

Carl kept it a secret, but he arranged for someone from Yale Records to come one night and hear us perform. He didn't want to tell me so that I wouldn't get too nervous. He told me the next day. The exec was impressed enough that he let Carl know the label would consider me as a studio musician in the future.

I spent the remainder of the holiday break at home and went to the shop to visit with Gordy for an hour or so each day. I hadn't seen that much of him lately. I told him about my new name and his only response was, "Congrats the suits took over." I think he was being sarcastic, but he let it all go quickly. I still didn't know why he had such anger about either the music industry or something else, but he was always a private person. I had never been to his house even though he had come to my parents for Thanksgiving and once for Christmas dinner. He would always change the subject when it became too personal about his past.

I have sparse notes about the second semester of my junior year. I remember Carl got me sporadic jobs on weekends at various clubs, but nothing exciting. I did obtain a studio job playing rhythm guitar on an album by the next overnight sensation, and greatest singing group. They were so overnight, I don't even remember their name, but it did give me some experience in a studio working with a producer and put a few bucks in my pocket, after Carl's cut. My advisor at school was very pleased I was able to get the experience.

Scott was considering transferring to Ohio State to finish his degree in education. Elise was offered to play in a small orchestra for an off Broadway production. Between our schoolwork and her practice time, we rarely saw each other.

I felt isolated, even though I was still on campus and Scott was still my roommate. The only good thing was that my grades were the best they had ever been, even the business classes I took during nights and weekends.

With no full time jobs arranged by Carl for me over the summer, I went home and played occasional weekends with Debby. I also went back to the shop with Gordy giving lessons and concentrated on my songwriting. I got a few tips from Gordy after he hinted he had written a few songs in his past.

I assumed he was involved with music somehow, because I would see envelopes delivered to the shop from The American Society of Composers, Authors and Publishers or ASCAP.

Skunk once told me that Gordy, "Made a few bucks from royalties, but the store kept him sane."

Thinking beyond my senior year and graduation, I had no idea what I would be doing the following year. I only knew it couldn't be giving guitar lessons snot nosed brats, who had no idea how to appreciate a fine instrument. Gordy had worn off on me.

Elise convinced me to come and visit her in North Carolina for a week near the end of the summer. It was like another world to me. I had no idea there were actually that many stars in the sky and the air could be so crisp and clear.

She was so much more relaxed and almost a different person at home. She wasn't nearly as shy and I noticed one very important thing. She would play the violin like a fiddle. Meaning no more Chopin at home, she was playing down right foot stomping Dixie style music.

Seeing another part of the country also opened my mind to the idea of seeing more of the world. If a day's car ride could expose me to that much transition, what else was beyond?

CHAPTER EIGHT

The start to my senior year stunk like rotten eggs. Scott transferred to Ohio State and never called to let me know. Pissed off would be an understatement. Upon dumping my things in my dorm room, I met my new roommate. Craig something. I never bothered to learn is full name. The kid wore eye shadow, played the flute and didn't like the Rolling Stones. I wasn't a fan of his Cher shirt either.

Lucky for me, he lived nearby and slept at home three nights a week. It saved me from having to find a beach to sleep on. Craig admitted, despite having turned twenty, this was the first time he ever slept away from his home. Ever. His parents forced him into the dorm for one year, even though he lived three subway stops from school.

I immediately called Scott and ripped him a new one for not having the balls to call me. He admitted his fear in letting me know and apologized. It didn't make up for the fact I had to share my room with a someone who's lifelong ambition was to play flute on a Barbara Streisand recording.

I struggled without Scott being around and keeping me focused on schoolwork. He called me a day after our initial dust up and explained to me how he needed more credits than Julliard could offer to graduate with a degree in education. He wanted to leave after his sophomore year, but hung in one extra year taking education classes at the same school I took my business classes.

We promised to stay in touch and attempt to write songs long distance, but some promises are destined to be broken.

My school advisor asked about my future. Me too. I wanted to take my guitars and tour the world. He chuckled and asked if I had a backup plan. Not really. I trusted that Carl would find me something locally that I could make enough money to scrape by and not have to move home after graduation. Ultimately, I wanted to put a band together and see the world.

My advisor asked if I was interested in staying on as a teacher at the school. At first, I thought it was a practical joke put on by Elise and Scott, but he was serious. "You have a wonderful patience about you," he said. "I know you give lessons where you learned to play. It's something you should consider. You would have to work your way up and start as an assistant and take more classes, but one day I would think you would make for a fine instructor."

I politely declined the offer. Elise on the other hand compiled contacts from her last off Broadway show and gained a position as the second seat violin with an orchestra for a large Broadway show opening in November. She had no idea how long the show would last, but it was a big opportunity for her. Carl worked out the details for her. Originally, she had planned on moving back to North Carolina after graduation.

I took one more business class at nights to appease my father. It was an economics class. I struggled, but I did learn a lot. Most of my classes at Julliard were a breeze. It allowed me time to focus on my songwriting. I would call Scott now and again to bounce off some ideas, but he was taking more than a full load at Ohio State and didn't have much time to help me. So much for promises.

My goal became to play half of my own music while playing for an audience. Between lessons from school and Gordy's help over the summer, my ability to create music grew exponentially. I wrote about twenty originals in three months. I earned the highest grade in the music production class. We were required to write all the lead and rhythm sections as well as write several different styles of music.

My professor was impressed enough that he asked if he could send one of them to a friend of his in the industry. I assumed nothing would come from it, but I was pleased he thought that highly of my work.

A chill began to fill the autumn air when Carl called telling me to rush over to an audition for a four night a week job at a successful club in the city. I would be playing for an hour, early in the evening, but the timing was perfect for me. I had all morning classes other than my one night class, which was two subway stops from the club. I would have time to be to class on time. I auditioned and got the job.

It resided in the snobbish section of the city, where mostly Wall Street executives would go to kick back and have a beer and small dinner. Big money, but casual. My contract ran from November through the end of March. It meant I would only be home for three days around Christmas, but I had to start planning a future beyond living in a dorm and playing with second-rate bands.

One night in late January after my set, a young man approached me about joining their band on weekends. It had been a trio, but they lost their lead guitarist. He got married and his wife didn't want him out playing weekends. They played blues. Nothing more. He said they had been playing at the same place for a year, but had to find a lead guitarist within a month.

Never having played much blues in the past, I had to think about it. That was until he told me they played in front of a raucous crowd every Saturday and Sunday nights. My current gig was ok, but it didn't push me musically. I jumped at the opportunity.

Mark Simmons and Phil Glass played loud and took no prisoners. Out first practice together led to instant chemistry. Elise was working every weekend with the orchestra including two shows on Sundays, so she couldn't complain that I was now playing Tuesday through Sunday. I was lucky in that most of my classes that last semester were easy for me with little homework. I knew I was stretched thin, something I had fought against earlier in the school year. However, I needed to play in front of a rowdy crowd to keep me motivated.

I quickly learned several new songs. I had the best of both worlds. I could play my originals during the week and kick it up a notch on Saturday and Sunday with the blues band. Part of my deal with the blues band was that we performed at least one of my originals every night. I reworked a few to make them fit in with a more edgy blues feel. The other guys wanted to play some originals anyway. It worked well. I really enjoyed being a part of their band.

Mark was an overstuffed fella, who had been friends with a slimmer Phil since both were kids in upstate New York. They both graduated from City College in New York and worked during the week as stockbrokers. They enjoyed playing music, but also did well as brokers. They offered me a few tips, but my pockets were empty.

Mark's father was a lover of the blues. Mark grew up listening to it all the time. He had played in a high school band with Phil, so when they moved on to college they kept finding ways to play music. Both were competent players, but neither had the training that I had received in school. I think they both realized in short order that I was the polished musician in the band. I played longer solos and was front and center, even though Phil, our drummer, did most of the vocals. I sang a few numbers, including my personal songs. Mark would take lead vocals on one song a night. We all sang backups when needed, but really none of us would be mistaken for Howlin Wolf.

I graduated with honors in May of 1977. I think my parents were happy I graduated, but didn't like the fact that I didn't have what they considered a secure full time job. Granted, I really didn't know what I was going to be doing much longer, but the downtown club extended me through the summer and the blues band had their contract extended too.

After graduation, finding a place to live was a bitch. I had little money. Elise's Broadway show was a hit. She too needed a place to crash. We found a small apartment on the edge of the town and split the expenses. Between the two of us, we barely had enough to live, but we survived. We rarely saw each other except on Mondays and early in the afternoons. I was home before her most nights and did manage to go see her perform one evening. She never did get to see me perform, since she was doing eight performances a week and even more over the holidays.

As the summer heated up, Carl, who I hadn't heard from in week called. "Uhm, my idiot client songwriter, have you ever bothered to copyright your songs"?

I replied, "My over compensated manager and agent, how was I to know to do such a thing unless you told me."

He was not happy with my response, but I was starting to grow tired of Carl since as soon as he got his law license and downtown office, I became way down his list of his priorities. When I gave my songs to my professor, I had joked that if ever anything ever came from it all, he should just contact my agent. I must have given him Carl's card. Being young and stupid was no excuse for not taking my former professor seriously, or not paying attention of the section in class about the legal matters of music.

A small record label from the Los Angeles signed a new female singer from the west coast and they handed her two of my songs. They called Carl to see if they could use one or possibly two for her to record. Carl said I was very lucky that there was one honest person in the music industry, because they knew the songs did not have a copyright. However, knowing they came from my professor they wanted to do it legit. Carl applied for a copyright later that day.

However, the big news, they wanted me to fly to Los Angeles and see if I would work with her to write a few more songs. They would pay for all my expenses for two weeks, including a round trip plane ticket. I would get songwriting royalties if she used the songs on the album. Carl handled all that for me and to this day, I really don't know the agreement. I jumped on a plane without asking any questions.

CHAPTER NINE

Linda Sweet had an incredible voice, but the record label really didn't know how to position her in the market place. She had one album on another label with limited success. They tried to make her into a smooth jazz sounding singer, but she had a raw quality about her voice. Born in Southern California to an American father and Mexican mother, Linda was only nineteen when her first album hit the streets. The new record label wanted to give her one more shot at stardom before they cut her loose.

I had never seen a palm tree before except on television. I had never seen many things I saw in Los Angeles, some of which I didn't care to see again. Drugs were everywhere, including inside the recording studio. I got along well with Linda. She was a sweet girl, who I think just wanted to sing, but was pushed and pulled in many different directions by the record executives. I stayed my two weeks and we wrote three more songs that I felt fit her voice and style. We wrote more of an upbeat rock and roll song and one that was pure blues. I reworked the song they originally called me about, and all three ended up on the album.

The record people were unaware that I played guitar until I arrived. I ended up playing lead guitar on five tracks on the album. Carl negotiated an extra bonus for my playing. I think Carl was happy he was finally helping me like a real agent and I was happy I had someone, who I trusted to handle it all for me.

Despite learning basic business skills in college, I wanted to play music and write songs. I didn't want to worry about the business side of my career. I trusted Carl knew what he was doing.

Linda asked me to stay in Los Angeles longer, but the record label was only going to pay my expenses for the two weeks. Besides, within the two weeks, we had finished work on the three songs that were mine and the studio work they hired me for was complete.

Linda and I hit it off so well, she asked me to join her band. However, her manager stuck his nose in and told me, "I'll decided who Linda allows in her company."

He made me feel like garbage. I knew Linda wasn't thrilled she had turned over so many rights to others. I don't think I looked the part of who they wanted in a band anyway. While we were recording Linda's album, down the hall recording in another studio were, "The Eagles." They championed long hair, torn jeans and big mustaches. The big wigs envisioned the new, "California Look" for Linda. Mom would have disowned me if I wore jeans with holes in them and Dad never allowed my hair below my ears as a kid.

Linda was stuck in a bad contract. The record label owned everything about her, down to what she wore on stage. I felt bad for her. I gave her my number back in New York and we did call and talk after I returned home.

My weekday gig fired me for leaving with no notice. I can't blame em much, but I didn't have time to wait for them to find a replacement for two weeks. I realized the only job I had was the one on weekends. That wasn't going to cover my end of the bills. Elise realized it too. Upon my return home her first words were, "Now what are your plans my traveling roommate?"

I knew deep down she was upset I had to quit my job to go to Los Angeles, but she also knew working a club for an hour a night wasn't a long term career. I did have some money saved up, but I knew it would dwindle quickly if I didn't find a job.

Debby and Kevin gave me a call when I returned from California. They wanted to come to New York and hang out with me for a few days. They asked to stay in the apartment with Elise and me. It was not ideal, but I couldn't turn them away. I didn't have any work for another two weeks since the blues band had a one month break and Elise's Broadway show had a twelve day vacation as well. It was her first break in over a year. She had planned visiting her folks back home in North Carolina, but I convinced her to hang around with us for a couple of days before heading home.

Kevin was heading off to law school in the fall. Debby passed her test to be a licensed nurse in New Jersey. She had moved back in with her parents. Ugh. I think she wanted to get out of the house for a few days. We went to a few clubs at night and visited the museums during the day to keep Elise happy. There was a bit of tension between Elise and Debby. I realized it was the first time they had met. They knew about each other, but Debby was never in New York while Elise was in town and in the summers, Elise was either playing with her orchestra or home in North Carolina.

I realized Elise had only met my parents at graduation and the one weekend I dragged her to my house for Thanksgiving. I needed to do something with our visitors before it all exploded. I had practice later that day with the blues band and there was no way I was letting those three stay together, even for a short few hours. I talked them all into coming with me to practice.

Neither Elise nor Debby had seen the blues band and Kevin

had nothing else to do. I asked Elise to bring her violin. I had an idea lingering in my brain for months, but never had the time to see if it could work. About thirty minutes into the practice, I asked Debby to sing one of my originals that she and I had done for two years.

Mark and Phil were stunned at how well Debby fit in with the band. The look in Elise's eyes told me she was caught off guard too. I knew Debby singing would blow them away with one song. We had performed it many times. She did it so much better than Phil or me. I could see Elise squirming in her seat, anxiously waiting for me to ask her to join us. The master plan was in full effect. We did one more song with Debby on vocals, then I sheepishly with a Cheshire cat smile, asked Elise if she wanted play.

We jammed on a few songs that everyone knew. It sounded better than I had anticipated. I had wondered ever since I heard Elise play her instrument at home how Elise and I would sound in a band together. That was the first chance we had in all the years of knowing each other to play in the same group. I'm sure the other two in my group had no idea what my ultimate goal was in getting them all in the same room.

Kevin clapped from his seat, though he quipped how we needed keyboards. We had a 4-track recorder with us, since Mark and Phil would record us to see where would could improve. I asked them to record a few tunes. We played my original again, only this time with Elise playing violin.

I knew right off, we had the makings of a great band. I don't think anyone else was thinking in those terms. We went back and forth for maybe two hours showing off for each other and trying to find songs we could all play. I was thrilled my little experiment had paid off big time.

We got back to the apartment and I floated the idea that we should play together like that again before Elise left for North Carolina. "Don't get any ideas," Elise said. "I'm a classically trained musician and that's the way it will stay."

Debby just mumbled, "I didn't realize what we just played wasn't classic music."

I smiled and let the comment float in the air like a wounded butterfly.

I called Skunk to see if he knew of any keyboard players looking for a gig. Even if we didn't all get together again in that format, Kevin was right, a fat sounding organ would fill out the blues band.

I also called Carl and asked him to start thinking about finding a bigger home for the blues band. I went over to his office the next day and played him the tape. His eyes lit up like fireworks in early July.

I did convince everyone to play one more time as a group. By now, the other two knew I intended to ask Debby to join us on Saturdays. They didn't know I was starting to put out feelers for a keyboard player. To them, the blues band was a hobby. I needed it to be a professional band or I was going to find another outlet for my talent. Plus, I needed more money. A two nights a week fun band wasn't going to cut for me any longer.

Elise went home to North Carolina for a week and wanted me to come along, but I needed to find work. Kevin and Debby went home. I did ask Debby to think about playing with us until she found work. She agreed though, Mark and Phil put up a fuss. I threatened to walk if they kept objecting.

I had a long sit down with them and told them I needed them to start thinking about taking the band to the next level. Mark was happy with his life. He was moving up within his company and didn't want to commit to more, but Phil was open to playing to a larger crowd and more nights. I really liked those two. We mixed well as a band, but I hungered for more exposure and money.

We went back to playing at the club the next week. Debby came back and played on about ten songs the first weekend. She needed to learn more of our set, so it was a good way of slowly moving her into the band. I landed a gig filling in for a solo artist, who was on vacation for two weeks. I had Debby play with me on those nights as well. She was staying with Elise and I and that didn't make Elise very happy, but I really didn't care. I was intent on making a band and finding a new place to play.

I began to convince Debby that I could put a professional band together and find us steady work. She looked into taking the nurses exam in New York State. Now that I was playing with Debby on stage again, Elise stomped around the apartment for days. Elise needed to understand my desire to become a professional around town, not a weekend wannabee.

Elvis Presley passed away in August at his home in Graceland. Gordy hit a low. I had never heard in his voice so dejected over the phone. I went down to see him a couple of weeks later, but his depression hadn't faded. Gordy traveled to Graceland for a couple of days to pay his respects. His bond with Elvis was evident, but Gordy refused to expand. I only knew that for some reason he felt he owed all he had to Elvis Presley.

Junior Johnson called me the day after Labor Day in 1977. The funky delivery in his voice struck me right away. He was looking to play the blues again. He had recently toured for two years with a musical production of, 'Hair.' He knew Skunk from years ago and when Skunk contacted Junior, he called me up.

"Loookie here boss," he said. "I ain't looking to hook up with some suburban white boy band that never heard of Muddy Waters or Albert Collins. You boys gotta prove to Junior that you got the chops to play the blues before I'ze committing to anybody. You dig?"

I knew he was the missing ingredient to offer our band an edge. I assured him that we played hardcore blues, but we were also, "suburban white boys." He agreed to come over and practice with us for one session.

Mark nearly quit the band when he heard I had invited Junior. Mark hated change in the band. I'm sure he felt threatened knowing he had lost his grip on control of it too. Junior smoked on the eighty-eights. He was a tall black man from Mississippi, who was from the old school when it came to playing blues.

Mark was concerned Junior's age could become a factor. Junior claimed to be fifteen years older than Mark. To me, his playing had no age. The grey hair at the temples and lines on his face told me Junior either spent far too much time on the road or lied some about his age. It made no difference to me. After one song, I wanted him in our band.

He knew every song in our set better than we did. He was a pro's pro and I was shocked he would even considered playing with us. "I need to find my mojo again," he said. "The blues has a way of bringing you home. My mind needs a rest from the road and me fingers need to play some real music again."

I spoke with Junior about my plans to record one day. He gave me the same look my father gave me when I told him at graduation I would find a way to pay my way through music. I think he changed his mind after Debby showed up and wrapped her voice around a Big Mamma Thornton number.

Later in the session, I cut loose in an attempt to impress Junior. No doubt we were a better live band, since we fed off our audience. I knew I performed better live, but we put forth a solid effort. Our four member band expanded to five, however the club refused to raise our fee.

I got on the horn with Carl and told him if he didn't find us a bigger place to play, I would find another agent.

"Don't tell me how to do my job, asshole," he said. "You're welcome to find another agent any time you like."

I didn't want a new agent and he didn't want to lose his very first client, but I needed cash and fast.

The Elise and Debby feud continued. My two week job ended, so Debby went back home. It was obvious to me how much the band missed her, and how much I did as well. My relationship with Elise became strained, almost beyond repair. We had never talked about much more than the next day's job or her wanting to perform with the New York Philharmonic Orchestra.

My mission continued to be to create a professional band, find a larger audience and make our way into a recording studio. Elise had more on her mind than staying on Broadway. She wanted to know where our relationship was heading. I only wanted to know why Carl wasn't returning my daily calls.

Any commitment beyond my music at that point was a dead end discussion. I think she nudged me only because she wanted to determine how distant our relationship really had become. Marriage never entered my mind. I was broke, had no real job and most of the time walked around feeling sorry for myself.

No doubt, Elise wanted something more concrete than being roommates. I cared for her a great deal, but my entire focus centered on writing songs and making the band successful. We barely had enough money to pay the rent and buy food. We were in no position to get married, or start a family.

My problems mounted with a phone call the following day. "I quit," Matt said. "I don't like the direction where we're heading as a band," he added.

"You mean successful?" I asked. He realized it was now my band and I had designs to make the band much more than it was currently. He made constant excuses as to why he couldn't practice, even once a week. The exit of Matt made me worry about Phil since they had been best friends since childhood. However, Phil expressed his excitement in finding a larger audience for the band.

Replacing Matt was easy. I called Junior and he told of his friend Duke Bryant. Duke was an excellent bass player, who played with Junior off and on over the years. He had played the blues among other genres of music. The transition took two practice sessions.

I think Matt thought we would shut the band down, but even if Phil exited, I would have continued. I asked Debby back for the weekend. Duke was a competent singer, so he took over Matt's singing parts as well as the bass lines. Phil began to feel slighted because he was losing most of his singing duties, but he knew the other two were better. Even I was stronger vocally than Phil was. However, I wanted to play and not sing much, other than back up.

The band was tight. Musically the best it had ever sounded.

Junior and Duke were real pros, my confidence had grown to where I knew I could play with just about anyone and Phil was an average drummer. He wasn't as good as the rest of us a musician, but he could keep a steady beat. We were now ready to move forward as a band.

The missing piece was still Elise and her violin sound. I knew I could not ask her to quit a steady paying gig for a band that was still forming. Besides, we needed her pay check. However, my long-term goal was always to add her to the band.

As shy, reserved and respectful as she was of others, she for some reason became a music snob. I could never really put my finger on why. She was very good in her orchestra role, but when she let her hair down and played her instrument like a fiddle rather than a violin, the woman rocked.

She would always tease me, "Even your own father knows that if you can't play the 1812 Overture you are not truly a musician." I think she was only partially teasing me with her words.

I would always counter with, "That might be true, but I think Paul McCartney and the Beatles have sold more copies of Yesterday, and I can play that really well." I was never sure which had sold more copies, but it was the only comeback could unleash.

Carl gave me a call and told me that the Linda Sweet album was about to be released. They asked me to go out on the road for a fifteen stop promotional tour, mostly in the western part of the United States. He also said that if all went well, they would be adding more stops. I guess I had made a good impression with Linda and the record execs.

Linda made a huge fuss about me being the lead guitarist for the tour. The record label liked what I had done on the record and gave into her demands. It turned out that the manger, who was so against me joining the band in California, was the uncle of the original guitar player in the band. He remained Linda's manager despite the disagreement over the lineup of the band.

Linda later told me she wasn't happy with his guitar work or his songwriting style. She had threatened to find new management if he didn't back off as to decisions about her band. A favorable review ran in Rolling Stone magazine, so the record company wanted to keep Linda happy and get her on the road as fast as possible in support of the record.

Call me crazy; but I had momentum with my own band. Leaving them was something I had to think about, even if I was being handed almost everything I had ever wanted. I was loyal to my mates. I spoke with them. They understood. We decided to go our separate ways for sixty days. We would then see where we all were after that, but would keep in close contact.

Phil needed the break to concentrate on his day job as a stockbroker. Debby had started to work part time in a hospital. She asked for more hours once I gave her my news. Junior wanted to take a long vacation back to Mississippi to see his aged mother and Duke had offers to play in other bands. He was fine with it as well. Before we all disbanded, we made a few tracks that I took with me to California.

Elise said she needed a little break from me. I had to admit, we were getting on each other's nerves. I needed the money and Carl reminded me, "This is your shot, don't screw it all up." He always had a way with words, being a hotshot attorney and all.

I spent Christmas day at home with the family and took a

flight out the next day to Arizona. The record company had arranged for the band to do rehearsals in a converted ranch house. We had two weeks of rehearsals before hitting the road for sixteen stops in thirty-one days. At first, a few in the band didn't warm to me much since they were buds with the fired guitar player.

One night at dinner, Linda let them all know, "The tension stops immediately or you can get your asses on the next flight out too."

I was happy she did it, but I was hoping my playing abilities would have eventually won them over. The album came out just in time for the holidays and received favorable airplay.

By the time we hit the stage for the first time at the University of Arizona, the students knew some of the words to the songs, including mine. Talk about an ego trip. We headed out to Phoenix on a cramped tour bus, but I was on such a natural high that others were singing the words to my songs that I couldn't sleep. We stopped in Las Vegas and played at the Sahara, where none other than my dad's idol Frank Sinatra had played in recent years and the Beatles had stayed overnight.

I called Dad to let him know I had just played and stood on the same stage that Frank did, he mumbled, "When you can play the 1812 Overture on that stage let me know." He was miffed that I wasn't some middle management trainee for Sears and Roebucks. Mom was impressed.

The tour headed to Reno, then San Francisco, Seattle, Portland then back down to end with some stops in California. We ended at the Hollywood Bowl. By the time the tour ended, Linda's album was number twenty-two on the charts and climbing with her first single at number three on Billboards Top 40. The single was one of the songs we co-wrote earlier in the year. The second single was my song.

Before the tour ended, there was already talk of an east coast tour and the record label requested Linda to start on another record. Linda asked me to stay on and help her write more songs and be a part of her band full time. I knew I was stupid not to accept on the spot, but I wanted to regroup at home for a week and then let her know.

I told her I would assist in writing more songs with her no matter what I decided about the band. She was a bit hurt and disappointed with my response, but once I told her about my own personal goals of having my own band she understood. I did however, leave it with her that I was ninety percent sure I would go back on the road with her. Once we made our way back to Los Angeles, I passed along my tape of the blues band to the record labels executives.

I went back home for a few days to see the family and Gordy. They were pleased I had a taste of success with Linda. It can be so funny how just a tiny bit of success will change things. The restaurant that we lost the open mic night at a few years back called Debby and begged her to come and play one night while I was in town. After Linda's song started to climb the charts, the owner had been calling Debby to see if she could get me to play there again with her.

I think it was maybe a personal satisfaction thing for Debby, but she asked if I would do it for her. Her family and mine all came for a free dinner. I even talked Gordy into coming over for a free steak. Our fee included dinner for ten. I invited a couple of friends from the old neighborhood and even though we had only originally planned performing for an hour, we ended up playing for over two hours. I had a top 40 song on the charts with another one climbing. The restaurant filled every seat the entire night.

I went back to New York to see Elise and catch up with her. Her show was starting to slow down with ticket sales. It was obvious they would be closing in the near future. They were in negotiations to take the production on the road, but the orchestra was going to be much smaller. She wasn't sure she wanted to continue with the production or find another show. For the first time, I think she was a humbled with my current success and her possibly being unemployed.

CHAPTER TEN

Linda demanded an answer about my future with her band. I said yes, but only on the condition that my band could open up for her on at least three nights when the tour was in the New York area. She didn't take my request well, but agreed. We were no Lennon/McCartney songwriting duo, but we did have momentum with her new album now sitting at number ten on the charts and close to going gold. I used my advantage to get my band an audience.

Her first single topped off at number twelve and the single that I wrote was now at number three. The Bee Gees owned about every other position on the charts that year. Linda was growing into the leader of the band and taking more control over her career since the previous time I had seen her. I think a few hits will do that to people, or maybe she needed to mature. Either way, she was far more secure in who she was as a musician and leader of a band.

The east coast tour would begin in sixty days. Rehearsals and writing for the new album would start in thirty days. The record company wanted her next album out before Christmas. The calendar read February. I had a few songs ready to go, but I preferred to keep them for my own group.

My bandmates weren't ready to rehearse. Junior was in Mississippi with his mother, Duke was in the New York area working as a studio musician. Debby was at home and Phil hadn't touched his skins since I left town. I called them all and told them we had an opportunity to play a few gigs in front of 7,000 to 10,000 people a night, but we needed to put it all together quickly. I also told them I was working hard to get us a record deal.

Junior balked at returning to town, but I told him if something happened with his mother, we would understand if he had to split. Debby worked double shifts so she could come to New York and rehearse. I had written a few new songs and wanted to work them into our upcoming shows. I talked Elise into coming to one of our sessions on her off day to learn one of the songs with us.

Phil's playing had become subpar and disinterested until Duke gave him a talk about being a pro or moving on. I only had three weeks before heading back to Arizona for rehearsals with Linda. The club where the blues band played for years had us back for a weekend so we could work out some of the songs. Our set opening for Linda would include six songs. I demanded perfection on each one. I had made them each a promise that once this part of the tour finished with Linda, I would concentrate on our band. I doubt they believed me. However, it was the only way to get them all to commit to all the practice for three shows with little money involved for anyone.

While in town, I contacted Carl to find out why I had not received a penny from any royalties yet. "It's complicated," he said. "The record company has to make back all their expenses before you're paid a dime."

"The frigging album was a hit and my single has made it to number three on the Billboard Top 40. Don't tell me they didn't make any money," I yelled into the phone. We exchanged a few more not so pleasant remarks before I told him, "Make sure I don't get screwed on this next album or I'm not getting on the plane to record another one with Linda."

I also wanted to know how Yale Records liked the recording I had sent to Carl to pass along for me. "I didn't like the sound quality, so I didn't send it," he said.

I was pissed. Carl kept assuring me that my checks would come eventually and to be patient. Easy for him to say sitting in his New York gold and leather office. He didn't understand that I needed the royalty money to buy studio time. I had promised the band we would be in a studio one way or another after the next tour with Linda wrapped.

Because I was the one writing the songs, doing the promoting and struggling for the cash for studio time, I would name the band. For me there could only be one name, Dylan James and the 1812 Overture. I did give in slightly when they all griped.

"Sounds too classical sounding," Duke said. We settled on Dylan James and The Overture. None of them, except Debby, thought our new band would last beyond a few shows with Linda, but they didn't realize how hard I was working behind the scenes to be successful. I had grown from a nerdy pimple faced kid with braces to a polished musician, who took this all very serious. I was in command and earned their respect.

Linda Sweet's east coast tour started in Miami and worked its way to Tampa then up to Jacksonville and on to Atlanta before getting a few days off. Linda and I started to write the next album on the bus and on days off. We worked well together, but one thing was starting to bother me about her. The band smoked pot on the bus many times on the first leg of the tour, but had always kept it away from Linda and me.

On the second leg, she was now in the back with them at times and I suspected was having a love affair with the road manager. They were starting to be more open with it, despite my efforts to get her to focus on her music and career.

She was now a twenty-year old star in the making, with much to achieve. I had hoped she wouldn't toss it away for drugs and people who wanted to use her. I suspected it was more than just pot they were inhaling, but I really didn't want to get too involved. I had nightmares about my summer with the beach band and didn't want to repeat it.

We played mostly colleges and venues that held crowds of about seventy-five hundred fans, but in Atlanta, we were the opening act for the Grateful Dead. That was really an odd scene with people getting off buses, who would follow the Dead all over the country. I was in the parking lot getting some fresh air after the sound check and watched as "Dead Heads" would open up the bus doors and chickens and goats wandered off the bus along with half-dressed girls.

A longhaired, skeleton looking man, who also got off the bus, acted as if all the ladies were his personal harem. I watched as the man clapped his hands and three of the women began dancing without the aid of any music. I walked over and asked them what they were doing and they said, "Living life man. What are you doing?" I joined in until it was time to go back inside the venue.

Before the show, I was eating dinner with the rest of the band, when Bob Weir from the Dead joined us. I told him what had happened outside and he anointed me an official Dead Head. So. I have that going for me.

The tour weaved it's way through Tennessee and Kentucky before getting back to the east coast of North Carolina. The album had gone gold with three singles having made it to the Top 40 with the big stations in New York, Chicago and Philadelphia all playing it in heavy rotations. The record label wanted to push up the next album to the fall, but it was going to be difficult to get it recorded and tour at the same time.

We arrived in Baltimore with two days off. I met the band in New Jersey for a day of rehearsals before we were to play in Philadelphia later in the week. I had asked Duke to keep an eye on Phil for me to make sure he was practicing, but he still didn't have his chops on the new numbers. Either that or I was now used to a professional drummer. Phil admitted he was nervous, as was Debby, but the other two had done this before and were ready to perform.

Carl knew he had let me down. He had his dad call in a favor and would have someone from Yale Records come to our show in New York. I didn't dare tell Phil or Debby since I knew that would frighten them too much. I told the other two, so they would be mentally ready to perform for a New York audience. They each reminded me they were far more seasoned playing to large crowds in New York than I was.

We played well in Philly as Dylan James and the Overture, but not perfect. I was happy we still had another night to play before heading to New York. We had a tour date at Princeton University where my family got to come back stage. I ended up having to get twenty free tickets for people from my past. I think they were still stealing my lunch money.

The band played better, but not perfect. I needed perfection for the next night in New York. Playing doing double duty forced me focus harder. After the first night, Linda asked Debby if she would come on and sing back up on the songs she knew of mine.

Debby was thrilled. I wasn't sure if Linda did that as a favor to me, her attempt to steal Debby into Linda's band.

Two nights later, we were playing on a college campus on Long Island New York. On the off day, I practiced with the Overture. I let it slip that not only did we have someone from Yale coming to the show, but also someone from Linda's record company, who was there to see how our writing for the next album was coming along.

Phil freaked. I asked him to do his best and not to worry. Debby seemed much more at ease performing to larger crowds. Elise sat back stage and joined us for one song. The timing worked since it was a Monday night and her night off from the Broadway show.

I was happy to see her and I think she was happy to see me as well. We did four songs of mine and played two blues standards Phil had played for years to keep him confident. We opened with one of those. Debby stepped up her performance. Duke and Junior were rocks, solid pros. I will admit I had some extra adrenaline that night and maybe missed a note or two, but one song received a loud ovation and gave our band a taste of success.

Overall, I knew we could have done better with more practice time, but we performed a good set. After the show, the only two things the executive from Yale would say to me was "Nice show. Lose the drummer and why didn't you have the fiddle player on stage more?"

I told Elise what the man said. She sneered and said, "I am a violinist. It's too bad a record executive cannot see a difference."

We crammed on the bus and headed for one of the last shows in upstate New York. It was bittersweet to leave my band.

We got three hours out of the city when they turned the bus around. We woke up the next morning still in the city. I didn't know why. The lead singer for The Who's opening act had had an emergency appendectomy a few hours earlier.

Linda Sweet would open at Madison Square Garden for The Who. Phil's butterflies from the night before found my stomach. I would share a stage with some of rock and roll's all-time greats, including Pete Townsend of The Who. I noticed goosebumps on Linda's arm during the sound check. I wasn't the only one giving the moment a second thought.

I met Mr. Townsend back stage after their sound check. There was no way I would miss an opportunity he hear their sound check. I wasn't sure if we could stay and watch the show.

We were playing an afternoon show the next day in upstate New York. Mr. Townsend was very polite and offered ten minutes of his time to speak about his songwriting. He took great pride in his ability to deliver classic songs year after year. It was by far the highlight of the tour, other than playing with my own band.

We walked onto the stage to a half-full house. People were filing into their seats and most were not expecting us to be playing at all. There should have been no pressure, but this was my moment to shine. The tiny lights from the ushers putting people into their seats started to bother me, when I turned and saw Elise give me thumbs up off stage to my right. I knew I had to focus and show her and the Madison Square Garden audience I had arrived.

All I could think about was the time I was in the same spot Elise was standing watching Skunk rule the arena. My turn. I strummed the first bars to the hit song I had written. Linda belted out the vocals. People began to cheer. My moment had arrived.

When my solo came and that spot light hit me, I didn't care that people where there to see The Who and Pete Townsend do his famous windmill leap across the stage. I was going to make them talk about me the next day.

I went into a trance maybe like Skunk. My brain and fingers became one during my opening solo. I stared at a beautiful woman in the front row and pretended like I was only playing for her. That was when my eyes weren't closed. I had a habit of closing them when I would concentrate on a solo. I was no longer playing notes on the neck of my guitar. I was creating a melody like never before. My mind was nowhere but making sure, I was one with my Les Paul.

After our performance, I was cleaning the sweat off my guitar back stage. Mr. Townsend came up to me and told me that he heard part of our set and he that was impressed with my solos. I got on the phone and called Gordy. He laughed at me some and said, "Great, kid, but don't lose your soul over what others think of you." He loved to talk in riddles.

The tour ended. My concern over Linda intensified. She offered excuse after excuse as to why she would miss our scheduled time to sit and write together. She would wander off with people who I didn't recognize. I fought against my better judgement in calling the record label and keeping them informed. Looking back, it was a mistake in not alerting someone.

What we had written together sounded weak. I reworked them alone. We were supposed to be in the studio in two weeks. I went back home to finish the songs and spend time with Elise. She dragged me off to an opening at the museum. I didn't mind. I knew I had been away and needed to build our relationship again, if one still existed.

I also tried to contact my band mates. Junior was back in Mississippi attending to his mother's affairs. Her health was in deep decline. Phil claimed to be excited about getting into the studio, but I was not convinced. Debby immersed herself into her nursing job and even had a new boyfriend. Duke was back with his part time band waiting for me to make good on my word. Getting the album done without any delays with Linda became imperative.

When I arrived in Los Angeles to make the record, Linda was a mess. It was obvious she was into drugs in a big way. I was upset the record company ignored the problem and refused to offer her help. They too only wanted a finished product.

I tried talking with Linda, but she wanted no parts of my lectures about being a professional. The album became a giant nightmare for everyone. I spent hours with the producer over dubbing the tracks of her guitar with mine. Her work was sloppy.

Finally, a top record executive showed up and realized how far Linda had declined and promised to get Linda into rehab once we finished our work. I objected, wanting to get enter right away. "You don't get it, do you?" He asked. "There is too much money at stake here. Finish up and we will get her some help."

"Her life is at stake too," I said. "And far more important than a few tracks on a piece of vinyl."

After we each calmed down the following day, he pulled me aside and told me he was impressed with the songs I had done for the album. "Do you have any more ready to go," he asked.

"Some, however, they are reserved for The Overture." I had lived up to my obligations with Linda and wanted to concentrate on my own band. Besides, they were in no hurry to release my royalty checks and I had done everything expected of me. I felt I owed them nothing more.

He knew we were the opening act for Linda a few times, but had not heard any of the tracks. He assured me if I helped Linda finish the album, he would take a hard look at helping out The Overture. I became torn ethically. I wanted to stop with the recording process to get Linda help, however my priority had shifted to my own band. Everyone wanted this project completed, no one more than me.

"Dylan," he said, "Drugs are far more common than you know. I've had this experience with other entertainers. There's only so much we can do. Do what you can to finish up and I won't forget it."

We put the final touches on the album with Linda cleaning up long enough to finish her vocals. As promised, they told her she had to go to rehab or they would not release her album. Her career would be over. The rehab center refused to allow me to see her, so I flew back to New York. I called to check on her almost daily, but they wouldn't give out much information.

Carl contacted me a few days later with what he thought was his big news. I had received my first royalty check. I flew over to his office and found out it was for $312.50. I was ready to buy my downtown Manhattan apartment and I could barely pay my half of the rent with Elise.

I think the real reason why Carl to see me in person was because he had an offer from Mountain records to record in a studio. The executive had come through on his word. He wasn't promising a record deal, but did make it possible for us to go into a local recording studio in New York City. This was not just any studio, this was, "The Electric Lady Land Studio" made famous by

Jimi Hendrix.

There was one caveat to the offer. We had to use a new drummer at their choosing. He had done his homework on the band and heard that we needed a professional drummer. I was not happy and asked Carl to handle it.

"Get the new drummer or lose the deal, Stu. I know you're a loyal guy, but they're adamant on a new drummer. I asked Carl to contact Yale to see if they were interested in offering us a deal. He gave me the history lesson on Mountain Records. Mountain began as a jazz label and newer acts, which was how Linda started. However, the parent company was Yale Records.

Mountain forced my hand into informing Phil he was out of the recording, or wait to find another opportunity. Carl told me that he would tell Phil, however I knew that was my responsibility. I wasn't about to kick Phil out of the band while touring.

I called Gordy for advice. "Don't lose your soul over music, kid." I began to see what he meant.

As expected, Phil took it hard. I assured him that he was not out of the band and that I had seen the Grateful Dead play with two drummers. Maybe we could do that type of thing. My stomach twisted in knots over the decision to bring in a new drummer. I called the other band members with the good news. They weren't as excited as I had hoped, other than Duke. Junior's mother passed away. Debby loved her nursing career as much has her boyfriend.

I had to drive down to New Jersey to talk her into understanding this was what I had been working towards for us for years. She had been with me every step. She couldn't quit on me now. It took several weeks, but we finally all arranged our schedules to get in the studio. Elise's Broadway show had ended. I asked her to come and play on the tapes. She was very hesitant at first, but I convinced her she could stop at any time if she wanted.

Mountain sent over a drummer, who had played with some very successful country acts. He was hired to work with us in the studio and really didn't want to be a part of the band. I was happy with he didn't want to continue with us beyond the recording. It would diffuse later drama with Phil.

We had enough time in the studio to record five tracks for Mountain's review. I requested more time to polish the songs, but it was denied. It was now sit and wait yet again. I had to admit the new drummer enriched our sound. Duke and Junior always sounded professional in or out of the studio. Elise played on three of the tracks. Debby's voice was strong despite not singing for weeks. I think Elise was a bit more at ease around Debby since she had a boyfriend.

However, we had a new problem. Debby's boyfriend tagged along and didn't know when to back off. I didn't want to upset Debby since we had very limited time in the studio, but her beau kept telling her to take breaks and not strain her voice. Time for breaks, we didn't have.

Irving Altos was the executive at Mountain who made it all possible for The Overture to get studio time. I owed him one and he knew it. It didn't take him long to cash in when he called me and asked to return to California to work on two of the songs on Linda's album. She was out of rehab and seemed ready to restart her career. I was skeptical. Her road manager Dirk Kalen was still hanging around. His influence on her was never a positive one.

I hinted to Mr. Altos that Dirk might be an issue. "Relax, Dylan," he said, "We're keeping a close eye on him. Linda is a big investment." I wanted Dirk fired, but that was not my call, nor did I want to hurt Linda.

She had made it all possible for me to get my own career off the ground and I and I felt I owed her a great deal. We recorded three of the tracks over again with some minor changes to the lyrics. It made a positive difference. Linda wanted to get back on the road, but Mr. Altos would not schedule any more dates. Linda had to could prove that she was ready. She wasn't.

During my time back in Los Angeles, I spent a fair amount of time with Mr. Altos. He was old school, like my father. His handshake meant everything. He shared with me his philosophy on how to be a success in the music business as well as a person. I had grown to find out he was a man of integrity, despite my initial reactions when he wouldn't push Linda into rehab right away.

I think he was searching to find out more about me, and the goals I had for my own band and career. It was good that he took a personal interest in my music more than being a moneymaker for the company. I did tweak him about all the costs they tacked on the recording sessions before I could get some real money in royalties. He did his best to justify it. I now had an ally with power in the recording industry.

CHAPTER ELEVEN

Mountain agreed to put Dylan James and The Overture back in the studio to finish an album and release it on a limited basis. "Let's put out a single and put you in front of an audience and see how it all plays out," Mr. Altos said.

The thrill flowed through me faster than water over Niagara Falls. One problem, we needed a drummer. Mr. Altos would not agree to have Phil be the main drummer. However, he did agree to allow Phil to play some type of percussion on the tapes and have his name in the credits. I thought that was a fair compromise, but Phil remained upset.

Mountain allowed the band to audition a few drummers. After sending Mr. Altos a tape, we decided on a young drummer with little experience, but who blew us all away in the audition. The kid was a natural. Mr. Altos agreed the kid had talent.

Billy Nash was a brash twenty-one year old from the Chicago area. He came to New York to finish his degree at a local college. His father was a well-known drummer in the Chicago area for many years and knew his son wanted to get out of his shadow.

Billy lacked any discipline. We were a professional working band. We had to scold our newest member a few times for being late for rehearsals. Phil reminded me that he was always prompt. Billy would adjust or we would move on without him, no matter how much talent he possessed.

Elise lost it one day when Billy pinched her on the butt. "There is plenty more where that comes from, sweet thing," he told Elise. I almost stepped in, but after Billy got a knee in the midsection from Elise, I figured she had lived in the city long enough that she could handle herself quite well.

Our allotted time in the studio would be three weeks. We cut twelve songs with Mr. Altos picking nine for the album. He picked six original songs I wrote, one of which was on Linda's album, and three cover songs. Mr. Altos was pleased with the final product entitled, "First Time Heard." Our first album hit the stores for holiday shopping in 1979, mostly along the east coast. The band had an upbeat funky sound due to the influences of Junior and Duke along with the fiddle sound provided by Elise.

Because of our unusual sound, the record label didn't know how to classify us. The radio stations refused us airplay, since we didn't fit into anything they were used to playing. The Overture wasn't like the band "Kansas" with a violin player, nor did the sound resemble the, "E Street Band" who had Clarence with the sax. We were our own sound.

We started out playing college campuses in the area on weekends. Debby had to decide if she was going to make this her career now or not. She was still driving back and forth from New Jersey and changing her schedule to do it all. Her health declined with the lack of rest in between band duties and her full time job. Her boyfriend voiced his displeasure with me more than once. I didn't care about him. I knew Debby could do much better than that egotistical jerk.

Linda Sweet, "The Third Time is the Charm" was released about the same time as The Overture's first album. Linda's first single was met with mild success and a tour was being planned to promote the album. I hadn't spoken much with Linda in recent months, since I was busy with my own album.

"She's working her way back," Mr. Altos informed me. "It's a daily struggle to keep her clean." Soon after that phone call, I received another. Linda's tour hit a snag when she privately put herself back in rehab a second time. The second single entitled, "Mystery to Me" started high on the charts and pushed the Village People out of the way on its way to number one. As happy as I was to have written a number one song, I privately wished I had saved it for my own band.

However, the royalty checks cashed the same way, no matter who sang the song. More importantly, I proved to myself and to the record label that I could write hit songs. That was the second time an album that I wrote songs for had hit singles.

The success of my tracks on Linda's album convinced Mr. Altos to toss more dollars at promoting The Overture. College radio stations began playing our album cuts all around New York and New Jersey. I would do an in person interview in the afternoon or on the phone earlier in the week and we would play at that college the same weekend.

WNEW and WMMR, two rock and roll oriented stations in New York and Philadelphia started to give the band airplay. Once Linda's single hit number one and radio insiders figured out that I was the songwriter, The Overture benefited. Our tour expanded to fifteen cities along the east coast. Debby took a leave from her job for thirty days.

"You're chasing an empty dream with a bunch of no talent bums," Debby's non-supporting boyfriend told her. It led me to dismissing him from my path as much as possible.

Mountain soon released our album in markets along the west coast. It peaked at number eighty-four on the Billboard top 100. The band became popular in the Washington DC to New York corridor, which pushed sales. It was enough to get Mountain to commit to a second project. The band developed a cult following with college students along the east coast.

After our tour, I visited Linda. She was home from rehab for a second time. She finally distanced herself from the people who were only interested in keeping her high and latch on to her fame. She was now healthy enough to tour. A short tour was planned for the west coast.

I spoke with Mr. Altos about having The Overture be the opening act for Linda on the entire west coast tour. He agreed. It meant double duty for me again, but I was ready for it this time. Linda hired Debby as a backup singer and Junior played keyboards for Linda on a few songs as well.

Phil wasn't invited along for the west coast part of the tour. He had become a constant complainer and didn't attend any shows outside of the New York to Washington area. He never took any time from his stockbroker position. I did all I could to soothe Phil, but I knew our old bandmate Mark had poisoned Phil's thinking.

I kept my word with Phil. He played tambourine and congas on the album. He received full band payments for touring and band royalties. In my conscience, I felt I had done enough for him.

Before I left for the west coast for rehearsals with Linda's band, Elise told me she was going to accept an offer to be the violinist in another Broadway show. I flipped out. I really didn't understand why she would want to do that since we were getting along as a couple and the band was now coming together. We stayed up all night with a long conversation.

"I grew up with very little, Stu," she said. "When I play classical music, it takes me to a place and time where I feel like royalty and important."

"Money won't make you rich," I told her. "Having a relationship with your God, being true to yourself, loving others and being a good person will do all that."

"That's easier to say when you can put food on your table," she said.

We were doing fine financially. Royalty checks began to arrive and we put some cash in our pockets from the tours.

"When I dress up in a black gown and sit in the orchestra pit for a show, I feel like Cinderella at the ball," Elise said. "I'm no longer a poor girl the hills of North Carolina." She would be missed on tour, but she had to be who she was at heart.

We had two weeks to get ready for the tour with Linda and the band. Linda's singing and playing was uneven. Her mind wandered. We did our best to motivate her.

During the last three days of rehearsals with Linda, The Overture came out and joined us. Elise relented and made the trip while awaiting her show to begin rehearsals. I practiced with both bands for three days.

The size of the venues we would play had increased. The capacities reached fifteen thousand people. Dylan James and The Overture opened up with a forty- five minute set with the Linda Sweet Band playing a ninety-minute show. For the encore with Linda's band, the entire Overture band joined in and played a Beatles medley on the nights that the audience was extra supportive. We played part of the second side of Abbey Road.

Linda's third album turned Gold and headed for Platinum with four songs reaching the Top 40. My songwriting abilities were proven. The record label knew it. I began writing material for the second Overture album. I involved Elise and Duke in the process.

Duke Bryant was as much of a perfectionist as I was when it came to the sound of the band. He had become our musical director. I trusted his musical instincts. Even though he was an excellent bass guitar player, he was almost as good on the six-string guitar. He had written songs in the past with a former band and was excited to write again.

Duke grew up in New Orleans. His influences included Fats Domino and the Isley Brothers. His round face and gigantic smile reminded me of Fats. When I asked him why the bass guitar and not the piano he said, "The bass guitar was the only instrument the school had left when it was my chance to pick for the school band."

His other function in the band became to watch out for our drummer Billy. He had a habit of showing up five minutes before sound checks, with a new woman on his arm nightly. Billy was young and wild. He collected a new tattoo on his back or arms from each town we visited. Duke did what he could to make sure Billy hit his marks for the shows. Even though there was a song list on the floor next to him, many times I had to tell Billy the song before we started to keep him on cue.

This was the first time out west for Elise. When we had a rare off day, we would find any museum we could within one hundred miles. Not sure how she knew, but she could find something to see everywhere we stopped. I wanted to sleep all day, but at least for a few hours I would indulge her sense of history. It was my compromise to her since she came out west with us.

I will admit she found some good cowboy museums that were fun to see. Debby laughed at me and would always stay behind. Duke came once because we were trying to finish a song, but he stopped short of buying a cowboy hat and shirt for the concert. I did and wore that hat for both shows in Arizona. I tossed it into the crowd the second night. A gorgeous woman found us coming out of the arena after the show and had me autograph it for her. Elise made sure I never bought another hat.

The tour ended just in time. Linda refused to eat properly or stay on the routines her doctor had prescribed. The record company wanted her to tour Europe later in the year, but she needed to get well first. They also wanted to start working on the next album, but between her health and me wanting to put out the second Overture album, our time was short.

Mr. Altos knew my main goal was to make The Overture a success. Playing lead guitar and main songwriter for Linda allowed me the exposure to jump start my career, but my priorities were clearly with my own band.

Weeks later, our management arranged for The Overture to play shows in the Midwest to keep us busy while working on the new album. We played Chicago, Detroit, Cleveland, Cincinnati and a few other towns. While in Ohio, my old roommate Scott came to our show with his new wife. It was nice to see him again. I called him onstage to play piano on the song I had written with him many years ago. He wept. I wasn't sure if they were tears of joy or tears because he fouled up his part to bad, we had to turn down his microphone.

I told Scott, "The next time we're in town and you want free tickets, learn your song." We had dinner after the show with Scott and his wife and they gave Debby, Elise and I a tour of the town. Lucky for us, the museum had closed for the evening.

CHAPTER TWELVE

Dylan James and The Overture returned to the Lady Land Studios to record our second album, this time with an ample budget. Mountain allowed me to hire Linda's producer, who I became comfortable working with, because he knew the sound I wanted to create. Raised in the area, he had family residing near the studio. It gave him an excuse to visit his old home.

Phil came back for the first session since returning from the band's Midwest tour and started to whine about wanting more to do on the record. Our producer sent Phil packing with a warning to lose the drama or not return. Phil returned the next day with a better attitude, but had become a major headache. I came close to firing him from the band.

Elise had a friend of hers come in for a few days. We added a flute on two of the songs. The album sounded more polished than the first one. I think the songs we all had written were a bit more philosophical than my previous ones. I collaborated with Elise on two new ones and with Duke and Elise on two others. I wrote the others alone. I wrote one for Linda called, "Windy Days" though I never told anyone it was for her. It took us three months off and on in the studio and some final writing to finish it. I contacted Mr. Altos and he approved ten songs from the thirteen we recorded for the second release.

We had tour dates set up around the New York to Baltimore area since that was the largest pocket of a fan base. We were the headliners on college campuses and opened for acts in large arenas.

In my last ditch effort to please Phil, I allowed his new blues band with Matt to open up for The Overture when we were in the New York area. I was hoping that would mend fences with those two, but it seemed no matter what I did they were never happy. We played ten shows to put some money in our pockets. Elise skipped the tour to play with her production on Broadway.

Linda claimed to be ready for a European tour. I had made a promise to go out on with them one last time. We delayed the release of the Overture album until I returned from Europe. I wanted the band to hit the road upon its release. I flew out to California for rehearsals, but to me Linda was pale and lethargic most days.

She was distant with me and everyone else, but was drug free and sober. We had someone from the record label going on the road with us whose only job was keeping an eye on Linda when not onstage.

We opened up in Westminster at the Royal Albert Hall. I was afraid to move so that I didn't hurt anything. The building was a shrine to performers. The trip was complete for me after the first night of the tour. Thankfully, the tour was only fifteen stops throughout Europe ending in Rome because Linda's health was in steady decline. She could barely stand throughout the ninety minute set. I asked to have her checked for depression.

The European tour sold out every stop. Personally, I thought the second album was better, but the third one went platinum. The record label wanted another one, but when it was obvious Linda couldn't deliver another record in the near future, the label opted for a "Greatest Hits and Live with Linda Sweet" package to be released for the holidays. Another offering from Linda Sweet seemed unlikely.

Before leaving for Europe, time permitting, Elise suggested a couple of museums I check out. I went to one in Paris and later another in Rome. I was fascinated with the ruins in Rome and was thrilled we had two days in Rome before the concerts. While touring the ruins of the coliseum a long legged stark black haired beauty waltzed up next to me.

"Are you in the Linda Candy Band," she asked in broken English.

I smiled. "You mean Linda Sweet?"

"Yes. Sorry me English is not so good, no?"

I smiled back. "It's much better than my Italian. Si?" I said.

She let out a cute giggle. Finally, I thought someone appreciated my humor.

"Are you the Dylan man from The Overture, who plays the music with Linda?" The woman with the large green eyes asked.

Stunned someone recognized me in Rome; I could only utter one syllable. "Yes."

"So you are he? Si"? She asked again. I was still in shock.

"How did you recognize me?"

She rubbed her nose and stuffed her hands into her black jeans pockets. "My brother goes to school in New York. He sees you many times. Says you play good music. He sends me your music and a poster. I know you come to Roma. Mia amica knows hotel where band sleeps. She works at front desk. I follow you here. Ok? Si"? I no spy. Fan."

I was still unsure of it all. I was barely recognized in New York City, but Rome? I needed time digest it.

"So I show you the good places in Roma to see and not ones for tourists? Si?"

Lorenz and I spent the entire day touring Rome. We visited St. Peter's Cathedral in Vatican City along with the Piazza Navona. It was an area filled with cafes and restaurants with artists wandering all over offering to make a sketch of the two of us. We walked along all the famous streets for hours until my feet ached. We sat long enough for one of the artists to do a sketch of the two of us.

Lorenza was kind and very funny. I enjoyed our time together. She asked if we could do it again the next day. She offered take me to see other places away from the city. Still unsure of our meeting, I accepted anyway. She met me at the hotel with her tiny little car before daybreak and drove us to the Tuscany region.

We ended up in Florence with beauty I had never imagined seeing in my lifetime. The towns were built with architecture that I had never witnessed and people though incredibly nice to me, seemed like they were still living in a world that was only within their own line of sight. The natives didn't seem to have a care about anything or anyone outside of their personal paradise. We visited museums that I'm sure Elise would have loved to have seen. I felt a twinge of guilt while touring them with my new friend. The county side was nothing like I had ever seen in the Unites States. Sharing it with an incredible woman made it a day, I would never forget.

At day's end, she took me home to meet her family and have a real Italian home cooked meal. I could barely walk from the table from being so full from her mamma's cooking. There was chemistry between Lorenza and I that I wasn't sure I had with Elise. I was still a nerdy kid at heart and had never met many women over the years. Even while on tour, I shied away from the groupies or women hanging around the hotels attempting to meet up with the band.

This was a rare treat that someone was interested in me, and didn't want free tickets, or try to get me to introduce them to Linda. I don't think Lorenza once asked me about the band or music. She wanted to know what I enjoyed doing away from the band. She didn't ask what comes first, the melody or the lyrics. She seemed sincerely interested in only making me happy as some odd way of repayment for making her smile with my music.

As nice as it all was, I was still very cynical for two days waiting to find out her real motives. I hated feeling that way. All I could think about were my dying grandmother's words, "to be true" and Gordy's constant reminder, "not to let music steal my soul."

Had this business jaded me this much? Lorenza never asked, but I left her four front row seats for her and her family, who were so kind to me. I also invited them back stage for a few moments to meet the band. We exchanged telephone numbers and addresses and promised to keep in touch. After the show, the band hustled directly to the airport for an overnight flight back to the States.

On the way to the airport, rumors swirled that John Lennon was murdered in New York City. I refused to believe something like that could happen in the town where I resided. I had never met John, but I knew he lived a few blocks from me in the Dakota building. Sometimes I use to walk outside the front of his building hoping to meet him. I never saw him or Yoko.

It wasn't until we all got back to the States that I found out the rumors were true. I still refused to believe this could happen. How could anyone, who wrote songs about peace and love, be gunned down in cold blood? What had happened to our society? I went from being at my peak of happiness to one of my saddest days in an instant. It's interesting how life can change without notice.

After the tour, Linda asked me to come to California to write for the next album. I let her know how upset I was that we had the entire tour to work on it and she avoided me. I refused her request.

Promotion for The Overture album and another tour was on the horizon. Linda pretended as if she had no idea I even had another band. That only added to the tension between us.

I spoke with Mr. Altos and asked if he would have someone check on Linda medically. My gut told me something wasn't right. I had developed a trusting relationship with Mr. Altos. I wasn't alone with my concern. Everyone else in the band commented on how Linda wasn't herself. I went back to New Jersey to see my family and Gordy for a few days before heading back to New York.

Dylan James and The Overture, "Our Second Shot At It" was released in early 1981 and this time we had a full cross-country tour scheduled for six months. Phil went back to the blues band on weekends with Matt and was happy to do so. It saved me from having to tell Phil he wasn't coming on the road with us. We did allow them to open for us when in the New York area for two shows. I think they had finally realized I wanted a professional band and they were not either willing or good enough to take the leap.

The tour started in Vermont then Massachusetts before heading back to the New York area. Elise's show closed after two weeks. She joined the band on tour. We needed a few shows to get our sound back in stride. I got a note from the security guard in New York that Lorenza's brother was at the show and wanted to meet me. I agreed and even though I didn't have much time since I had to get on the bus, it was nice to have met him. I sent his family my regards and wished him well. Elise wanted to know how I knew him. I just said he was the brother of an old friend.

A few weeks into the tour, I got a call from Mr. Altos. "Linda has an issue surrounding her brain. We suspect that's why she acting odd."

"What? What type of brain disorder?" I asked.

"I can't remember the name of it. Trust me. She's getting the best of care. We have flown in the best specialist from John Hopkins to look at her. She's in stable condition and resting at home. I'll update once I know more."

I was deeply saddened, but knew she wasn't herself on the entire trip through Europe. I began to question how my God could allow things like to happen to people like Linda. She started out as beautiful nineteen-year old girl with huge dreams and when she achieved them, she couldn't enjoy the success. She was still in her early twenties, with so many years ahead of her, yet lost in her own mind. I barely performed in the show that night. I dedicated the entire night to her and when, "Windy Days" played, I cried on stage. I played that song like it was my last.

The tour hit a bump in Chicago after Billy found his way into a bar fight with some old friends the night before we were to play there in front of his home crowd. He broke his hand and was out for six weeks. We had to cancel two shows. I called Linda's drummer to fill in until Billy could heal up.

I did meet Billy's father. He struck me as nothing like Billy. He was very professional and actually thanked me for taking Billy off his hands.

"Thanks," I said. "However, I hired a two handed drummer, not this one handed son of yours." We got a chuckle over it. We both agreed Billy still had some growing up to do.

We left Billy behind in Chicago with his father to knock some sense into him. I knew I didn't want Billy in my sights. We still had more than half of the tour left and it took about three or four shows with our new drummer to feel comfortable again.

The album received good airplay across the country. The first single peaked at number 38 on the Billboard 100 with the second single in the wings. Elise and Debby were getting along much better and the tour was attracting a larger audience as the tour moved across the country.

I arranged for the band to visit the hometown or close enough for every band member to play in front of friends and family. We played in New Orleans during Mardi Gras for Duke. I had never seen so many women with bare chests in my entire life on one street. I made a promise to Duke that night that we would manage to make it back to New Orleans around Mardi Gras every time we could. I didn't like all the beads being thrown on stage at first, but I managed to pick up a few strands and keep them as reminders of our wild night in New Orleans.

We had four off days while the bus drove from New Orleans to San Diego for the second stage of the tour. I flew ahead to California to see Linda. She looked frail, but the doctors were having success getting her healthy. I visited with her for two days and even worked out the beginnings of a new song. We called it "A Beautiful Song."

She was under doctor's orders not to work too hard, so we mostly sat on the porch and relaxed. However, she seemed anxious to write again, which was a good sign.

Linda had given me my start. We were very close friends until she became ill. I owed her a huge debt. She had a caregiver, who was with her all the time. Linda's job became to heal and rest.

I didn't know until I arrived in California, but what I was told was her, brain disorder, had actually been a tumor that was removed with a ten hour surgery. Linda had lost some memory, but she was healing nicely. The prognosis was better than it had been a month before when I got the call that she was ill. Her smile had returned and she seemed at peace. We opened our shows with "Windy Days" every night of the tour from that day forward.

My body told me it needed rest. I had been on the road quite a bit over the previous two years. I had written songs for four albums and needed a mental holiday. While on the tour, I planned a nice trip to Hawaii with Elise. I tried to get the management company to let us end the tour Hawaii, but our sales didn't warrant a stop there.

While in Los Angeles, Linda came to see our show. Everyone greeted her with big hugs and large smiles. She only stayed about half of the show, but it was still nice to see her.

We were on a bill with Journey and Reo Speedwagon. Both were successful bands, but our sound differed from them. However, it exposed us to a new audience. We had one more show with them a week later at an outdoor show in Las Vegas. I only remember thinking why would the promoters make us play outdoors in a desert.

Since we were the first band to perform, we had to come on stage before the sun had set. I was sweating before the first solo had finished in front of a near empty crowd.

The tour ended in Seattle Washington with the album peaking at number eighteen on the charts, and one single making it inside the top ten. We ended up having four singles released with three making it inside the top 40. That was good enough to get another contract to record. This time Carl negotiated for two more albums, not one. We had a following on both coasts, though our main fan base lied in New York area along with a growing fan base in the south. I wasn't sure if it was because of the fiddle or exactly why, but we sold a lot of records in Georgia through Texas.

Elise and I headed off to Hawaii for ten days of relaxation on Waikiki Beach. We did all the tourist things and enjoyed time away from everyone.

"Look at that sunset, Stu. Wouldn't it be wonderful to be married with a sunset like that on a beach?"

"Be careful or our next album will be called, 'The beach is a hot place for a wedding.' My idea went down faster than the Titanic. She didn't appreciate my humor and let me know it. Our loud discussion overflowed into the streets of Honolulu. Maybe it was a good thing we didn't have a fan base there, since neither of us was recognized. However, her point hit home. She was at a time in her life when she wanted more than tour buses and recording studios. I cared for her very much. We had been together for many years. The time had arrived to determine our future as a couple.

Elise headed back to North Carolina for a few weeks with her family. I left for Los Angeles to meet with the record label about the future of The Overture, as well as the Linda Sweet Band. I worked with Linda's producer on the live recordings for her Greatest Hits and Live Songs release. Later in the week, I bopped over to see Linda.

She had made great strides since the last time I had seen her. She asked about writing for a new album. I let her know I was heading back home to write, then off to Europe for a vacation. After that, I'd be back in the studio with The Overture.

Letting her down wasn't an option. I told her I would start to writing down some concepts and mail them to her. I thought we could work that way until she was at full strength. I made a promise that when I got back from Europe, I would visit and see what she did with my initial ideas. From there we would try to finish a few songs.

"Ok, Dylan," she said. Her bottom lip almost hit the floor. However, after more yacking, she understood it would be months before any doctor would clear her to work full time. We had time to work on music. Besides, the Greatest Hits package would need time to run its cycle on the market.

I went back home to see the family and Gordy. Debby and I played a private party for an old friend of hers who turned thirty. It was hard to turn down favors for Debby since I had put her through a lot in the beginning, running back and forth trying to record, and rehearse while she worked as a nurse.

Her father wasn't happy to see me since he too was certain she was chasing an empty promise and her future was more secure in nursing. "She's a big girl, who made her own decisions, Mr. Fletcher," I said. "She's made more money in the past six months in six months on the road and royalties from the albums then she would have with years of nursing. Plus, she saw the country side."

My father busted my chops too, even though it was obvious I was having a lot of success as a musician. It was all starting to get very old, not having people see I could make in the music world. I reminded them all about something a teacher taught me as a kid when he said, "Chose a job you love and you will never work a day in your life."

I loved being a musician and felt that God had laid out a plan for my life and had given me the talent to live that life. I was at peace with who I was and what I was doing with my life. It bothered me when others told me that one day it would not be enough for me to survive.

My brother was an accountant with some big company and my sister had completed law school. To my father, my life was being wasted. That's one reason I stopped in to see Gordy so often. Even though I still didn't know all about his life, I knew he could relate somehow. Gordy looked worn to me.

"I've reduced the hours of the store," he said. "Business is down with all these big discount shops opening up in New York. People are running up there and picking up instruments after I spent hours in here with them teaching em about what is best for them. It's starting to wear on me. I'm thinking about charging consulting fees now. However, I'll stay here forever. This store was always my destiny."

I headed off to Italy to see Lorenza. I had called her to let her know I was going to be in her homeland and she told me that she could not take too much time off from work, but she wanted to see me again. She was my one salvation, who seemed to understand who I was with no pressure to change anything about me.

I convinced her to come with me to Venice and then to the Swiss Alps for a few days. Her dad voiced his displeasure. Young women did not travel with near strangers in his world. I had to respect his thinking and showed him reservations for two rooms on the trip.

The trip was only for four nights, but the tension her father and I flared. He was old school and some musician wasn't going to dirty his daughter. Lorenza was twenty-five. I left it up to her with no pressure. I stayed in her area for a few days trying to calm nerves.

Our chemistry came alive the moment we were together again. She rarely asked me about touring or my music. She tried to show me her country and make me laugh. On the drive back to her home from the Alps, she hit me with an awkward question. "Do you have lover at home, Dylan?"

Lying to her would have cut my heart out. I told her about Elise. "We had a big fight in Hawaii. She went home to her parents and I'm not sure where our relationship is heading."

Her silence during the remainder of the drive home said it all. I was falling in love with Lorenza and didn't know what to do about it. I suspected she felt the same.

I stayed in Rome for another week to spend more time with Lorenza, until her father kept pressing me about my intentions with his daughter. For a person who wrote words for a living, I had none for Lorenza or her father. My one escape in the world had dissolved into more people wanting commitments from me beyond music.

Leaving Italy and Lorenza shredded my guts. Finding women

with no strings attached would have been as simple as grabbing one outside our hotel doors on a nightly basis. That type of relationship was never for me. However, committing to either one of the two women in my life who I cared about seemed oddly foreign to me too.

Songs for the next Overture album popped in my brain in two weeks. I wrote ten songs almost instantly. Most were about loss and confusion over a lover. It got to the point where I had to call Duke and ask him to write an upbeat song or two for the album. I did however think about when I had met Pete Townsend. He spoke about conceptual writing like he did for "Tommy and "Qaudrophenia."

Loss would be the concept for the next record, despite the fact I hadn't lost anyone or anything in my life. However, it was the first time in my musical life that my personal emotions seeped into my writing. As odd as that was to me, in the past, most of my songs were about other people and their loss or happiness, rarely mine.

Duke passed along two songs that were really better suited for a Sly and Family Stone recording, but since we at times had that same sound, it was maybe a good idea to break up the album with one or two of his ideas. Elise too had written a song about her home while she was away. We had enough material to head back into the studio.

I flew to California for a week to see Linda before recording the next Overture album. She could still only work about two hours at a time before needing rest. Writing with her became a slow process. We did manage to write two songs and I wrote another on my own.

It became more and more obvious to me that she might

never be in the studio again. She claimed she was progressing and wanted to resume her career. I prayed she could recover enough to sing and record, however touring seemed very unlikely. She constantly talked about how much she missed the road and an audience.

It was not common knowledge in the industry that Linda had brain surgery. They had kept it as much as possible from the media. A press release only said that she had suffered from exhaustion and was taking a hiatus from recording and touring. The rumors were out there that she had brain cancer and was near death, but they did what they could to keep Linda from the spotlight.

While leaving Linda's home one day, a local newspaper writer cornered me. He asked about Linda's life and recovery. I told him how well she was doing and that I was in town to write with her again. Big mistake. The next day in the paper reported how Linda was working hard and that the new album near completion. My words were twisted. Lesson learned. Mr. Altos scolded me for stopping at all.

CHAPTER THIRTEEN

Dylan James and The Overture were back in the studio to record, "Love Songs and Other Stuff" with Billy back behind the skins. Another stern warning was issued, but no doubt, he barely heard a word. Billy would show up with his girlfriend of the day for the recordings before heading out on the town for the evening.

Elise asked questions about why I had to go to Europe alone and why letters from Italy were arriving at our apartment. I only offered vague responses. She made it well known that unless I became married to more than my music, she would find a new place to live.

Debby inched closer to marriage. She would arrive in time for her recording sessions, then head back to Jersey.

"My clock is ticking," Debby said. "I want to be a mother and wife. I'm not sure how much longer I want to be on the road away from home."

I wasn't thrilled with her attitude, but there wasn't much I could do about it. I had wild man Billy on one side and two women with biological clocks ticking like time bombs in my ear. I thought about asking Duke and Junior to fill out the band with their friends, but I knew that would change our sound completely.

Tim, our producer, suggested more strings and wind instruments on this album and even though it pushed us over budget, he was right. We added a saxophone and strings on a few of the tracks. We still had the raw sound of Elise on the violin, but the new instruments added a real richness to our sound. Junior assured me he could duplicate some of the sounds on the road. However, we decided to add another person, who could play several wind instruments for the tour to make it sound as close to the album as possible. They wouldn't be made a full member of the band, only tour with us.

Tim Dowdy had produced several successful albums. I had worked with him on Linda's albums as well as The Overture. He was originally from New York, but kicked around with some bands in the south, before finally settling in Southern California. He worked odd jobs in a recording studio and eventually worked his way into producing albums. Never seen without a cigarette in his mouth gave his voice a raspy sound.

The doctors tried to convince him to quit before he died of throat cancer. He never enjoyed anyone telling him how to live his life and certainly didn't like anyone not working hard in his studio. He was fortunate enough to have worked with George Martin, who had produced the Beatles and Alan Parsons for one year when the record company offered Tim a job in England.

You could tell where Tim's influences had come from when adding classical sounds to a recording. However, he also influenced with the raw country sound from the Deep South here in the States. He knew exactly what I was looking for and by the time we had finished recording the third album, he had nailed it. Everyone was excited with the finished product.

I knew it hit a home run with Mr. Altos too. For the first time, he was going to give our album a large promotion campaign. It meant all of us had to do radio interviews and even travel into the radio stations, but I was ready for the task. I was very proud of this album and wanted airplay on major radio stations all across the country.

We planned hitting the road for most of 1983. We kicked off the tour at The Bottom Line in New York City. It was an invitation only performance. We recorded it for a possible later release. Most of the executive big wigs brought their mistresses and girlfriends for a night out. Debby had eloped days before the tour started and wasn't focused to begin the tour.

Her husband would come and go from the tour as much as he could and still keep his job as an IRS agent. Just what we needed, someone counting every t-shirt we sold on tour. Debby got upset at me when I told her husband to leave band business alone. He was boring and slightly obnoxious. I had to dig at him somehow. Her new husband upset me hanging around and being negative all the time.

Elise commented about how this would be her last tour with the band. She wanted to go back to playing with an orchestra and was tired of being on the road. I told her she still had many more museums to visit and couldn't quit the band. She still never appreciated my attempts at humor.

I grew weary of listening to her complain about the road and how she wanted a family. I recognized this would be her last tour, unless I married her. I thought I could get her stay in the band as my wife. However, I'm sure she missed playing with an orchestra. I guess I was being selfish, but I didn't care.

The album flew up the charts. The first single went to number one three weeks after being released. The second one did the same. Not an empty seat was found when we came to town. The band had reached highs so few every reach. We added second shows in many cities. We were in huge demand. Elise and I couldn't walk the streets without being recognized. Debby was easy to spot with her red hair. She ended up wearing ball caps when outside of our hotels.

Elise and I could no longer visit museums without an autograph seeker stopping us. It changed how we conducted our daily lives. However, all the fame only encouraged Elise to want to quit the road. She was a very private and shy country girl and didn't like all the attention. We went from being the opening band in small halls to being the top bill in famous arenas across the country.

When the tour made its way through California, I stopped in to see Linda. Her improvement continued. She wanted to get back into the studio. She asked if I had more songs ready. Writing songs for her was the last thing on my mind.

"Linda, I can't get into the studio with you for months. Our tour has over thirty dates remaining and it's possible we're heading to Europe in the fall. I'm sorry to let you down, but I have to focus on my own music right now."

Linda had written a few songs on her own, but her best work came with collaboration. She wrote beautiful melodies, but her lyrics lagged behind. I told her that if she wrote out the music for what she had written, I would jot down some lyrics while on the road. I still had a great allegiance to her and did my best not to totally abandon her.

I called and spoke with Mr. Altos. He let me know that Linda had improved a great deal and there was a real possibility of her getting into the studio again. Her short-term memory had improved. She was able to remember lyrics from one day to the next. Something she wasn't able to do in our prior meeting.

As relieved as I was too hear the good news, I was also sad because I knew my days as her touring lead guitarist were done. I had too many responsibilities with my own band. Mr. Altos agreed. Linda and I had completed three songs and with the four she had given me, we had the making of her next album. Mr. Altos hired a songwriter to go and sit with Linda three days a week to finish writing the album. It removed a lot of pressure and guilt from me.

The tour felt endless. We played sixty-five shows in over fifty towns with only one short break in the middle of the tour. It was grueling. By the time it was over, we had a number one album with six songs making it to the Top 40, including one written by Elise and one by Duke. Both were thrilled to have written a Top 40 song.

Between Linda and The Overture, I had now written four number one singles and eight that had made its way into the Top 40. At the end of the tour, I bent a knee and thanked God for giving me the talents I had. I could never have imagined that I would have gone from a shy high school kid, to a shy guitar player and songwriter with that much success.

After touring the States, the band took a well-deserved month from the road. We would later head to Europe for our first visit as a band. Linda returned to the studio to work on her fourth album. I flew to California at the request of Linda and our producer Tim to lay down several guitar tracks. I really wanted to stay in New York and recharge my batteries, but I went for ten days as a favor to Linda and Tim. My work appeared on five tracks. Three of the songs I had written with Linda appeared on the album along with one I had written alone.

A tour was still beyond Linda's capacity. She would frequently forget the lyrics. The album was merely to put fresh music out and attempt to keep Linda Sweet in the public eye. It had been nice seeing her again. It was also a way of thanking Tim for all he did to shape The Overture's album into the monster platinum selling album it had become. Without many of his suggestions, there was no way that album would have been that successful, and I knew it.

I was looking forward to the European trip, since I had planned to see Lorenza. I had tried calling her a couple of times, but my calls went unreturned. I wasn't sure how I was going to spend time with her with Elise around, but I would worry about that later.

We started in Madrid, made our way into France and Germany before heading to Sweden. Later, we hit the Netherlands and Denmark. Next, would be London, before heading to Italy and end playing in Greece. It was a twelve-stop tour in less than a month's time.

It was easy to get Elise to come along since there were so many historic places for her to visit. She too was excited about playing The Royal Albert Hall. "You never did make it there with your orchestra. Don't worry. I'll bring you to all the finer places to play around the globe," I said. She still hated my humor.

While in Stockholm, we had a bit of trouble with Billy. We almost had to cancel our show. The night before the show, he was arrested and jailed. The chargers were for sexual battery. I woke up Carl back in the States. It was a giant mess and this time Billy was visibly shaken. We were on a foreign soil with little anyone could do to help.

After hours of interrogating Billy and his accuser, all charges were dropped. He had been out in a bar and had made advances with a young woman. However, there were no signs of abuse or any signs that any sexual activity had actually taken place. It's true she did go back to his hotel room with him, but he swore she left soon after and nothing at all happened between them. The hotel had cameras of the two of them entering the hotel and her leaving less than ten minutes later appearing exactly as when she arrived.

She later confessed that she really only wanted to meet Debby. The woman thought she could find Debby's room if she made it a far as Billy's room. Because Billy was too drunk to figure out it was a setup, she threatened to go to the police and claim he tried to rape her if he didn't take her to Debby's room. He refused and tossed out his accuser. She was foolish enough to attempt her ruse. It took about fifteen hours to find out she was making it all up as revenge.

Billy was finally scared enough to be more careful, at least while we were in Europe. He stayed in his hotel room the rest of the tour except when on stage. It was another reason why I tried so hard not to be in public alone with fans. You never knew what could happen on the road.

The tour finally landed in Rome. I snuck out to see Lorenza. She wasn't home, but her brother met me at the door. It was the same brother, who I had met in New York. He was aware of my calls, but was afraid to tell me the news. Their father had told Lorenza that he would never approve of her being with me. His word meant everything to her.

It wasn't that he didn't approve of me or my work. It was that he didn't like the idea that I would come and go from her life and leave her behind. He saw the pain that I had caused. I guess I was too selfish and driven to notice what I had done to her.

She had married and moved to the Venice area. Her brother

asked that I not contact her. Lorenza was aware the band stopped in Rome. She called and asked her brother not to tell me where she was living. She was trying to forget me and move on with her life.

Her brother handed me a small brown envelope with my named marked on the outside. When I opened it, there was no note, only a small charcoal sketch of the two of us made years earlier in the plaza. Pain hit me harder than a Nolan Ryan fastball. I teared up all the way back to the hotel. I had never felt loss like that before, except for when I had lost my grandmother. A vastly different type of pain. It was starting to hit me about how much I had lost in my personal life, while being driven to achieve musical stardom.

I took time to reflect before reaching the hotel. It wasn't about the stardom really. No, I don't think it was ever about becoming a star. It was about being true to who I was, like my grandmother had always told me. It was about doing what made me a better person, or so I thought. Yes, the money poured in. Yes, it was easy to have things I never thought I could have in a materialistic way. I owned several guitars and a nice shiny sports car back home.

I wanted my own personal peace and happiness. However, I realized every choice in In life comes with a cost and consequences. I really didn't have to suffer a loss in being emotionally connected with Elise and not Debby. Both remained close. In some respects, I was still as close with Debby as I was with Elise, despite Debby's marriage to her ever increasingly boorish husband.

Ever since the day, my dad paid Gordy to teach me that first scale; I was doing what I wanted to do. At times, it wasn't easy like my summer at the beach, or playing for little pay to drunken Wall Street Execs or the endless tours. However, I chose the life I was now living. I never regretted anything until the moment I found out I had lost Lorenza.

I left four tickets for her family at the ticket office in front of the arena. They went unused.

Our management had left several free days in and around near the end of the tour in Italy and Greece so that Elise could visit the historic sites. It was my way of thanking her for sticking with me through all the years. It also made me open my eyes to what a loyal partner she had been for over a decade. Here was a woman, who had given up her strongest desires to play in an orchestra, and I had never given much thought as to how much she sacrificed to stay near me. I needed to be more aware of the people around me.

After receiving the news about Lorenza in Italy, my body reacted poorly. Something was wrong, maybe nerves, stress, maybe I was just exhausted, but something wasn't right.

Elise and I were visiting the Acropolis in Athens when I stumbled to the ground. The heat was excessive. However, Elise thought it was more than the heat. She suggested I seek medical attention. We went to a hospital in Athens, where I sat in a small waiting room.

My blood pressure spiked. I had regular checkups before each tour, because when you tour Europe or certain countries, you have to have shots for diseases that maybe no longer exist in the States. I knew what my blood pressure should have been and mine was dangerously high. The doctor agreed. He wanted to hook a monitor on my heart to make sure I either had not had a heart attack or was not a candidate for one shortly.

Doc left me in the hands of a nurse, who did her best to hook the crazy wires across my chest. I started to feel worse. My head felt a watermelon sledgehammered by Gallagher.

The nurse kept fighting to get the tape to stick to my chest and kept pulling the chest hairs off every time she tried it. That only adding to the misery. Finally, she got it all hooked up correctly and turned on the machine.

The machine rattled. The nurse muttered in bad English. "Oh no, oh no, no, no, gud."

The thought of dying in a half painted room on foreign soil pulsated through my brain full of smashed watermelon. Sweat beaded across the nurse's forehead. Her hands began to shake. None of that calmed my shattered nerves.

The heavy set, bow legged nurse wobbled into the hallway screaming what sounded like Yiatpoc, bonoeia, though it was very hard to tell at that point the exact words. She screamed at the top of her lungs until finally the doctor came back in to the examining room.

I knew death could happen any second. I began confessing all my sins. The doctor read what the machine had spit out and proceeded to yell at the nurse in his best pissed off Greek doctor tone.

Now I was freaking out and rattling off my prayers in machine gun fashion. I'm praying to anyone who I thought would listen, including Zeus. I figured he was in earshot. The doctor in a calm tone, explained to me that they were having an issue with the heart machine. They were doing construction on the floor above and that was affecting the results on the machine.

The nurse was not aware of the machine problems. The print

out stated that I had died. I assured him I thought I was still alive, but he was the doctor. He didn't appreciate my humor either and made me wait an hour until the machine was working properly.

After examining the new results, the doc diagnosed me with heat exhaustion and high levels of stress. He gave me a few pills to lower my blood pressure until I could get back home and have a more thorough exam. I guess Asclepios the Greek God of medicine looked favorably on me that day. We finished the tour the next night and flew back home to the States for a long vacation, or so I thought.

The flight home was exhausting. I never could sleep on planes. However, the long flight offered me time to reflect on who I was as a person, who was in my life and what plans I might have in my future. I think God had sent me a wakeup call to reflect where my next journey would take me.

I was nowhere near ready to quit the music business, stop playing music or creating music. I came to realize there was a void in my life. I had never felt that until I had lost Lorenza. What would happen if I lost Elise? Would I feel the same loss? What would happen if I could no longer play music? What if Debby chose family life and quit the band?

I had always been so sure of my life and now on that long flight home and for several days later, I sat in my new Manhattan apartment and questioned it all.

Carl had become a successful agent and upper manager within his law firm. He was making them so much money they made him a partner. Not only did he represent me personally and the band, but many top professional athletes, television and movie stars as well as my old roomies mouthy soap opera drama queen. He had a holiday party and invited all his clients. Elise and I attended. The drama queen was there hoping to meet a movie producer and being as arrogant and divisive as I had remembered her in school. I called Scott to let him know just how lucky he was later in life with his lovely bride. He still defended her despite not seeing for a decade. Once again, proving love truly is blind or deaf.

Carl had taken care of my money. His firm had a financial management division that did investments on my behalf. A young hotshot broker named George McAdams had invested my funds in Disney, Coca Cola, IBM, Apple computers and several other stocks that did very well. He also talked me into investing in real estate by purchasing a Manhattan apartment overlooking the skyline of the city.

I had my family over for Christmas dinner and asked Dad if he thought that maybe I could pay my own bills yet. "Money does not make the man, son," he said as he walked into my kitchen.

I still didn't know what I had to do to prove to him that I could be successful as a musician. Both of my siblings were doing well and had families laying all over my new leather sofas. Dad still frowned upon my career choice, despite me having been on magazine covers and had a secure footing with my investments. At least my brother was happy with his Christmas gift. Carl arranged for me to get a signed Oakland Raiders football helmet from the era of when they had beaten my Miami Dolphins. I had gotten Mom and Dad front row seats to see Frank Sinatra and his only comment was, "That might be too close to enjoy the show."

"Really, Dad?"

Elise went to North Carolina to spend some time over the holidays with her family. I had promised to join them in a few days. I had more shopping to do before I left for the Carolinas. It was time to step up and ask her to marry me. I also needed to tell her that I would be ok if she hooked up with another orchestra and retired from the band. I searched high and low across New York City to find the perfect diamond ring and headed on down to Carolina.

CHAPTER FOURTEEN

When I arrived at the family farm, Elise had a surprise for me. "When we have a private moment, I'll tell you," she said with a large smile plastered across her face.

"The pig won the blue ribbon at the county fair?" I asked. The fact that the smile instantly disappeared told me that either I was wrong about the pig, or she still didn't appreciate my humor. I went with option two and remained quiet for several minutes.

Later, Elise told me she had a special place she wanted to take me. This time I kept my county fair jokes to myself. We drove to a site overlooking the Smokey Mountains. It was an impressive view as the mist dangled from the tips of the hills in the distance beyond a valley below our vantage point.

"Elise, I have something to talk with you about as well."

Before I could say another word, she blurted out, "I'm three months pregnant. I went to see the doctor just before I left New York because I was having what I thought was morning sickness."

"That's wonderful news. I thought it was my cooking making you sick," I said. I became convinced she really didn't appreciate my finely tuned humor as she punched me in the gut.

"Is that your only comment," she said wearing her evil stare.

I knew it wasn't the best way, but I decided to do my very best Sylvester Stallone imitation in the original Rocky movie.

"Well, if you don't have nuttin better to do, I thought maybe you wouldn't mind marrying me so much, especially now that you're all knocked up and your father owns a gun." Not quite like Stallone, but it was the best I could do while still looking at her glare. I wasn't that surprised by her news. I heard her in the bathroom several times a day puking her guts up, before she left for Christmas with her family.

"You, Mr. Songwriter," she said. "you have to do a Rocky imitation to ask me to marry you?"

"Well if it will help, we can get married on a hot sweaty beach," I said.

I'll never be sure if she was happy or wanted to toss me off the side of the mountain, but after an endless, "grrrr" and stare, she grabbed the ring and slammed it on her finger.

"It's about time you asked me, my daddy was cleaning his best shot gun this morning you know," Elise said.

We made the announcement about the wedding plans to her folks, but not the other news. I wanted her to wait until I was out of shotgun range until that bit of news dropped over the town.

A month later, we were married on St. Thomas in the Virgin Islands, on a hot sweaty beach. We remained there for a month long honeymoon. I flew my family to the island, as did Elise. We rented cottages for the two families and had a wonderful week with both families in town. Invitations were extended to the band as well as Mr. Altos, Linda, our producer Tim and a few friends from the past along with Scott and his wife. Mr. Altos made the wedding day, but left for New York the following day.

Linda came for the week. It meant a lot to both Elise and I since she rarely left her home. Someone from the media spied her and me sitting by the pool deck with pad and paper. A news story hit the papers that we were writing for her next album. We were writing, but not for a new album.

A big reason why she made the long journey was because MTV had an idea to do an acoustic set of videos and they wanted Linda to rework her songs. There was a possibility of a live album with the same songs as the videos. She wouldn't promise a full out release of an album. She did however, promise at least one new song along with a few older tunes reworked acoustically.

She didn't enjoy working with her new songwriting partner, so she came to St. Thomas to write a new song with me for the videos. Songs played acoustically was right in my sweet spot. She knew I would have a hard time turning down a chance to go back and reworking our old songs on acoustic guitar. She did however have to talk me into being in the videos, which meant more work while I had planned on being acquainted with my new furniture in my Manhattan apartment. However, I never was one to sit on the sofa for long, or turn down my dear friend Linda Sweet.

Older music showed up on tiny little silver platters called compact disks. All of us in the music business loved that since it meant our older albums would be released in a new format generating new sales of old music. I had to fly to Los Angeles to work with Tim to rework the old tapes for the new format. I spent another few week working with Linda reworking the songs and doing the videos scheduled for release later in the summer.

Our first child, a daughter was born in August of 1984. We named her Diana Anne after Diana Ross of the Supremes. Elise and I were living in New York, but we had planned to buy land in North Carolina, near her folk's farm.

Carl requested that I to take up residence in another state, though he preferred Florida for tax reasons. I wasn't going to move away from New York forever, but he was trying to save money on my tax return by taking up legal residence elsewhere. We chose North Carolina. Elise wanted to raise our daughter away from the big city.

Linda's acoustic videos were a huge hit on the network. We recorded a few more songs acoustically, which MTV later called, "Unplugged." The compact disk version, as well as vinyl were released with much success, even though Linda hadn't produced much music in the past few years. Her fourth album had been out for months. It reached number twenty-seven on the charts; however, the record company was disappointed with the sales figures. The new acoustic only album sold better than her previous album.

There was talk of Linda playing live shows in the California area, but I had no time to devote to sporadic concerts. I was a new father, a new husband and I had to get started on the next Overture album.

Elise was busy with our child, but did say she would record with the band. However, touring was out of the question. Junior began squawking about his cranky knees and bad back. He no longer wanted to go for longer than four months total on any tour. We were still considered a great live band, so to quit touring wasn't an option for me. Debby was now pregnant and wanted to shorten our tours too.

Gordy called me and asked me to come back to Jersey to see him if possible. Since I hadn't seen my family for a while, we made the trip down to Jersey to take the grandchild over to see my parents. I went over to see Gordy at the shop. He did his best to remind me of a time when he was getting me quality guitars that one day he would ask me for a favor.

At first, I didn't remember, but after a while, he convinced me that I had made him that promise. He wanted to know if I would play a concert with the entire band or in the least with Debby and myself and donate the proceeds to a veteran's group of his choosing. However, his name couldn't be associated at all. I agreed in an instant. He was thrilled and I called the management team to set up shows in New York and San Diego.

I talked it over with the band members and they all agreed, including Elise, to do the shows. Billy made a crude comment that had to do with a female soldier, but I ignored it and thanked him for his support. It was good to know he was back to his old self after being back in the States. Not.

Dylan James and The Overture, 'Back in Town' landed us back at Lady Land Studios. Tim wanted to expand the string sounds and make even more of a Sgt. Peppers sounding album, much to the delight of Elise. I was a bit unsure, but agreed to go along with it.

For the first time, I hadn't written all the songs in advance of going into the studio. I was writing some with Duke and Elise, and had written a couple before arriving for the first day. It was not going well. Maybe the time away had decreased my desire to succeed, or maybe I had run out of things to write.

For the first time, the songs were slow to come and I wasn't always pleased with what I had finished. There was a parade of string and wind musicians coming in and out of the sessions. Tim and I argued over our new sound. I think being a new dad had changed my priorities. My attention was divided between my family and working in the studio. Then it struck me, write about my new daughter. Write her a love song and stick it on the album. What better way to have strings and wind instruments, but a love song to your own child.

Within moments the words were flowing again, 'She cried a little and smiled a lot, my emotions I'd never fix, I told her I loved her but she didn't care, she was so young and so unaware.' The song, 'August Morn' was born.

I continued to struggle with Tim. He wanted the entire album to have an orchestral sound. I wanted a few songs that would hit you in the face with raw power. I had Duke and Billy on my side. Billy always wondered where his thirty-minute drum solo was going to be on the recordings. Debby, who was popping the buttons on her maternity dresses, sided with Tim and Elise and loved the softer sound for the album.

It took over four months and a scolding from Mr. Altos to wrap up the recordings. We had ten tracks. Seven pleased me. I wasn't happy, but the record company was screaming for new material. We wrapped it up and released what I considered an inferior project in the spring of 1985.

The tour had to wait. Debby gave birth to her first child and was in no condition to hit the road. We had a tour planned for the summer, but became and on again, then off again tour. We would hit five to seven cities before heading home for two or three weeks. It was the only way to appease Debby. Junior enjoyed the new touring schedule too. Junior had a new home in Mississippi and flew home every chance he could get.

A few days before we were to start the tour, Debby's husband called me. "Why does your band have to record and go on tour?"

I peeked behind the curtains for Alan Funt and the, 'Candid Camera' show. I was amazed at the question. After I refused to answer, he continued, "Can you all just put out old material and stop recording now?"

I banged the phone on the desk and shook my head for a moment before responding, "Is this a serious question? Why does a band have to make music?"

"Well yes. Let's face it. The Beatles haven't recorded or toured for years and they still sell records."

"Do you know any differences between us and The Beatles?" I asked.

"What do you mean?" Debby's irritating husband asked.

"Well for one," I said, "we are all still alive and we have yet to go our separate ways."

"It's very hard when Debby is away," he said.

"For you? Or for her? Does Debby know you are making this call?"

"No of course not," he said.

"I suggest you speak with her and get off my phone." My dislike for Debby's husband grew with each passing day.

Keeping my promise to Gordy, we played a show at Radio City Music Hall to start the tour with all the proceeds going to the Disabled Veterans Fund. Elise joined us for the show, even though we had hired a new violinist for the tour.

We played many of our past songs and sprinkled in a few new ones. We ended the show with John Lennon's, 'Imagine'. I told the audience, "Imagine a band that no longer made music or a world where we didn't fight wars. Unfortunately, I can't. Thank you to our troops for keeping us safe so that bands can continue to make music. Good night and God Bless America." I doubt Debby's idiot husband had a clue I was talking directly to him.

CHAPTER FIFTEEN

Our new violinist could have been confused for a model, and was a first rate musician. She played with the same fury as a hurricane ripping up beachfront property. Sasha Meronyanka defected from her homeland after playing with a Russian orchestra in New York. She said it was always her dream to play until her fingers bled from playing too fast and too much.

Classical music bored her. She wanted to come to the USA and play rock and roll. Be still my beating heart. I had someone who wanted to play her instrument the way Elise could, but never really would in concert. Sasha wanted to be front and center and perform solos. She also played alto sax and dreamed of being a star.

The record company didn't know what to do with Sasha when she showed up at their New York office soon after she defected and was granted asylum. Carl happened to be in the record company's office working on our next recording deal when Sahsa arrived. He knew Elise wanted off the road and called me. I auditioned and signed her for our tour the same day.

Almost immediately, during concerts, we picked up the tempo on a few of the older songs and I allowed Sahsa and Billy play off each other a couple of times a night. The crowd stood cheering every time they did it. We found the energy we had been missing while recording the last album.

I had to keep telling Elise that Sasha was only fair musician. She knew better. She read the clippings from Rolling Stone Magazine. Since it was a limited tour, I didn't want to add extra musicians on the road. The fact that she could play sax, helped us from not having to hire an extra musician. I would have instantly made her a full member of the band, but I wanted to allow some time to pass not to hurt Elise or the other band members.

We changed the song list some so that Debby didn't have to sing lead on every song for the tour. Duke sang one or two a night and I sang two of my older songs. We also let Billy sing, 'Yellow Submarine', before intermission.

Debby was still not back in peak form. Usually worried about the baby, who was back stage on the tour, she would sneak off stage while others sang. We tried to keep her engaged with the tour, yet not wear her out being a new mom and lead singer in a rock band. We had hired someone to care for her son, but Debby was still never far away.

Elise and our daughter moved to North Carolina with her parents while I was on tour. I joined them during breaks. On the first break, we looked for some land to build a house close to her parent's farm. I wanted to be closer to civilization, but I could always go back to New York to visit when I needed the comfort of concrete and faceless people.

One day while searching for land, we met an elderly white haired woman, who had been a real estate agent in town for over forty years. She gently reminded us of that fact every thirty seconds.

"I know where every stick in the county is and everything about everybody," she said. She showed us a gorgeous thirty-acre plot of land that overlooked the river. Trees lined the lot, except for a small clearing for a house. Electric and sewer system were foreign to the lot. Only one dirt road, which became an instant mud hole after every hard rain, circled our potential home site.

The land had remained in the hands of one family for three generations, the future tax value wouldn't be easy to determine. Few lots ever hit the market. I asked our agent, who claimed to know everything, what she thought the taxes would be, should we purchase the land.

"Well, sir," the lady with a southern tone, "since the land is priced over thirty-thousand dollars, I expect the taxes to be quite high."

I wondered how high could the taxes be. To our agent, the land was expensive, but for me, I could pay for the land after three weeks on tour. I looked at her as she took a step back and lowered her head.

"I'm embarrassed to say they might be as high as twenty-four dollars."

In my head, I was multiplying that per week. "So roughly twelve hundred a year then, not too bad," I said.

The poor woman began to fan herself with the sheet that had information on the properties we had looked at, "Oh, no, sir. The twenty-four dollars is for the entire year. We don't have high taxes round here."

I could only laugh. Elise hit me in the ribs because she thought I was being rude with my snicker. Everyone taxing authority had found their way into my pockets once the money started to roll in. Paying a small amount in taxes was good news. The tax comparison between an awesome swath of land in the mountains, versus a concrete box in Manhattan once again opened my eyes to the tax system.

Elise and I bought the land. She hired an architect to design a home in the clearing. I requested running water and electricity. Another shot the ribs from Elise came with my comment.

I did have my standards when it came to my home, but not my brother and father. They were hunters and since the mountain was full of wild turkey and deer, they were welcome to come and stay on the land. I told my dad and brother that they could pay us rent while they were in town, since there was no way someone who plays music could ever afford a place to go hunting. You would think that after thirty years, Dad would appreciate my every improving humor.

The album ran up the charts, but not as high as the last one. It went gold. We had two Top 40 hits. The one about my daughter, 'August Morn' reached number two. I was happy the album was selling as well as it had, since I was never pleased with the product. It's sound never grew on me. We played four songs from it on the tour, but we relied on material from the past, along with a few cover songs, for our roughly twenty-six song set on tour.

Sasha flashed signs of being a real crowd pleaser. I wanted to make sure she felt at home in our band. I wanted her to stay long term, since it appeared Elise wanted to be a mother and wife. She had even stopped auditioning for Broadway shows or any orchestra work. Motherhood had really changed her back to the shy country girl I had met in college.

The marketing boys came up with an idea to make a logo for our band. They called it branding. It would be a black silhouette of a violinist with a curvaceous look. I was fine with it, until I learned that the ball caps and shirts would only display the logo. Our band name wasn't featured anywhere.

My ego needed time to soothe. I spoke with Elise about the change. She wasn't happy that the violinist used as the logo wasn't her figure. The dropped name was secondary to her. We all have our priorities.

Debby grumbled, "Why is our logo fashioned after someone not even an official member of the band?" She had a point. Everyone had to swallow some ego and move on. Duke, Junior and Billy didn't care as long as their checks kept cashing from merchandise sales. In the end, it turned out to be a good idea. The ball caps were an instant success at the concerts as well as in selective stores. I had to pay for diapers and the excessive twenty-four dollar tax bill somehow.

I noticed a change in Debby's attitude during the second leg of our tour. Debby mentioned a few times how she looked fat and the boys in the front rows were now drooling all over Sasha and not Debby. She went home during the break, and went on a crash diet. She also a hired a personal trainer. I never said a word to her about that kind of thing, I only cared that she did her part on vocals.

Since Sasha defected just weeks before joining us and heading out on tour, she had no place to live. She temporarily had stayed with a friend of a friend while in New York. Once off the road, I invited her to our place in North Carolina. We rented a home near Elise's parents while our home was built. Sasha had never seen goats or pigs up close. It became a culture shock to me at how much she had never experienced. Touring with a rock and roll band across America was only a small slice of her new experiences.

Sasha Meronyanka spent her first twenty-four years in Moscow. Her talents allowed her to fly through the music programs in Moscow and wore the label of a prodigy. She mentioned that she had to leave her mother and father behind as well as an older sister. She wrote them often to let them know about her new experiences.

It worked out having her stay with us for the three-week break. It offered Elise time to get to know Sasha better and not make a fuss when I made her a full member of the band. Sasha would be on the next recordings, not Elise.

We stayed in North Carolina for half of the break until Sasha and I visited my parents for a few days. My brother wanted to meet Sasha. We then headed to New York to find her a place of her own. I contacted Carl about getting her a contract to be a formal member of the band. He was also helping her start the process of becoming an American citizen.

Sasha was anxious to become a United States citizen. It didn't take her long to become acclimated to our culture. We scheduled a stop in Tampa, Florida with a few off days around it, so she could visit Disney World in Orlando. I figured once you've ridden, 'Space Mountain' and wore mouse ears, you've experienced American culture.

We did the third leg of the tour on the west coast for four weeks. As promised, we ended in San Diego where we played a free concert on the navy base in San Diego for the midshipmen and families. I don't know how many they packed on the site, but the local authorities in San Diego wished we had played in the local stadium so they didn't have all the headaches of parking and traffic issues. Apparently, the navy miscalculated our popularity.

We stayed after the show for hour hours signing autographs and speaking with the men and women, who were about to ship out on a tour. Knowing how hard leaving families behind can be on people, we did what we could to make them know they were appreciated. Sasha and Debby were both a big hit with the single men. It made the end of the tour a memorable stop. It also was the perfect location for me to walk the beach and give thanks to my maker, who had given me so much.

The news of our San Diego trip pleased Gordy. The next time I saw him, Gordy threw off a genuine smile. Gordy smiled as often as solar eclipses. I didn't tell him, but we already had plans to do it again on the next tour. The band loved the idea of giving back. In fact, our stop made such an impression on me, I asked Carl to make contact with some of the army brass and arrange it so that I could take my acoustic guitar over to the local Veterans hospital and sit and play for the soldiers and staff. I don't know how many times I would later make visits, but every time Elise had a, 'honey do list,' I remembered I had planned a last minute visit to the hospital. While in New York, I would take Debby or sometimes Sasha along and give the veterans something to talk about around their Veteran's hospital.

During the last tour, we had changed up the set list more than usual so that Sasha and Billy could offer some incredible solos. We recorded a few of the shows for a future live album. I recognized that no one had an appetite to record other than Sasha. Putting out a live release, gave us time to get our lives settled before coming back with a strong effort.

I also wanted to give Debby time to be a mother and me a father. We all decided to take a year off as The Overture. Junior went back to Mississippi, Debby played mommy and Billy wanted to start his own band. I couldn't sit that long. I just couldn't. After three months of picking floor tiles and looking at color chips, in North Carolina, I came up with a new project.

I called Linda and told her I was heading out to California. I scooped up Sasha and Duke for the trip. We joined with Linda and a couple of studio musicians and we recorded an album of entirely old 1950's hits. We never used our own names on the album. The album hit the stores as, 'Ignoto' a new band rediscovering hits from the 1950's. Ignoto is a loose translation, meaning unknown in Italian.

The radio stations would run contests for listeners to see if they could figure out who all the band members were on the record. It was eight songs, sold at a discount price, but it sold over 100,000 copies. It kept us all busy for a few weeks and put Linda Sweet's name back in the public eye. Eventually, the main musicians were discovered. We had all come up with silly names. Me, I used my real name, but only my first and middle name, Stewart Patrick. Since so few knew my real name, and even Elise and Debby called me Dylan on the road, it worked. I was happy to spend a month with Linda and it gave Sasha some studio experience, as well as a few dollars in her pocket, while we were on break.

We talked about playing one show at the Hollywood Bowl on the day the album was released, but we were afraid we wouldn't sell any tickets since we didn't use any real names. While there, Linda asked if we could write together again. I promised I would make time in the future.

CHAPTER SIXTEEN

Elise became pregnant with our second child. It became imperative our home in North Carolina was finished. I didn't want to live in a cramped house any longer. Elise firebombed the idea of moving back to New York. Her due date was the same time the band would be back in the studio and later touring. Our year hiatus evaporated in a hurry.

My mother retired and wanted to come to North Carolina more often. I convinced her to come stay with Elise while I would be away. She agreed. Elise wasn't thrilled with the idea at first, but later realized an extra hand with Diana couldn't hurt.

The next few months, Elise and I went back and forth from New York and North Carolina until our house was completed. I made a real effort to write again and felt more comfortable working in New York. Duke infused some confidence back into my songwriting.

However, something felt wrong with my new music. Debby, Duke and Sasha joined us for dinner while in Manhattan. We concluded the lyrics were strong, but melodies needed work. I could always trust Duke to tell it to me straight. He was the first to speak up at dinner that I needed to improve the sound. That's when it occurred to me.

I asked Linda to join me on the east coast. Her doctor cleared her to travel, though she rarely left her home. Mr. Altos called me to let me know, Linda's doctor thought it was good for her to get away from California for a while. I really pushed her into joining me for an extended visit.

Linda Sweet came to New York for two months. She would visit museums with my pregnant wife. Neither had the energy to be out for more than a few hours, so it worked well. It also got Linda to break some of her routines.

Linda admitted the new sights and sound inspired her writing. Our creative juices churned like it hadn't in years. She pushed me. I pushed her. Duke joined in on a few sessions. Over the course of two months, we banged out fifteen songs new songs that made us proud.

I called our producer Tim and the rest of the band. The time had arrived to hit the studio. When they all arrived for the first session, I dropped the news on them that Linda was going to participate in the recordings. It made perfect sense for Linda and for me. Linda didn't have the pressure of being out in front, and it gave us each an excuse to record together again. The record label loved the idea.

I focused on returning to our old sound and making a very upbeat and fun sounding recording. Tim had other ideas. He still wanted to use orchestral sounds. I explained to Tim it would be my way this time, or I would find a new producer. We were going to make a high-energy release. Period. Tension filled the room like low hanging smoke in a barroom for several days. Tim came around to the idea. I reminded everyone that, Dylan James and The Overture was named that for a good reason. I was in control.

At first, I wasn't sure if Debby would be ok with the idea of having Linda sing some of the vocals. Not only was Debby happy, she encouraged Linda to not only perform on the recordings, but join us on tour later in the year.

Linda considered the idea after all the band members encouraged her to stay on for the entire session. We enjoyed a great group of people as musicians and great chemistry. Yes, Billy had his issues, but after trying to put together his own band and seeing what it was all about to lead a band, his attitude changed. I think he realized how good he had it being in a hit rock and roll band with few responsibilities.

Debby was thrilled to share singing duties with Linda. I never knew how close of a friendship they had developed over the years, until we that time in the studio. I think part of it was that Debby wanted to have another child and was looking for an excuse not to have so be in the studio every day. Her husband had gotten use to her being at home.

I begged Debby to time her pregnancy until near the end of the tour. I think Debby had it in the back of her mind, that if she got pregnant and needed to stop touring, Linda could fill in for her. However, there were no guarantees Linda could hold up for an entire tour. Besides, Linda hadn't agreed to doing a full tour, even if she only sang a few songs a night.

Adding Linda's voice and Sasha's fire, the band had a much more energetic sound than the last recording. The new recording pleased me a great deal. We sent a few demos to Mr. Altos. He agreed with my assessment. I knew we were about to deliver another hit record.

We didn't have to rush this time. The live album was in stores and selling well. We had earned the right to spend real time in the studio to create something that in the end everyone would be pleased to release. I wanted to tweak our fans a bit with the name of the record. My idea was to title it, 'Dylan James and the

Overture, Not Your Average 1950's Band'. No one seemed to like the idea but me. I pushed hard until I got the name. Had Linda not been with us, I might not have pushed so hard, but I wanted to play off the last recording Linda and I had made together.

Billy ripped into me. "Dude, we're creating a digital recording now and not an analog tape one. Stop calling it an album." To me they were still albums and always would be. Billy reminded me constantly that we used those new fangled apple computers that George McAdams had heavily invested my money. Billy was ahead of the technology curve.

The album or compact disk, if you prefer, took four months to record. Elise was ready to give birth to our second child and was back in North Carolina. She had moved into our home there, but I wanted her to deliver the baby in New York in case she delivered while I was in the studio. I lost and we stopped the sessions for two weeks. Our second daughter, Deborah Lynne, arrived in April of 1987. She was over eight pounds at birth and came out screaming with a yell reminiscent of Roger Daltry on, 'We Won't Get Fooled Again.' My mom stayed with Elise, while I rehearsed in New York with the band for the upcoming tour and the final touches on the new release.

The band seemed excited to hit the road again. We had been off the road for over a year. We added enough off days so Linda and Junior had time to rest between performances. Junior had kept it quiet from us. However, he had been diagnosed during our last tour with early stages of prostate cancer. That was a big reason why he was so tired on the last tour.

He believed the doctors had caught it early. With the year off, he had time to rest from the treatments. However, we still had to consider his health. Debby delivered the news that she was pregnant. I started to wonder why I had started a band with two females. With her news, the band had now lost one to motherhood with the other waning in her desire to continue touring.

I knew her husband was in her ear constantly, but Debby made a very nice living from the band. He lived off many of the benefits too. Her husband and I exchanged unpleasant comments pretty much every time we saw each other. I got along with almost everyone, except three people in my life. Billy Potts from my old beach band, my senior year roommate Craig, and now Debby's husband, who I refused to even recognize by name. The idiot had the nerve to drive around in his new Porsche that Debby bought him for Christmas, and criticized the way his wife made a living.

The tour ramped up at Trenton State College in New Jersey, not far from Debby's house. The band name wasn't on the ticket. The school billed it as a Fifties Night in a hall that held three thousand people. Tickets were handed out freely at the student center, two days before the show. We all wanted one night to warm up with the new lineup and this was an easy way to do it.

I gave my parents and family fifty tickets for their use or for friends as did Debby. I saw some old friends like Kevin, who I hadn't seen much of over the last few years as well as Gordy. He didn't have to drive far, so I called him in advance. I asked if he would come on stage and play the encore with the band. He played the lead on, 'Blue Suede Shoes.'

At first, he turned me down. Once I told him the next night we were playing Madison Square Garden and all the proceeds were going to the Veterans Group of his choosing; he couldn't refuse my request. He knew not only myself, but the entire band had given a lot to the Veterans and it was all started because I had made a simple promise to him many years ago.

The audience must have been in shock when we took the stage. You could hear crickets when we played the first song to a near empty room. By the time we started the third number, the place was standing room only. It didn't take long for the word to get out what was really going on in the hall. The crowd was just as stunned to see Linda Sweet playing rhythm guitar and singing lead vocals. Since the album hit the market that morning, it wasn't yet common knowledge that Linda was playing with The Overture. I prayed her association with the band would last longer than a few nights.

Gordy tore up the encore. I invited him to do it again the next night. He declined since he rarely strayed far from his home in Princeton. However, his smile after walking off stage told me all I needed to know if he thought it was worth it or not.

Word spread like wild fire that Linda had performed with us. The few tickets that had remained for our show at Madison Square Garden sold out. The band busted with energy. It was the beginning of new tour and Sasha had never played inside the Garden.

She had been looking forward to it for months. She had a one of a kind, skintight red, white and blue latex costume made only for that show. She filled it perfectly. Linda was excited just to be back on stage. Nervous, however, within the first few songs she had calmed down. Debby sang lead on the first three songs to give Linda time to adjust to the sold out crowd.

When Linda sang the first single off our album, the place erupted. I knew we had a successful tour coming up if Linda could hang in there for the long haul. Towards the end of the show,

Linda came over and said "I had no idea how much I've missed this rush until now. Thank you."

We played for well over two hours with three encores. This time I welcomed Skunk Baxter to play the lead on 'Blue Suede Shoes.' Gordy had called Skunk that morning to tell Skunk that Gordy had performed on stage with us. Skunk contacted me and asked if he could do that same. I jumped at the chance of having him perform with us.

The New York media gave the concert rave reviews and said that the band had never sounded better. Sasha's profile plastered across the local papers the next day. We all accepted that her image had become our visual identity.

The album flew off the shelves. Radio stations made it sound as if Linda had joined the band permanently. Our press agent had to release a statement letting everyone know that Linda was only a temporary member of the tour. There was no guarantee on any given night she would be performing with the band. We didn't want to mislead the public. After that night, Linda wanted to finish the tour, but no one really knew if she would have the stamina from night to night.

We had a night off, before heading on into Boston, to play outdoors at the Boston Commons. I was a little concerned playing outside in the heat, but it wasn't the desert. We played to another sold out show with thousands sitting outside the venue in the park. Linda and Debby started to work together better and Sasha wore a green Boston Celtics jump suit for the show.

Sasha understood marketing. Her image highlighted the papers in every town we entered. The rest of us counted the proceeds as another thousand caps flew off the sales shelves. The tour took us to Montreal Canada for the first time. We had a bit of a hassle when Billy's arrest report showed from years ago. We played two shows in Canada before taking a week off and starting up again in Philadelphia.

Linda Sweet had become a walking contradiction in life. She was still young and successful on many levels, yet seemed lifeless at times. She was young in age, yet the drug addiction and brain surgery had sapped much of her youth. She loved to entertain, yet claimed she no longer had the energy to perform, even though her doctors told her there was little reason why she couldn't function at a high level. She was a very passionate and loving person, but shut most people from her life.

The only person she claimed to have loved; got her addicted to heroin and stole much of her money. Linda built a wall around herself after the addiction. Trust became a huge issue for her. Who could blame her? She trusted me, but mostly as her writing partner. We were friends, yet didn't share real personal experiences, unless it was in a song. Our relationship with each other was on display in our music, yet in some regards Linda and I were strangers with each other.

She told me about five stops into the tour, she wanted to finish it, yet she missed her home in California. She wavered back and forth after each stop if she would play the following show. I would get frustrated, but Mr. Altos told me that it was possibly effects from the surgery. I did my best to be patient, but much of my patience was lost on being a father and leader of a band.

I had little time now for people who wanted to bring negativity to my life, or my band. We were successful in my mind, because everyone in the band wanted the same thing. We all wanted to make great music free from the trappings of the music business. A near impossible task, but we tried.

One trapping I refused to tolerate was drugs in and around the band. Even smoking one joint by a roadie led to their immediate expulsion. Everyone when hired, signed a paper designed by Carl, outlining all the rules surrounding the band. I considered people who used drugs, to be weak minded. I wouldn't stand for it, even in a small way.

I never forced my religious beliefs on anyone, including my own wife. I always believed that your relationship with your God was a personal matter. However, if someone asked me about my views in an interview, I would share my perspective. I never claimed to be the easiest person to work for, but I expected lofty goals from everyone around me. No one was going to stop my pursuit of the perfect band and song.

One day Linda and I were overlooking a calm ocean in Ft. Lauderdale. We had a show scheduled for the following day at the Hollywood Sportatorium. "I've seen you pray before shows, Dylan. I know you believe in God. Look at me. I'm a decent person, yet so much pain has come into my life. Why should I believe in God?"

"Look out at the vast ocean," I said. "Smell the salt air. Look at the palm trees swaying in the breeze. Pay close attention to the small children playing in the surf with their parents not far away. Listen to the sea birds talking with each other. Did you create all that's around us?

Linda giggled. "You know I didn't and neither did you."

"Then who or what did?" I asked. "Whoever or whatever did, that's who I pray to when I speak with my God." We sat quietly for hours listening and sharing in the nature that surrounded us.

The conversation I had with Linda that afternoon, allowed me to reflect on my life. I had a wife and two little healthy girls, a home in two places and career that seemed to still be on the rise. I worked with people I could trust and respect. Even Dad was coming around to the fact that I could not only care for myself, but provide for a family with music as a career. Elise's family treated me as blood and cared for my wife and kids when while I was on the road.

Many blessings were bestowed upon my family and myself. I lived a blessed life, but I felt earned my position. I worked hard. I stayed true to myself. I lived what I thought was a good Christian life and felt like all was a byproduct of living that way. I had inner peace.

The album and tour were wildly successful. We played in sold out arenas every night. The album was number one on the rock charts as well as the country charts. Linda and Debby had become great friends and enjoyed sharing the singing spotlight as much as Billy and Sasha shared solo spotlights.

I took my turn at solos as well, but we all seemed to understand our place in the band. Once it became apparent that Linda was staying on throughout the tour, we added a three-song set after the intermission. Linda and I came out and played her biggest songs acoustically, like we had done for MTV. Then she would take a breather backstage while Sasha had her time in the spotlight with Debby singing. We timed the show so that Debby and Linda could rest during the nearly three-hour show with one fifteen minute break.

We toured for the better part of seven months, with a few breaks scattered throughout the tour. We traveled to cities we had not visited previously, like San Antonio, Portland, and Lincoln, Nebraska.

We ended the tour in San Diego the same way as the last

tour, only this time our show was in the football stadium. All the tickets were allocated to the US Government to distribute to the local naval base as well as veterans in the area. The idea had caught on so well, that other bands wanted to be on the bill. It became an all-day event with The Overture closing out the night. Another chapter in my life ended when I walked along the beach and I thanked God for all my many blessings.

CHAPTER SEVENTEEN

The band members went their separate ways for a month, to reenergize before our scheduled stops in Australia and Japan. I headed back to North Carolina for a family reunion. They were with us on parts of the tour closer to home, but they didn't come with us during the west coast swing. I hadn't seen them in over a month.

Kids grow so fast at a tender age. I felt like I had missed out on something I could never get back from being on the road so long. I had two families. My band family, as well as my wife and kids. Elise understood. She had experienced it, but she would only be happy once the upcoming Australian tour would be complete and I could return home and play husband and dad for a while.

The tour of Australia would be short. However, it was long plane rides. It wasn't until a week before leaving that Linda agreed to participate. She had always wanted to visit that part of the world.

Our larger issue was Debby. Being near the end of her pregnancy, her doctor highly recommended she skip the tour. We had to make a decision to either cancel the tour or find a replacement for Debby. Since Linda was on board and it was only for seven stops between Australia and Japan, we found a replacement singer who looked and sounded enough like Debby.

Debby's fill in had played in the band we used as our opening act for half of our tour, so she was familiar with our songs. I also wanted to have an ace in the hole, just in case Debby decided not to return after her second child. We changed the set list to include a few more of Linda's songs. Since she had never toured that part of the world, it seemed appropriate and put less pressure on Debby's replacement.

It revived Linda's sales down under and in Japan. Despite being a short trip, it became a profitable one for Linda and my songwriting royalties. The tour ended in Osaka Japan, where I found an ancient site called, The Fujii-dera temple. I once again counted my blessings at the base of the temple, which had become my custom to end a tour. I wanted to give thanks for all I had.

Upon returning to North Carolina, it was turkey season in the area. My dad and brother were in town visiting with Elise and the kids. Mom was there I think to make sure the other two didn't upset Elise. We had a houseful. It was nice to see them, but I wanted to relax and see my wife and kids. They stayed a few days before heading home. Elise showed a great deal of patience with a full house. I think she did it because for many recent holidays, we had spent them with her parents. She knew I was very good to her parents. I think she knew enough to put up with dirty boot prints in the front door way for a few days.

Debby had her second child before I returned from Japan. My family and I drove up to Jersey to see her and the baby. Debby gave me the honor of being the child's Godfather. They named the child Michael Dylan, after her husband, who's name I never cared to know, and of course yours truly. Her husband put up a fight about the name and myself named Godfather, but it was Debby's child too. I brought my best behavior to the Christening, even though Kevin was there trying to egg me on to get into an argument with Debby's husband. I paid for the dinner party after the baptism. I think that soothed ole' Michael just a bit. Getting him to spend money was more difficult than hearing Sinatra sing a sour note.

We headed up to New York for a few days. I had some business with Carl and Mr. Altos. I wanted to see them both. While in town, Carl and I had lunch at the same restaurant where I played years ago. It was funny how I recognized a few of the faces in the crowd, though no one recognized me, which was perfectly fine. They had some poor struggling kid playing piano. After lunch, I introduced myself to the pianist and told him I had started on that same stage. He was a student at Julliard. It brought a smile to his face and mine.

During lunch, Carl told me that the Veterans Group that we had donated to many times with our concerts, wanted to give the band, 'The Freedom Commendation Award' offered from the Secretary of the Army. It was a nice gesture, but I declined. "We're not in this for awards," I said. "Only in a small way to give something back to our community."

"No way, pal," Carl said. "It would be a great insult if you say no. Show up. Smile with your plaque. Take the photo and go back to North Carolina."

The band agreed we should accept, but only Sasha and Duke wanted to go with me and pick up the plaque. Junior's health issues had returned. Debby wanted to be a mommy. Billy was getting his band back together and was going into the studio to record. He said he would come depending on his recording schedule.

I called Gordy to get his take since it all started with a favor for him. "Go smile and get the hell out of Dodge," he said. He knew we weren't looking for credit, but it was a nice gesture to offer the award. The date was set for two months later in Washington D.C.

We now had at least six months off from recording and touring. I planned to do nothing, but stay at home in North Carolina and be a dad and husband. I again peered at my life and realized that even though I was still in my early thirties, I was blessed with so much. I was looking forward to what else God had planned for me.

I realized the band might need some changes. Junior talked about retiring during the tour of the Far East. Debby claimed she didn't want to hear the word band anytime soon. Her husband told her that if she didn't stay home for at least a year, he would leave her. I was furious when I heard, but it was her life. I knew deep down I had to stay out of her married life.

I had to spend my time off wisely with my daughters. I had never changed a diaper. I had never been alone with my daughters. Elise asked for some, "me time" one day to get her hair and nails done. She left me alone not having a clue what to do. I was more petrified being alone with my own children for a few hours, then I ever was standing on a stage with fifty thousand sets of eyes staring back at me.

I didn't want to have to call Elise's mother, who was only ten minutes away to come and help. Nor did I want to call my own mother for advice. I was sure Elise's sudden request to be away for a day was a payback for when I told her that she didn't have nearly the pressure on her to perform day in and day out, like I did in my career. I understood the snarl and it only took one dirty diaper.

At first, I figured the dirty diaper could wait until mommy

came home. Then the thunderous noise hit me like an AC/DC concert and it was coming from one small child. I had no choice, but to do something. Besides, the wrath from Elise would have been even louder had I not tried to soothe my child. It began to upset my older daughter. It was time to be brave.

I gently lifted her from the crib and laid her on the changing table. Her poor eyes were the size of marshmallows from all the crying. I was now feeling bad for not trying sooner. Even at a young age, the female sex knows how to put a guilt trip on the male variety. I slowly pulled the tape from the sides of the diaper. How could one little girl create a smell worse than fish guts baking in the sun?

I glanced quickly to see if Elise had a gas mask nearby. None was in visual contact, something I thought we should alter. I cleaned her off with the messy diaper before finding a tin of wipes. I used half the box wiping her backside. With my other daughter watching wide-eyed, I managed to tape on a fresh diaper on my youngest. Eventually, the scream that I don't even think a mother could love, ceased. I managed to make it to the kitchen with the two of them in tow and found a juice box Diana and a bottle for Deborah. We all sat on the sofa and watched some purple dinosaur sing to my daughters about love and peace. I thought calling the station manager to see if John Lennon had been reincarnated singing about peace, but I knew they wouldn't appreciate my humor.

When Elise arrived home with a few shopping bags and her newly styled hair, the three of us had one eye open and one eye on that purple creature on the television. It was the first time I had started to bond with my own children. It felt good.

"How did it all go", Elise asked.

"Piece of cake," I said. Elise didn't need to know that I had been in sheer panic mode while she was away. I took her out to a fancy dinner later that week to let her know what a good mother I thought she was and bought her a new necklace. I knew she wanted the acknowledgment more than a necklace, but it made me feel less guilty that I had not told her for many months how much she was appreciated and loved.

The next several weeks, I stayed in North Carolina, which was the longest I had been in one place in years. I spent time learning about how to be a dad and husband and tried to become part of the community. Elise took me the center of town one Saturday night, where the people from the town gathered to play music at the end of the street. Elise told me that I stood on the exact spot, where she started to learn how to play in front of others. I was embarrassed that I didn't know how to play any of the songs, but I did strum along with one or two. One of the older men teased me.

"Some music star you are. You can't play any of the classics," he said. I smiled and kept on strumming a few chords trying to make it look like I was keeping up. I failed, but it was a nice evening.

The night before leaving for Washington, I received a call from Dad. "How are the kids? And by the way, you don't visit your mother enough," he said. "I heard about this award. I had no idea how much you and the band donated to the different veterans groups, or how many times you played privately in VA hospitals."

"How did you find out?" I asked.

"An old army buddy of mine read about you in The Military Daily News. They ran a full- page spread about you and the band. I had no idea, son. I'm pleased you found a way of using your music to help others. I'm proud of the man you have become, even if you still can't play my favorite song." Dad and I had a nice conversation before I headed upstairs to pack and get some sleep.

Leaving home became more difficult with each trip. However, the time had come to head off to our nation's capital to pick up our award and smile. Debby changed her mind and decided to join up with me, Sasha and Duke. Billy was paying for studio time and Junior claimed to be too tired for a plane ride. They each passed on the trip. I kissed all three girls good-bye and headed up I-95 to Washington D.C.

A local radio station knew I would be in town. The station manager called to see if I would do a live interview at the station while in town. I agreed to be in studio for an hour to take calls and answer questions. They asked if I would bring along other band members, but I never passed along the request.

I arrived the night before the ceremony and caught up with Duke and Sasha. Debby and her husband stayed in the hotel across the street. Her husband was being his usual miserable self and wanted Debby to keep her distance from the band. We went out to dinner and talked about ideas for the next record. I asked Duke if he wanted to add some tracks to the next album. He was pleased I asked. Sasha had recently returned from Russia where she visited with her mother and sister. She took all the newspaper photos and reports as well as all the magazine stories about her and the band. She also told me she had an offer from Playboy magazine. She told me they were doing a, 'Women in Rock and Roll' issue, and wanted her to be included. I explained to her what photos in Playboy looked like, but she assured me she would be wearing clothes.

"Shoes don't count," I said. She too never appreciated my

humor.

The next morning was a beautiful spring day on March 25th, 1988 with a bright blue sky and little humidity. The ceremony was scheduled for 10 am, which is early for musicians. However, being a father of two young girls, I discovered that 7 am did exist. After all, watching, 'Sesame Street' and 'Big Bird' had become a tradition in our home.

A driver from the armed forces was expected to pick us up in the hotel lobby. Debby met us at the hotel lobby and waited with us, with her husband. There was obvious tension between them. I shied away from both of them.

Sgt. Adams with his neatly appointed pants and shirt picked us up and drove us to an office building near the Reflecting Pool, with the Washington Memorial in plain view. The view alone made me happy that we decided to accept the award in person. Debby and her husband were arguing in the back. The rest of us pretended not to hear.

We arrived just before our scheduled time. Several well-dressed army brass offered a firm handshake and hearty hellos. Introductions came with the greetings, but all I noticed were medals and ribbons on their chests. I figured the men and women with the most decorations were the ones I should smile for the most.

Each one went out of their way to make us felt welcome. Sasha kept talking about how she was going to tell her mother and sister she had met the President, but they kept correcting her. She knew she wasn't meeting the President, but they obviously didn't know her like I did. I think she was starting to pick up some of my humor as she kept asking them which medal was the medal that only the President could wear. I think they finally caught on after Sasha's giggles filled the room.

We were ushered into a nice room, where the photographer stood waiting. After another minute, the photographer lined us up the way he wanted, a man covered in medals and ribbons, handed me a plague, and after several snaps of the camera, we had done our duty. A few in the room asked us to sign a photos and old album covers. We all kindly obliged every request. Sargent Adams was instructed to take us back to the hotel. I however, had promised to go by the local radio station after we were done. I walked the room offering good-byes to everyone. One of the soldiers invited Sasha to tour the Capitol Building. Duke managed to tag along with them, much to the dismay of the man wearing the fancy uniform. Debby and her husband disappeared after the last photo. I went down to the lobby awaiting my ride to the radio station.

A few minutes later, a kid who didn't look any older than seventeen, showed up in front of the building, driving a beat-up Chevy. He introduced himself as the intern from the station. He would be my ride. He seemed excited to meet me and had our biggest hit blasting out of the car windows.

I carefully entered the car on the front passenger side. "Awe, Mr. James, I can't tell you enough what a thrill this is for me. I'm a songwriter, just like you. My band, The Stinging Bees plays around town here. Hey, do you think you can come hear us play this weekend and get it us a recording contract? My mom would love you forever if you helped me."

I tried to be polite and listen to his tale, but I would have preferred to be touring the Capitol with the others. We made a turn onto Constitution Avenue. As we did, I spied the Reflecting Pool that looked amazing against the brilliant blue sky. The future songwriter of the year was going on and on about something, when I looked and saw a car speeding through a red light at Constitution Avenue and 17th Street. In a blink of an eye, I knew we had been hit.

The speeding car punched into my side of the car. I could feel our car sliding through the intersection. The car didn't stop until we were wrapped around a pole on the other side, with the car that hit us, punctured into my door. I have no idea how I stayed awake for most of the ordeal, but I did. In mere moments, I could hear the sirens heading in our direction. My young driver went silent.

I tried to get him to speak, but I was so twisted around, he was no longer in my line of sight. All I saw was blood on the windshield and parts of another car, inches from my face. Moving became impossible. All feeling in my arms and legs was gone. I could move my fingers, but I was so wedged in the car, I was afraid to try to move.

I started to think about my daughters and my wife and if would ever see them again. I thought about the fact that I had no feeling in my legs. I then started to pray and ask for help, then forgiveness of my sins. I didn't know what else to do until finally I heard someone trying to speak to me.

A deep voice asked if I could hear him. "Yes," I said.

"Don't move," he said. As if, I could. I could hear what sounded like them trying to move the other car away from me. It seemed like hours to get that done, though I later learned it all happened in three minutes. I could hear a cutting sound, metal on metal. It felt like an eternity. Someone strapped something to my arm. Then, nothing but total darkness.

CHAPTER EIGHTEEN

My eyes struggled to survey the surroundings. I heard the voices of Elise and my mother call for help. The sounds registering in my brain told me I was in a hospital room. I attempted to speak, but I heard nothing. Something felt lodged in my throat.

Three unknown faces, one man and two women hovered over me. The man rattled off a series of questions before squeezing my hand. I did my best to respond. Nothing. I wanted to go back to sleep. The questions continued. Why were they testing to see what I could move and not move?

"Do you feel anything, Mr. James?" The prodding stopped. Finally, I heard a man's voice speaking with Elise. I knew the sound of Elise's sobbing. I had heard it many times. I tilted my head ten degrees to the left to see Elise smiling at me with teary eyes.

"Welcome back, sweetheart," she said. "It's been a long two weeks. Now rest. The doctors are going to fix you up. I promise."

I didn't remember anything from those two weeks. Over the course of the next days, the doctors described to me the surgeries they had performed. The first stabilized my back, the second removed my spleen and to stop the internal bleeding. A third repaired my broken pelvis. They had yet to perform surgery to fix my broken left hand.

My initial reaction to hearing about my broken hand hit me harder than the bad back. I could still be Dylan James with a bad back, but a smashed up left hand was close to being the worst nightmare for a right-handed guitar player.

For days, I laid awake questioning why something this drastic had to happen to me. I wasn't like Linda. I said my prayers. I lived a good life. I had a good family. I didn't deserve such a fate. I wanted to join Dr. Who in the time machine and rejoin my life from a month earlier. I was facing over a year of physical therapy. I had major damage to my back. They performed a laminectomy to relieve pressure from my spinal cavity.

I grew angrier by the day. Taking a year from my musical career couldn't happen. I had just come off a high from the last tour that so few will ever understand. I wanted my life back. I refused to allow my daughters see me as crippled in any way.

The two times I attempted to move from the bed, I experienced pain that I wouldn't have wished on Billy Potts from the band at the Jersey shore. I asked about the young kid who picked me up that fateful day. I was told not to worry about him, focus on my own wellbeing. Answers like that fueled my rage.

Every day was the same routine. Steal my blood; shove a pill down my throat. Wake me up from a sound sleep to see if I felt someone tapping the bottom of my feet. Everyone from my mother to Elise to the nurses to the doctors told me how much I had improved. If so, why was I still strapped to a frigging bed?

I pushed for answers from the doctor. "You're a very lucky man, Mr. James," he said. "We thought we had lost you several times in those first few hours. You must be a fighter, because you suffered injuries many others wouldn't have survived. Take my advice. Stop asking so many questions and do the therapy the staff requests. We want you home as fast as you want to be home."

I wasn't feeling very lucky. I only felt anger. Anger was an emotion I hadn't known well before the accident. Oh, I would find some silly reason to be upset with something or someone from time to time, but not the anger that pulsated throughout my entire soul. I turned to the one thing that I thought would relieve some of my anger.

"The girls are in North Carolina with my parents," Elise said. "I told them that you are making music and will be home soon. Mom and Dad send their best. They call twice a day for updates."

"Please tell me the truth as to what happened, Elise. Did that young kid survive the crash?"

"The driver of the car who hit you was fired the day before the accident. He was on an all-night binge. He died at the scene."

"Good, he got what he deserved," I said.

Elise frowned and took my hand. "Your driver Sam, he was thrown from the car and survived, but is still banged up. The paramedic who removed you from the car couldn't believe you survived that wreck. He came by a few times while you were in the coma."

"I wanna go see Sam and let him know none of this was his fault."

"I've told him that," Elise said. "He felt very guilty over the accident. I'm told they're treating him for depression as much as his physical injuries."

"Please write a note to Sam for me. Let him know that when I get outta here, I'll get together with him and we can write a song about this whole mess. Better yet, see if they can wheel him to him, since the doc won't allow me to move more than my arms yet."

"Sweetie, I know you want to do what you can for the man. However, he's been moved to a rehab center somewhere. I need you to worry about you and get better for me and our daughters."

More days passed of lying still, except for the occasional sponge bath. Nurse Kate did her best to care for me, despite my constant complaints. No doubt, I uttered a few words that I wish I could have taken back. I'm also sure I played my role of the spoiled rock star perfectly.

I watched television until I was too bored to think. The problem was; all I could do was think. Why and what had I done to receive such unfair treatment from my God. I never claimed to be a perfect person, but I tried to live a clean life. I stayed clear of drugs and alcohol. I never once cheated after I had married Elise, even if I could have most nights on tour. I gave back to the community. I had done my best to respect others.

I stayed awake at night constantly asking myself what I had done to deserve my punishment. Nothing made sense. Everyone kept telling me how lucky I was to be alive. If strapped to a hospital bed was being alive, I no longer wanted to be alive. I wanted to patrol concert stages far and wide. Having people tap my feet and extract blood in the middle of the night wasn't being alive.

One drunken bastard had taken away mornings learning the alphabet with my daughters and seeing their beautiful faces at dawn. Even the thought of changing diapers without a gas mask was far more appealing than sponge baths before dawn.

Sasha and Duke came to visit me the day before therapy was to begin. Elise had combed my hair and had the hospital put on a clean shirt before they arrived. I felt embarrassed they had to see me in that condition. However, seeing my bandmates lifted my spirits.

"Billy will be along in a few days," Duke said. "Junior has some issues he's dealing with and can't travel right now, but sends his regards."

Neither of them mentioned Debby. I was maybe too afraid to ask. Elise added, "Linda calls for her daily updates from California."

Duke offered a wicked smile on his unshaven face. "I've taken up chess and since I hear you have some free time on your hands, I'm gonna come back and teach you how to play."

"I've got no time for games, Duke," I said. "Bring paper and pen so we can begin writing the next record. I wanna be in the studio before our fans forget about us. I intend to lick this therapy thing much faster than they're telling me."

Elise let out a huge sigh, but I shot her a look and continued. "The moment I can stand or sit up long enough to play, we begin to lay down tracks."

Sasha began crying and left for the hallway. Elise followed her. It wasn't my ears that were broken, it was my back. I could hear them both sobbing. Duke did his best to divert my attention from the emotions, but the idea of anyone feeling sorry for me, other than me feeling sorry for myself, brought back my anger.

"Elise told me that you were asking about the driver of your car," Duke said. Elise has enough going on right now. I'll find out where they transferred him and let him know he's got backstage tickets to our next show in the area."

"Great idea, Duke. Thanks for handling that for me. Tell him, I'll give him a call as soon as I'm feeling up to it."

The next day was beyond painful. Agony was the word of the day. We had one goal for the day. The hospital staff wanted to raise the back of the bed and have me sit up for ten minutes. The doctor poked and prodded me as they adjusted the bed. Every touch felt like my bed had become a bed of spikes.

"This is great news that you're in a lot of pain," the doctor said. "This shows the healing process is coming along nicely."

"Easy for you to say," I managed to say in between screams of pain.

During the next week, the goal was to sit up longer each day. Eventually, I could hit the buttons and sit up for as long as I wanted. The pain, though still pronounced, alleviated some each day.

Nurse Kate was a tough woman, who had worked twenty years in that hospital. Her demeanor was sympathetic, yet firm. Her main mission became to keep my bedsores to a minimum. She reminded me all the twisting and turning to get to the hard to hit places were for my own good.

A huge day occurred when I could wiggle my toes. Who knew such a small accomplishment could bring a grown man to tears? Only Kate Nurse could share in the moment. Elise had returned to our daughters for a few days.

The next big step became getting from the bed. Summer was near before I managed with help to move from the bed to a chair, with assistance of course. I kept telling both Kate and my night nurse Emily that once I could stand on my own, I was heading home.

"Yeah, I'm pretty tired of your sour attitude too," Kate said.

I deserved every sour note from my nurses and then some. I

wasn't the best of patients.

Once I could sit alone for an hour, the plan was to move me to a physical therapy center, where I would learn to walk. I didn't need some girl just out of college teaching me how to walk. I knew how to walk. I lost the battle. Our insurance found a facility only forty-five minutes from home. Elise went through hell for months, driving back and forth from North Carolina. I wanted to shorten her trip.

Before leaving the hospital, Elise arranged for all the nurses and staff to get a dozen roses and a nice gift certificate for each of them. It was her idea. She knew the disaster I was as a patient.

To my surprise, Kate informed me that she had seen the band several times. One reason she pushed me as hard as she did was so she could see me perform again.

"Many of from friends are huge fans," she said. If I let you leave here not doing everything I could to fix you, my friends would never forgive me."

"So you don't try to fix everyone who comes in here?" I asked.

She laughed. "You really do intend to be a major pain in the ass for your entire visit, don't you?"

Elise bought copies of all our records and had the entire band sign them all for Kate and my night nurse. I had yet to sign them.

"Write something special on there for me, will ya?" Kate asked.

I don't remember what I wrote, but I remember Kate bear hugged me after I handed them to her.

The people at the rehab center weren't as pleasing as the

nurses at the hospital. They expected me to work and work hard. Taking a simple step, even with the aid of bars and a therapist was much harder than I ever imagined. Putting one foot ahead of the other became harder to me than writing a number one song.

Rehabbing made me feel worthless to my family and band. It ignited the anger once more. The staff insisted I was ahead of schedule, but their words meant nothing to me. Maybe the anger worked against me in my recovery, or maybe it was driving me to get home. I didn't know. I only knew I the anger sizzled on a daily basis.

The pain in my back was masked somewhat with strong medications. Atrophy had set into my legs while in the hospital. It made learning to walk again even more difficult. Every morning they would take me into a room where parallel bars were set up. If I managed to straddle ten feet, the therapist promised I could return to my room. The first time I made it the full ten feet, it took almost twenty minutes.

Duke rented an apartment in the area. He ran errands for Elise when she needed help then would come and harass me until I agreed to play chess. Every time I tried to talk about the next album, he would shoot me a dirty look and say, "Your move sucker." He had grown to be my best friend other than Elise. I was too angry with the world back then to understand how much so many people had sacrificed for me, including Duke. It was many years later before I thanked him.

One day while playing chess, Duke had a tear in his eye. "Dylan," he said. "I have to tell you what my greatest fear was when I heard you were on death's door."

He had my full attention for the first time since our last tour. "What's that?" I asked.

He sighed and glanced out the window. "I played in three bands before I joined The Overture. You were the only person who treated me like a brother. Everyone else looked at me as the bass player. Nothing more."

For a short time, the anger lifted as Duke continued.

"You took me into your band and listened to my ideas. You asked me to write music. No one ever wanted anything more from me than to show up, bang on my bass and go home. I owe you a great deal and was afraid I'd never be able to tell you."

"Oh, get over yourself," I said. "I even listen to Billy and we both know he's an immature idiot."

We both laughed. Duke didn't always enjoy my humor, but he understood me. The jerk still took my king in thirty moves. You would think since I had done so much for him; he would have let me win just one game of chess.

CHAPTER NINETEEN

Walking the hallways with a walker hit another milestone. Eating afternoon ice cream in the little café at the opposite end of the hallway became a big deal to me. My therapist Samantha refused to bring me any.

"You want some, get it yourself," she would tell me each day when I hit the call button.

After being able to get out of bed on my own and enjoy afternoon ice cream, an older woman, who I chatted with a few times, asked me a question.

"I told my daughter about you. She thinks you're some hot shot rock and roll star. I told her you don't look so hot to me. How come I never hear you playing in your room if you're such a big shot. She wants to know if she can join us for ice cream one day and hear you play a tune?"

"As complimentary as your offer is to me, you can tell your daughter that along with my other injuries, I broke my hand. The doctors tell me I have to have therapy on my hands before I can play again. Healing my back has been hard enough."

Mrs. Hood licked the last of her chocolate ice cream from her spoon. "I figured you wouldn't play for her. But, I thought I'd ask. Hot shots like you don't care about us common folk."

It only took me five minutes to race back to the room. I called Elise and by dinnertime, my guitar nestled in my fingers. The doctors warned me it would be a slow process with the guitar too. My hand had broken in several places.

I strummed a few bars. Maybe it was a good thing to play, because I didn't notice the pain in my back and legs as much. I noticed it in my hands and fingers. The calluses that had been built up over several years weren't as pronounced. I wasn't sure I had the will to want to fight the pain in another part of my body, not counting my ego. The idea that I could no longer play guitar depressed me. The anger and depression had changed me.

I guess the rehab center recognized my depression too. Twice a week Dr. Summers would come to the center and would talk to me about life. We spoke about my anger. Talking with her only fueled my anger.

We conversed about how I would occasionally get angry with Elise. I had no reason to be angry with her. The Pope should have granted Elise Sainthood after putting up with me. None of that mattered. Once I realized I would even have to relearn the guitar again, I considered life no longer worth living. Dr. Summers wanted to pursue that thought. I didn't. I wanted my life back before I hopped into that old Chevy, or end it.

The only reprieve was the time Billy showed up. He sat there for hours telling me dirty jokes. He tried to make time with every female who dared to walk within twenty feet of my private room. He reminded me again about the time he too broke his hand in a bar fight. Billy assured me it was only a matter of time before I got all the dexterity back in my fingers.

Billy wasn't a hand expert, but he had experienced breaking his hand and having to go through therapy to get it back to full strength. His words hit a mark with me. At least that's what I tried to convince myself.

Billy stayed overnight and stopped by again the next day. We talked about his blues band. He claimed they were a big hit in the Chicago area. He had produced the first album with the band with his own cash. He released it with a small blues label out of Chicago. For two days, I released some anger. For all his shortcomings, Billy knew how to light a room.

Linda called once a week. I knew she called Elise most days. Linda claimed she didn't want to interrupt me from my therapy, so she would get her updates from Elise. When we did speak, we would mostly talk about music and how happy and excited she was after joining us on the last album and tour.

She spoke as if she would continue making music with The Overture and not worry about being a solo artist. I was thrilled and assumed the rest of the band would agree to make her a full member. She asked about visiting so we could start writing as a team again.

"I'm not the greatest company, however, I'd love to see you," I said. "Duke comes around most days. Even he can only take me for an hour or so each day."

"I'll come see ya then. I know you're mostly talk, Dylan." Near the end of her call, I asked her if she had spoken to Debby. "Uhm, well, no. Well, every once in a while. Sorta. Why do you ask?"

Linda always was a terrible liar. "It's been months since the accident and not even a card or a call from her. Don't you think that's odd?"

"She's asked me about you. I know she's spoken with Elise a bunch of times."

"How do you know that?" I asked. "I've asked Elise and this is the first I have heard anything about her checking on me.

A hush came over the phone. Several moments later, Linda said, "My dear friend, you need to worry about you right now, the rest of us will take care of Debby. I've said too much. I must go. Worry about you and not the others for now, please."

Linda hung up the phone. What did all that mean? I called home. At first, Elise pretended to know nothing. "Linda has already let on that something in going on with Debby," I said.

Elise took a long pause. Then a short sigh. "Debby has hit a rough spot. She's being cared for and didn't want you involved. I give you my word that she's fine. That is all you're going to know for now. Worry about yourself. When you leave the center, Debby has promised to come and visit with us at our home."

Fumes spewed from my ears and nostrils like one of those raging bulls in the Bugs Bunny cartoons. I could barely walk ten feet without needing a rest. I again felt totally helpless and worthless to others. The idea that no one would trust that I could help a lifelong friend, raised my blood pressure so much that it registered later in the day when they hooked me up to check my vitals.

I wanted to say a prayer for my friend. However, the anger raged inside me so much against God for putting me in my situation, that I didn't dare ask for help. I struggled through the pain of getting out of bed and putting on fresh clothes. I had every intention to leave the center and try to be a use to everyone again.

Where and what was I really going to go or do? I didn't know where Debby was living. One other big thing. I had no car. I rang the number that I thought was Debby's home. No answer.

The next morning was my visit with Dr. Summers. I opened up

about the situation with Debby. I wondered why would others wanted to keep the news about her away from me. The only reason I spoke up with Dr. Summers was that no one else cared to listen to my story. The staff pretended to listen. I knew better. Duke had returned to New York for a few weeks. He picked up work as a studio musician to keep his chops.

After pouring out every detail of my relationship with Debby, Dr. Summers admitted she intended to change my prescription for the anti-depressant I was taking. She wanted to make them stronger. I hated being a test rat for drugs. I had taken very good care of my body over the years. I ate properly and never ingesting drugs or alcohol. After all the medications they shoved down my throat, I felt my body slipping away a tiny bit more each day. Who wouldn't be depressed over not being able to do things they took for granted a few short months ago?

I begged to be taken off the anti-depressants. "It will help in your complete healing process," she said. "You have been through a dramatic time, Mr. James. We have your best interest when we prescribe any drug."

"Have you ever tried to work when your brain was altered with chemicals?" I asked. I need to experience life in order to write music. You must understand I can't do it when I feel like my body is in slow motion."

"Take the medications, Mr. James."

Three more months passed. I could walk short distances with a cane. My hand had regained much of its strength. Physical therapy increased to three hours a day. My body's health had surpassed the health of my mind. I was convinced that my depression stemmed from being caged in medical centers for half a year and seeing my daughters. Doc Summers disagreed.

Even Elise sided with the medical staff that my fastest road to recovery remained staying locked up. I agreed to stay longer if I could see my daughters. Summers said I had too many anger issues to be around children, but Elise relented and finally brought them by to see me.

As thrilled as I was to see them, it again made me feel inadequate and less of a father. They were still too young to fully understand what had happened. They were told, I was injured working, but would be home soon. I sobbed for over an hour when they left.

My workouts picked up after I committed to being home for Thanksgiving. I worked harder for several works than at any time in my life. My legs were no longer an issue. They had regained their strength. I could walk around the grounds with limited pain in my hips to my legs. However, I would feel a pinch in my back if I pushed too hard.

One thing that motivated me was a surprise from the armed services. Despite the excellent care, I received from the staff, the army sent over a specialist, who worked with wounded soldiers. He monitored my progress. It was a kind gesture that the army took a special interest in my wellbeing. The doctor they sent was a hand specialist. He designed specific exercises to help my fingers regain dexterity.

"Hey, Dylan, good news," Linda said during one our weekly phone calls. "The record label asked if we would do a follow up to our 1950's album, only this time with 1960's classic songs."

"You do realize I'm still trapped in this hell hole, don't cha?"

"Well, Mr. Altos thinks maybe this will give you an incentive to keep working hard in therapy and get home soon."

"Tell him the doctors think I have another year before I can travel on planes without pain or stand for a long times."

"Oh, bull," Linda said. "Elise told me you should be home within the next sixty days. You were the one who convinced me the only way to really recover was to get in the studio and on the road and make music."

I hated when people turned the tables on me. "I'll think about," I said.

"Stop with the pity party, you always told me," Linda said. "I'm coming to see you next week to get your head right. You've sat on your ass long enough. Now get over yourself and start to think about not only the 60's record, but the next Overture release. You promised me I didn't have to start my own band again. I intend to hold you to your word. Let's hope your disposition can improve by then."

"Yeah, yeah," I said.

"And one last thing, life is going to keep going on, even if you don't want to participate in it right now, Dylan."

The next thing I heard was the click of the phone in my ear. I thought about calling her back, but I knew it was about time to take my vitals. I didn't want to spike my blood pressure and give them an excuse for more drugs.

Later in the week, my session with Dr. Summers was canceled because of visitors. Gordy and Father Daniel wandered into my room. I enjoyed seeing them both. However, I quickly became suspicious as to why they would come as a pair to see me. They claimed it was to save on expenses and to have a driving partner.

"Wish we could have gotten here sooner," Gordy said. "You know how I hate to leave the store or the area. You look better than I expected though."

We sat talking for hours about the weather, and how Orel Hershiser was having a great year pitching for the Dodgers. Father Daniel asked me if I would say a prayer with him and Gordy before they left.

"Why bother? God hates me," I said.

A more disappointed look, I had never seen.

"Why would ya say such a ting," the Irish priest asked.

"Because I did nothing to have this happen to me," I said. "I'm convinced I'm being punished by your God."

Gordy scratched his face and got up from his seat. At first, I thought he had intended to hit me. Father Daniel looked at Gordy and asked him to sit.

"Stu, ya listen ta me, and listen ta me gud," Father Daniel said. "Neider my God nor yours putcha in dat intersection at dat time a day. Your free will did. It twere your choice ta be in dat car, at dat time, and it twere an accident, pure and simple. It tweren't your time ta move on from dis earth. Did ya ever tink dat your God saved your dumb ass from more pain and suffering or death at dat corner?"

I have to admit I didn't think of it in those terms. We sat there for a few more minutes with angry stares when Gordy spoke up. "Stu I want you to move to the window and please and look as far as your eyes will take you."

I did. He continued. "Way out there is your soul. I warned you about losing it and you have."

It hit me hard hearing that from Gordy.

"If I have lost it, it has nothing to do with the music business and everything to do with the fact I'm pretty useless to everyone who depends on me right now," I said.

Gordy came over and put his hand on my shoulder. "My dear friend, Stu, you will never write a good piece of music, hug your wife and kids the same way or smile warmly again until you find your soul. A big reason why your fingers can't find the same rhythm, even though your hand is partially healed, is because you became one with your instrument, but without a soul, it's impossible. Music comes from the soul. You no longer own one."

I had no idea how he knew I could play notes, but not create the same sound I had on the last tour. I frowned at Gordy but he continued with his rant.

"When you want help in finding your soul, you know where to find me. Until that day, please avoid my shop and me."

Those words crushed me. Father Daniel tried to smooth over the tension, but it didn't work. They got up and left.

CHAPTER TWENTY

All the hard work paid off. Release day occurred. Therapy would continue on an outpatient basis, three days a week. The daily grueling grind had ended. However, once home, everyone kept a distance from me. No one would still tell me about Debby, other than she and her daughters were fine and had moved to another home. No wonder no one had returned my calls at her previous home.

Linda visited the second week of November. Her skin had a bronze glow. She claimed to be as fit as she had ever been. She had a daily workout she refused to miss. A couple of times, my daughters joined her.

After breakfast and the Mickey Mouse Club with the girls, I would sit on the porch with Linda and my guitar. Words and melodies came easy to me. However, my famous love songs turned into stories of despair. It was all my mind would conjure up. Elise and the girls would check on us and grab a hug. My body would go through the motions of holding them, but something was missing.

My mind wandered to what Gordy had told me. I wanted him to be wrong, but I knew he was right. Peace with my music and instrument would be impossible until I made peace with God and myself. Even Linda knew.

"The public will never accept this kind of music from you,

Dylan. They expect you to make them smile, not feel your anger."

I didn't care. "The public will accept it, because it's who I am now. If they're a true fan, they'll follow me down this path."

"Don't take your fans for granted, Dylan. They'll leave you the first time you fail them," Linda said. "There's a new shiny band in every bin of the record shops."

Duke and Sasha joined us for Thanksgiving in Carolina. Linda stayed. Billy declined, instead spending the time with his family. Debby was also spending Thanksgiving with her family, though I didn't hear that directly from her. Junior was too ill to travel. I spoke with him on the phone. I wanted to pray for a speedy recovery for my friend, but couldn't. God wasn't listening.

During Thanksgiving dinner, we talked about starting a time schedule for the next release from The Overture. Linda would join the band as a permanent member, which made me smile. A second female voice added so much to the sound. I tried to be excited about working on the next release. My mind refused to acknowledge that I would soon be healthy enough to make it happen.

We also talked about the 60's record. I wanted it to take back seat to The Overture's future. What I didn't know was the real reason why Duke spent time in New York. He originally told me he was working as a studio musician. Duke and Sasha, along with the studio musicians we had used on the 50's album, had laid down tracks for the new album. Linda added vocals. They were all waiting on me to add the guitar parts. I also discovered that Duke and Linda had written music for the Overture's next works without my knowledge. They said they were waiting on me to add to the list. I think it was their way of trying to get my lazy butt back to work.

After removing myself from the table in a huff, Elise came upstairs to speak with me.

"Honey, you shouldn't be upset. These people love you. You have done so much over the years for them. This was their way to show you how much they appreciate your efforts. You can add some of your music to the next album. Please. They are guests in our home. Don't ruin this dinner for everyone."

We hugged. I could feel the love coming from my wife. I could also hear the sob. I tried hard to return her love on the same level. I failed. We returned to the table. I explained how the news was a shock to my system and apologized. I promised to work on both albums after the first of the year. We finished a nice dinner with my mother in law's famous pumpkin pie and my father in law's nap near the fireplace.

The Friday after Thanksgiving dinner, we were sitting in the television room when Duke pulled up a folding chair and sat in front of me. "Dylan, I didn't want you involved. Debby had issues with Mike. He knocked her around a few times. Once we found out about it, Carl put a restraining order on the jerk. We hired security and moved her and the kids to a new home. Mike spent a few days in jail. The divorce will be final in January. She wanted to come this weekend, but we were afraid it would all be too much for you. She's anxious to see you and promises she'll be in the studio when you come to work on the new release."

I sat in silence for fifteen minutes trying to gather my thoughts. I had none. I had assumed the big secret had something to do with her and her husband. However, it still hurt that no one trusted me enough to able to handle the news. My mind shifted to wanting to hire my own security team and beat on her husband the way he beat on her.

I thanked Duke for handling the situation. I again felt helpless in not aiding my friend in time of need. Duke had visited with Debby a few times when he was in New York. Debby and her kids moved to a nice suburban home in Northern New Jersey. She moved closer to New York City, so she could go home at night during our recording sessions. Her parents had moved close to their home as well. Later that evening, Debby and I spoke on the phone for hours. We each promised to see each other very soon.

Everyone left the following Monday. I worked double time with my hand exercises and practicing the guitar. I also wanted to do something special for Elise for the holidays. She had been my rock during the ordeal. I made a call to Carl to check on finances.

He assured me the cash had continued to grow through royalty checks and with the stock portfolio. I arranged to pay off the mortgage on my in-laws farm. They had lived there for many years, but when times became rough, they were forced to refinance. I cleared all the loans.

It was the least I could do for them. They had looked after my daughters, while I was in rehab. It was more a gift for them, but it also gave Elise security in her mind too. I also booked a cruise to the Virgin Islands for the first week in February with Elise and the kids.

By early December, I was able to drive myself to therapy. Everyone was pleased with my physical recovery. On my off days from therapy, I would spend as much time as possible with the girls. The nine months absence were months I would never get back. Some days, it seemed I barely knew them or them me.

I would have good days, then bad. My mind took me to dark places. The anger for the drunk driver, and for the God who allowed it, consumed me. The pastor from the local church where

Elise and I attended would stop by to see me. I talked with him, but I knew my words were hollow. I suspect he knew too.

"Make peace with your life, and God. It's the only way to find your way home," he would tell me. I knew peace was impossible until I could stand on a stage for a two hour and thirty minute concert and not feel pain. The pain in my body had subsided for the most part. I could stand. I could play the notes. As much as I wanted the passion to return in my heart and soul, only darkness would surface.

My brother and father arrived for hunting season. Mom came along to see her granddaughters. Mom would follow me all around the house driving me more insane. My mind remained numb from the medications, the anger or both.

"You have a wonderful family and life, Stu," Mom said. "What's with all the moodiness? This isn't my son."

Mom did convince me to spend Christmas at their home. Elise and the kids would come too. It wasn't always easy juggling where we spent holidays. We had spent many of the recent ones in Carolina with Elise's family. Elise agreed to join mine in Jersey for Christmas.

We arrived at my parent's home on Christmas Eve. As usual, Mom had the place all decorated to the max and Dad had lights strung up on the outside. The cooler weather affecting my back, but I stayed quiet about it. My brother and sister came with their families.

"This is the first time I have all my children and grandchildren in the same room at once," Mom said. "This is the best gift anyone could give me for Christmas."

I would have expected nothing less from her. We let the kids rip into all the gifts early the next morning before heading to Christmas service. I sat staring at the stained glass window behind the alter counting the tiles almost the entire mass. I didn't feel anyone was going to listen to me anyway. What was the point? I only went to services to appease Elise and my parents. When communion time arrived, I sat firmly in my seat, despite Mom tugging at my sport coat to join her in line.

We had a lovely dinner. Late that night, I doubled up on my pain medications from the cold house. The kids were as exhausted, but overall it was a nice day with the family.

The next day some old friends gave me a call and wanted to know if I would go out and shoot pool at a local club. I agreed and we met up later that evening. I was having a good time shooting pool when this young looking girl came up to me and asked if I was Dylan James.

I intended to say no when my friend Danny blurted out, "Not only is it Dylan James, he's the best guitar player in the entire world."

"Well if you exclude Eric Clapton, Carlos Santana, Frank Zappa and about fifty others I might agree," I said.

The young girl smiled and said, "My brother's band is playing on the other side of the club. They want to know if you'll play a couple songs with them."

I politely declined much to her disappointment. I hadn't played for anyone other than bandmates or family since the accident. I wasn't sure I had the guts to play in public. Five minutes later, out of the corner of my eye, I caught someone calling me to the stage. My name blared over the sound system. My friends pushed me to the stage.

Fear struck me like a bolt of lightning. My playing ability had improved, but I wasn't ready for the public's eye. I hobbled up on stage and warned the small crowd that I had not played in public since my accident.

"What accident?" The lead singer asked through the microphone.

My body shook. Drips of perspiration ran across my forehead. I tried to get off the stage, but the crowd began to chant my name.

"You do know Johnny B. Goode don't ya?" The drummer asked.

I smirked at him and regained some confidence. What guitar player from my era wasn't raised on Chuck Berry classics? It was even one of the tunes on our 1950's album. I even had the original Chess label 45 stored away in my parent's attic.

One of the band members handed me a cheap guitar. I had no idea if the thing was in tune or plugged in. I picked a couple of notes to figure it out when the lead singer pronounced to the crowd, "Back away from the stage. It's about to get very hot up here, very fast.

I hated the sudden pressure to perform. However, I felt trapped. My only solace was that I assumed that even at eighty-five percent of my best playing ability, it would still better than anyone else in the club.

Adrenaline pulsated in my veins. I ripped into the opening riff the same way I had a hundreds of times in the past. The band followed my lead. Not my best work. I managed to get through the song. After the last note was completed, I handed the guitar back to the kid and thanked him for the invite. I was done.

The small crowd of maybe thirty people hooted and hollered for more. I waved and thanked them as I gingerly left the stage. I felt nothing more. For the first time, there was no rush from having been on stage. I would always get a rush, even from a small audience. The band announced they needed a break.

My hand reminded me that I hadn't been practicing long solos. That was as hard as I had played on a solo since the accident. Between that and the two hours of standing playing pool, my hand and back were sore. I headed for the exit. The young lady, who had asked me to play earlier, caught me on my way out. She thanked me for playing with her brother. The kid who lent me the guitar was her twin brother. She told me that he had a poster of me on his bedroom wall.

I felt obligated to thank him. I walked with her to her brother and wrote down words from my experience on stage on the back of a napkin. I handed it to her twin brother. I also jotted down Carl's office number. I told him to call that number. I invited him and his sister to the studio in New York to watch the band record. The smile on their faces was the best Christmas gift anyone had given me that year.

We stayed a few more days visiting with Mom and Dad, until the day, we were to visit Debby at her home in North Jersey. I hadn't seen her since the day of the accident. I wasn't sure how she would view me, since my walk still had a wobble to it. I no longer used a cane most days, but running or jogging was still months away.

Elise and the kids came along for the ride. The moment Debby and I saw each other, I wasn't sure if the tears were for her, or for me, but we both started to cry immediately. We both apologized for not being there for each other. We gave each other a hug until others started to take notice of how we stayed latched together.

After the initial tears, we sat for hours. Few words flowed between us. The three adults watched as the kids played together. As much as I wanted to stay calm for Debby, a rage came over me about her husband, who had hurt her emotionally and physically.

I eventually brought up the subject of making music, to try to wipe my mind clear of the anger. Everyone decided that I should finish work on the 60's album since it was near completion. They only needed my guitar and some overdubbing. Debby offered her voice as a backup singer.

She assured me her mind and voice were ready for action. She also told me that Kevin's firm handled her divorce. Kevin took watch over the restraining order and had her husband prosecuted. Debby assured me that Kevin and Carl were staying on top of her legal and security issues and I need not worry.

The next day, Elise, the kids and I headed up to New York for a couple of weeks. I would lay down my guitar parts for the 1960's album. I wasn't sure how much we would be staying in New York in the future, since our oldest daughter would be starting school in fall.

We had decided; well Elise decided; that the girls would attend school in North Carolina. She wanted a slower paced way of living for the girls. After having spent time in Carolina, as much as I loved New York, I agreed with my wife.

Besides, I had hoped my attitude and health would soon reach a point where I would be hitting the road. Elise deserved to be where she felt safe and secure with our children.

I talked with Carl about selling the apartment. He thought it was still a good investment. We decided to keep it, despite the expense. We discussed renting it out after I finished recording The Overture album in the spring. We left that decision for another day.

An odd thing happened to me while driving in the city. The congestion of driving in a big city scared me. More than one person had asked me if I was afraid to get in a car again after the accident, but it had never occurred to me to be afraid. I knew what had happened.

I was a control freak, who wasn't at the wheel at the time of the crash. I believed none of it was my fault. A drunk had struck the car and nearly killed me. It was the drunk drivers and God's fault. While driving in the city, I took long stares in both directions, on a couple of occasions, afraid to hit the gas. I blamed it on the pain medications.

After finding my way back at the apartment, I swallowed a Valium. It took off the edge from driving in the city. I knew better, however I had nowhere else to turn. I again thought about what Gordy had told me about how he would help me, but since this was the first time I returned to the area and didn't feel welcome in his shop, I didn't think it was appropriate to call him. I would fight my demons alone. I never told Elise about my fear of driving in the city.

The next day, I took the subway to the recording studio. Duke was already hard at work. He was helping to produce the album. He also wanted to know why two young kids were told they could come to the studio to watch us work. I laughed and told him the story. I called Carl to make sure it the arrangements were set for my new friends to come later in the week.

Duke played what he had on tape and explained what he wanted from me. Ten tracks needed my guitar sound. I had two weeks to complete my parts. That seemed more than ample time for me to finish my additions, even if after an hour of playing, the pain would flare up in my hand.

The hand specialist had assured me the healing was on schedule. Everyone had told me it would take a year to heal completely. I was still three months short of the mark. I was hopeful that by the time we returned from the cruise, I would be able to play for hours at a time with no pain in my hand or back. One doctor warned me that I would likely have some pain in my back for the remainder of my life. I was beginning to believe him.

The goal was to complete one or maybe two songs a day. I did all the guitar parts to my satisfaction in nine days. One day I didn't get much accomplished, since I played around with the brother and sister too much. I allowed Matt to play in the studio and try to mimic one of the solos. Duke and I took them out to lunch after the session and we talked music for hours. I enjoyed seeing Matt and Samantha again and wished them both luck. I think I had more than made up for the fact that I turned down Samantha's request the first time she asked me to hobble on stage.

January in New York City had its benefits, but the cold found its way into my broken bones and made my body ache. I set me back more than expected. I took more than my allotted share of painkillers too. I promised myself that once we hit the warm Caribbean weather, I would back off the drugs. We stayed the full two weeks in New York despite having finished my studio work.

Elise desired time to catch up with some friends, did her share of shopping and saw the new exhibitions at the museums. I sat home with the girls while she had some much deserved free time away from the kids. I never mentioned to her that my back was acting up. I wanted her to enjoy herself without me whining in her ear. I had done plenty of that for several months. We headed back to North Carolina the third week of January.

I decided on a family vacation because Diana would begin school later in the year. I assumed I be would touring in the summers, at least a few more years, so it might be one of the last vacations would could take without working around school days.

The cruise put a smile on everyone's faces. I was still my moody self, but I tried to minimize it for the girls. I wasn't sure why I was mad at the world. My hand felt like it had improved a great deal pain wise and walking had become less of a chore. I walked the decks of the ship and filled my lungs with fresh ocean air at least twice a day.

While lounging on the deck one morning, I thought about my life. Attempting to understand my anger and depression was a daily chore. The continuing sessions with Dr. Summers seemed to only ignite more anger, not lessen the burden.

Growing up, I was the wallflower. I thought leadership skills were part of me. However, they never emerged until I led a band. I never looked for confrontation. I read books on depression and self-help, but it only led to more confusion inside my brain. Dr. Summers claimed the medications were to aid with my depression. I didn't want to believe I suffered from depression. Yet, others around me claimed I had changed.

I now wrote moody, dark pieces of music. So what? Many musicians would go through stages of expanding their songwriting themes. I assumed that's all I was doing too. I gained weight. Who wouldn't if they were shackled to a bed for months? I had never been a health food person, but I did eat a proper diet. Even on the road, I ate well-balanced meals to keep my energy levels high. I also jogged quite a bit or hit the exercise rooms in the hotels. Therapy was tough, but it wasn't the same type of workout my body had been accustomed. I assumed that added to my bulging waistline. The only conclusion I could arrive at was that a drunk driver and God changed my life. If others didn't like that I was pissed off, tough. I would get over it when I was ready.

After the cruise, we headed home to North Carolina. Therapy continued, but only twice and sometimes once a week. The Doctor bitched at me because I hadn't kept up with my exercises while in New York and on the cruise as much as he wanted. I chalked it up to another person upset with me and didn't let it bug me.

Dr. Summers wanted to increase the doses of medications yet again. Elise begged me to follow doctor's orders. I cheated a few times in tossing the pills down the toilet, but for the most part, I took them. Elise claimed she knew when I stopped taking my pills. She said I was too miserable to be around when I tossed the pills away.

After sitting home for two weeks after the cruise, I called the band to schedule when we could hit the studio. Junior wasn't returning my calls. After three days of leaving messages, his nephew called. He informed me that Junior had moved into a nursing home. He could no longer care for himself. He also told me Junior's real age, which was twenty years older than even he told me. I had always suspected it, but his nephew confirmed it.

My initial reaction after speaking with Junior's nephew was, oh crap, we need a new keyboard player, not for Junior's wellbeing. It wasn't until the next day I took pause to realize my horrible error in judgement. I immediately called Junior. His voice sounded like the weakest note on the keyboard of life. I suspected that would be our last conversation. Junior would be a loss to our band and a lost friend.

I spoke with Duke. He already knew all about Junior's health. He had even traveled to see Junior.

"Why didn't you tell me and take me with you?" I asked Duke.

"He has enough pain in his life right now. Did you want to add to it be sitting there being your usual cheery self?" Duke said.

Point taken. However, it had still upset me that Duke had put a wall around me and didn't want me to have to deal with anything more than necessary. That too added to my inner madness.

I called Mr. Altos to see if he knew of any keyboard players looking for work. He arranged for auditions set for later in the month in New York. Billy called and asked if the keyboard player in his band could audition. Duke and I agreed, if only to keep peace in the band.

Junior passed away three days after I spoke with him. It upset me I never made time to go see him before his passing. It was a regret, I would never forget. Elise and I joined Billy and Duke at the funeral. I sat at the service doing mostly the same thing I did at Christmas mass. I counted stained glass tiles not wanting to speak privately with God.

I took time to think about Junior and the times we had spent together. I decided to remember Junior Johnson for who he was. He was a fine man, who lived life younger than his numeric age, and who never went without a smile etched on his face and a kind word for anyone who would listen.

CHAPTER TWENTY ONE

After the funeral, I laid low at home, trying not to upset the family. Peace reigned in the household until the time arrived to audition for a new keyboardist and record the new record. Duke and I auditioned close to twenty musicians, finally settling on Billy's band mate Jack Harrison.

Jack didn't distinguish himself, but he was as good as any of the others. Duke and I both knew Billy would get upset if we didn't pick him. I was worried that Billy and Jack were drinking pals away from the band. We took a chance and trusted it would not be an issue.

We hired Jack as a tryout for the recording sessions with no guarantee he would join us on the road. He had to prove he wasn't under Billy's command and would be show up on time in the studio. Billy put up a bit of a fuss because we didn't make Jack a full time member of the band. I reminded Billy we did the same with Sasha. He backed down.

Linda flew in the next day. I arranged to have my apartment cleaned so she could stay with me. We could write at nights if necessary. I could still only play about two to three hours at a time before my back and hand would start aching.

"It's not from the accident, you're just getting old," Billy said.

Recording was tough on people who were at full strength. The days were long and sometimes combative. Everyone now had an opinion as to how we should present ourselves as a band. I wanted to explore our dark side.

Linda and Duke complained our audience had no appetite for my moodiness in music.

"How would you know," I asked.

The battle over our sound lasted for weeks. Little progress was evident. No one could agree which music should make the final cut.

"Write 'Overture' music, will ya, Dylan? Billy asked. "Let's do this so I can get back to my other band. We have a tour around the mid-west planned for the summer."

Our producer sided every time with Duke and Linda. Billy would wander off with Jack when the debates began. Sasha sat quietly reading magazines. Fashion had her attention. Sasha fancied herself creating line of cosmetics and clothing. Her interest fluctuated between our recordings and taking phone calls about a fledgling business.

After the heat became too much in the studio, Mr. Altos flew in and invited me to dinner.

"Possibly, you rushed back too soon, my friend," he said. "Let the others handle the details. Duke did a wonderful job with the throwback albums. You should listen to his instincts until you recover. It's only been a year. Maybe take another six months at home."

"I'm perfectly capable of writing music and recording," I said. "Is it my fault no one else sees we need to expand our audience with a new sound?"

Mr. Altos took a sip of wine and gave me the same look Dad

gave me when I didn't take out the trash as a kid. I assumed it wasn't because of the wine.

"I've heard the demos, Dylan. I agree with the others that your current audience won't accept this from you. The one you have now has paid off in a big way. You don't need to find a new audience. Your music has always been about love. Oh, you threw in some suffering, but because of broken hearts, not broken spirits. You have a wonderful gift of hitting the formula that sells. Don't change."

I offered him the same debate I gave to the others, but he wasn't receptive.

"Don't allow one rough patch ruin all your fine work," he said. "Take all the time you need to make yourself well. I've heard the demos of the work Linda and Duke have done. Add some guitar. We can add your music again on the next release when you're writing like your old self."

Even Mr. Altos had turned on me. Why wouldn't anyone understand I wanted to try something new and it had nothing to do with my accident? It was all I could think about at the time.

Debby was the only one on my side. She voted to add all of the song about loss and despair. One of the songs was for Junior and was entitled, 'Lost Keys.' I thought that was an appropriate song for the record. The others in the group finally added it to the mix.

We added parts of three others I had written at home. Duke and Linda rewrote a few lines. Mr. Altos said that if I didn't allow the changes, he wouldn't release the record at all. Linda and I dug up two unfinished songs from our past and finished them. We added two that Duke had written. We also added two cover songs and added a song previously unrecorded that Billy and Jack were working on for their band.

The fighting ended when I agreed to allow the album be a mix of writers, more so than anytime in previous recordings. It took twelve weeks to record the album, which made its debut in the fall. We titled it, 'Busted Seams.' I suggested the title, 'Drunk Drivers Drink Too Much,' but I lost that battle too. We agreed on dedicating the record to our dear friend Junior.

Recording took its toll on everyone. No one wanted to go on the road to support the record until late fall. I was under pressure from Dr. Summers to continue therapy and not leave her care for months at a time.

Sasha found investors for her new line of work. Billy and Jack toured with their blues band throughout the summer. Debby refused to spend months in the studio away from her children only to hit the road. Linda missed her home in California. Duke was anxious to get out on the road again, but we all decided we would start the tour in late fall.

We didn't want to commit touring past the new year. No one knew if I would hold up, including me. We would decide what to do about extending the tour, as we got closer to the holiday break. Europe would be a possibility for the following spring. Too many in the band now had other interests.

I spent the summer with Elise and the kids in Carolina. Two days a week, I kept my appointments with Dr. Summers in individual sessions or group therapy. It made me more dysfunctional.

Our pastor would check on me once a week. One Sunday after service, Pastor George and I sat on the back porch watching the deer graze. He brought up the story of Samson.

"Samson had great physical strength and accomplished much with it. However," he said, "it was not until Samson trusted in what God could do through Samson that he could have his greatest victory."

I kept watching the deer feed until Pastor George nudged my chair and suggested, "Maybe God has a higher purpose for you other than playing music. Have you considered that you have a higher calling and now you're wasting the strength God has bestowed on you with your anger?"

I hadn't ever thought about it and wasn't about to start. He continued.

"The Bible is full of stories about healing. It starts with your soul. Seek forgiveness for your sins and God will reward you."

"Me? Me? I have to repent my sins?" I said it so loud that Elise came out to check on us. "What about the asshole who damn near killed me. What about his sins? What about all the criminals in the world. Oh, no Pastor. I'm sorry but there are so many others in this world who need to repent their sins. God needs to ask them long before coming to me."

I wanted to be left alone. I wanted to sit in the hills with my wife and daughters and not be bombarded with sermons and discussions about letting go of my anger or seeking a higher calling. His visit only wound me up yet again.

Summer turned to fall. Meeting with my shrink wasn't making me any better. However, Elise begged me to keep going. It was the only reason I went twice a week. To me, the entire, talk morphed into how I felt crap. It was all a giant money making hoax.

The band came to North Carolina for two weeks of band practice. The tour had been set. We were to begin in Atlanta and wind our way up the east coast. We fought over the play lists for the shows. The band refused to play any new songs of mine off the new record, except for the one I wrote for Junior. From the new release, we would play Junior's song, one of Dukes, Billy's addition and one of the older songs Linda and I had updated.

We would cover two from the sixties and two from the fifties albums as our encore. The only thing we could agree upon was that we didn't want to play the same set from the previous tour. We would play three different songs from Linda's back catalogue. The show worked out to just over two hours per show. My back could handle two hours on stage.

A month before The Overture album came out, the 60's release hit stores. Sales were brisk. It was titled, 'Ingonito, Not So Much.' It didn't have the same splash as the previous one, because the mystery was gone as to who was in the band. The novelty had worn off, but it was the first new music I had participated on since the accident. I figured that drove some of the sales. Neither the 50's nor the 60's records pictured as huge sellers. So really if they put a few bucks in everyone's pockets, we were happy, including our record label.

The Atlanta show came with an excited crowd. The band put on a professional show. I wasn't into it at all. As much as I once loved to hop on stage, it seemed more of an exercise to work through each individual song. My playing had become mechanical rather than the free flowing style I had for years. There was no rush. I had decided it was from all the chemicals my shrink had prescribed.

I began to forget where my fingers needed to land on the

neck of my guitar. I had practiced them all summer. I felt dead inside. I never asked the band if had seen a difference in my playing. I guess I didn't care. I kept telling myself it would get better. I'm sure after a few nights on tour, it did get better, but it wasn't the same.

When the tour hit Washington D.C, we had Sam my driver from the accident come backstage for the concert. We asked him to join us for the encore. He had admitted to me before the show he that had not picked up his instrument since the accident and was scared to death to try.

We spoke about life for several minutes backstage before I convinced him to join us onstage holding a guitar. He didn't have to strum along. He joined us onstage with a guitar. After the show, we spoke again. I told him that I had no hard feelings towards him. He needed to get on with his life and begin playing his music once more. I don't know if my talk did any good since that's the last we time we spoke.

We headed up to Philly for two shows at the Spectrum. My brother showed up backstage for both shows. The dope wore his Oakland Raiders football jersey to the first show in Philadelphia. I introduced him near the end of our performance. He walked on stage briefly, but he didn't understand why he was booed. Philly has always been notorious for their sports. Pointing at his Raiders jersey as he crossed the stage wasn't the best idea of his life.

Sasha gave him one of her famous football jerseys for the second show. It was the first time I had laughed on stage the entire tour watching him waltz on stage with Sasha's jersey draped across his chest. I told the crowd my brother was diehard Raiders fan. They booed until he left the stage. I loved it. I knew he enjoyed it too, even if he had pretended otherwise. All Raiders fan are a bit strange.

We had a day off before heading up to New York and the Garden. I knew I had to be at my peak mentally, if only for one night. All the proceeds would be going to the Veterans groups. I wanted to be at my best. I stopped taking all medications for a few days to see if it would help my playing.

We played three sold out performances in Madison Square Garden. The energy of the crowds each night forced us to add songs to our encore each night. My playing became more focused, however anxiety creeped into my senses during the second night. Sweat poured from me far more than normal. I asked if the lights were brighter during the first break, but I was told they were the same as the previous night.

The anxiety convinced me to restart the medications. I didn't know if the anxiety was from the lack of pills or something else, but I didn't want to take a chance that I would fall into a deeper hole. My hand worked well with little to no pain. My back ached after a long day, but I had accepted the pain as normal.

The third night had a different buzz in the crowd and with the band. Many celebrities joined the average fan for the evening. Duke and Debby both had friends and family backstage.

Skunk Baxter, who I hadn't seen in years, requested a visit backstage before the show. We stood overlooking the crowd filtering to their seats.

"Gordy is very concerned about you," he said. "We all are. Rolling Stone is running stories about you being a zombie on stage. They reported there are nights you don't move an inch on stage. Is any of that true?"

"Ah, you know they only want to sell magazines. No one from

there has spoken with me since the wreck. How would they know how I feel?"

Skunk circled me a few times. He peered into my eyes. I blinked hoping he would stop.

"Give Gordy a call," Skunk said. "He feels bad about the last time he saw ya. I tried to get him to come with me tonight, but you know how he is sometimes. It takes an act of Congress to get the guy to leave his house or that blasted store."

"Yeah well look, I ain't got much to say to Gordy. He can call me if he wants. As far as me standing in one spot most of the night, did it occur to anyone that my back barks at me if I move around with a guitar strapped to me? It's so much better than it was even a few months ago, but I doubt I'll ever be the same on stage."

Skunk joined us onstage for the third encore. We jammed on two Check Berry nuggets and one Buddy Holly selection that suited Duke's voice. Skunk could still control an audience. I stood off the side and allowed him to play lead while watching the faces of the people in the front rows. It did my heart good to see someone that connected with his guitar on stage. I knew I couldn't do it.

The album received mixed reviews. It sold well along the east coast, but not as well on the west coast of the United States. We always were far more popular east of the Mississippi River. Our current tour mostly concentrated in the areas where we were the most popular. However, we had a few shows scheduled for the west coast to end the tour.

Recent tradition had the band ending in San Diego. We would play a free show for any military or retired military person who wanted to attend. Carl and the Veterans Agency had it all down now as to how to give out the tickets. The record company loved the idea that we would do that on each tour. The marketing department with the label made sure the national media wrote stories of how the band would give back to the military community. None of us in the band wanted the publicity. We were all too happy to play for the vets and current military men and women. That tradition remained. After the show, I didn't walk the beach or thank God for my blessings. Some traditions were meant to be broken.

By the end of the tour, Duke knew my interest waned from night to night. I had made him the musical director of the band before the tour. He had control over who played what solo and when on every song. He also arranged the set list from night to night. My list of solos became shorter almost each night. Sasha, Billy and Jack were awarded more solos. I was becoming an ornament on stage and not much more. The worst part was that it never bothered me. Before the accident, that never would have happened, nor would Duke have taken my soaring solos from the set.

Dr. Summers and I had weekly phone conversations during the tour. Mostly I sat on the one end without much to say. She continued to claim I was making great progress. The only progress I knew was her bank account grew with each session. Each session was a waste of a phone call. Mr. Altos and Carl insisted I stay with the therapy on the road, or they would cancel the tour. I took the lesser of two evils and made the calls.

We did have one mishap on the road, not counting the endless times that Billy and Jack were either late for the sound checks or arrived just in time. We had another roadie use drugs while working for the band. I could put up with many things while touring, but I refused to deal with illegal drugs. It was doubly important, because even though Linda had been clean for many years, she was still an addict. I would never forgive myself if she started to use again while she was on tour with the band.

In an odd way, I did feel guilty about his termination. I was more dependent on drugs than he was, but my rationale was they were pain pills and meds for my scrambled brain. Either way, it was policy for everyone including band members, to sign a contract that if they were caught with illegal drugs, they would be dismissed. Carl handled all employment issues for the band. Carl had little choice, but to fire the roadie. He was arrested purchasing cocaine from an undercover cop in Cleveland near the equipment truck.

That was one area where we really missed Junior. He was the bands internal conscience. He made sure everyone was on time for sound checks and made sure everyone stayed away from drugs. I didn't mind the groupies in the hotels, or if our staff let loose with a few beers in the bars. I had few rules on the road. However, I was never going to bend my rules about drugs.

I did speak to Dr. Summers about my guilt over me ingesting drugs, yet not allowing others. She suggested my guilt was unwarranted. She thought there was a big difference between cocaine and prescription drugs. I wasn't convinced.

Maybe because Jack and Billy made a second career out of bar hopping after the shows, or maybe because for the first time, I wasn't writing on the road, but I noticed girls everywhere on tour. They were backstage, they were in our eating areas, they were in the hotels, and even once, one managed to get on our bus.

The bus was our inner sanctum and off limits to anyone not associated with the band. I even had a nude woman waiting for me in my hotel room after the show in Detroit. The temptations cropped up everywhere. In years past, I was focused on putting on the best performance I knew how. I was immune to everything else around me. My mind now wandered. I saw things I had not seen on other tours. Girls were always there. Once Elise started to tour with us, she made sure groupies stayed from my view. Even Debby over the years would shield me away from some of the trappings of women on the road.

That tour, they were all over the place, even showing up butt naked in my bed. I stayed true to Elise. Hurting her would have hurt me more than any pain I had ever experienced with my back and hand. She was a wonderful wife and mother and I had grown to love her more with each passing day. The only other woman I had ever felt strongly for remained tucked away in Italy.

I never cared who in the band did what with whom other than drugs before or after the show as long as it didn't affect their performances. Many times Billy and now Jack and occasionally even Duke would find comfort with a woman on the road. I didn't care. Imposing my ethics on my bandmates would never happen. It kept good chemistry within the band. I think Linda would sneak someone into her room now and again. She would have a sheepish grin the next day like the cat that ate the canary. Debby never did as far as I knew. Her jackass wife beating husband would be with us most tour dates. I think she was much more concerned with being a good mother and didn't have time for any other extra stuff on the road. Me, I just wanted to sleep and finish the tour.

The band took a break for Christmas. A tour of Europe would begin in March in London. The band would soon play seventeen performances in fifteen cities. I demanded the tour begin at Royal Albert Hall. The hall was built in the late 1800's. Everyone played there from classical composers like Verdi and Wagner to contemporary legends like The Beatles and Led Zeppelin. I really was hoping that playing there could shake me from whatever was ailing me. It was my favorite place to play in the world other than possibly Madison Square Garden. My desire in booking Albert Hall was so the ghosts that called the historic hall their home, would stir my passion to play more than notes once again.

Upon returning home for Christmas break, I received a full physical. My doctor was thrilled with my physical condition, considering all I had gone through during the year. He reduced my pain meds to almost nothing. He suggested I take them only when I deemed necessary. He thought I could afford to lose twenty pounds, but overall he gave me thumbs up with the progress.

Dr. Summers saw me on break as well. She on the other hand refused to alter my medications. The three times I had taken myself off the drugs, I became anxious. She scolded me for trying. I didn't know myself any longer. I had been such a happy go lucky nerdy kid. I hated being an angry adult without a plan.

I sat with Pastor George one afternoon as well. He once again tried to find ways for me to leave my anger for God behind. I tried. I did. I didn't want to be angry. I wanted my life and mind back. He asked me to pray with him. I couldn't bring myself to say even a simple prayer with him. I was convinced my prayer would go unanswered.

The remainder of the break was uneventful. We stayed in Carolina for Christmas Day. We headed to see my family for a few days before school began. The army arranged for me to see hand and spine specialists at John Hopkins. They both agreed I had healed remarkably well. However, the back specialist informed me that my back was about as good as it was ever going to be.

CHAPTER TWENTY TWO

Elise headed off to London with me for our European stops. I had bragged about Royal Albert Hall so much, she wanted to see it for herself. We made a mini vacation out of it going to London three days earlier than the shows. She pulled me along to the museums during the days. I arranged for a private tour of the Hall, but we had to wait until the day before the show, since Sasha wanted to join us. Elise and Sasha went on and on about all the violinists that had played there. I pretty much ignored them and harassed the poor cute Brit, Feona, who would be our guide.

Elise scolded me because I teased poor Feona for not knowing all the ghosts, who lived in the hallowed hall. Nor did she know the exact spot on the main stage that creaked when you hit it just right. I did. I teased her that all that information should be part of her tour.

I could tell she was a new employee. She flustered easily. I felt terrible when I found out it was her birthday, so I offered her two front row seats and enough money to have a nice dinner before our show. I was in such a good mood wandering around the Hall and listening to all the ghosts remind me of their past performances.

The band ignited a mellow crowd. Our performance was the best of the year. By the end of the evening, the crowd danced in their seats to, 'Twist and Shout' and 'Come Together.' The ghosts had indeed induced me to play with passion. The second night delivered another inspired set ending with 'Back in the USSR.'

Elise flew back home the next morning. The band flew to Holland. We had a day off before playing at The Paradiso in Amsterdam. It was another interesting site to me, since it was a converted church. The environment struck me as the complete opposite of London. The Dutch stood in a large open area inside the building for the entire show. Most never sat. The Dutch were lovely people. I enjoyed my time with them.

After Amsterdam, the funk returned. I think all the excitement of seeing London with Elise and playing Royal Albert Hall retained my focus. On the flight from Amsterdam to Munich, my brain was stuck in the mud again. We played shows throughout Germany, France and Spain before landing in Rome for three days of rest. Besides London, I always loved to visit Rome.

Rome was Linda's favorite stop on tour. We lost track of Jack and Billy. Duke flew to Venice and Debby visited Sicily. The first day in Rome, I wandered around with Linda and Sasha. We walked until our feet hurt. My diet was void of pasta, but it was not easy wandering around the shops of Rome. I bought a 35mm camera before we left the States and took the opportunity of seeing Rome to learn how to use it.

When I got back at the hotel, there was a note left for me at the front desk. Lorenza's scent and handwriting were evident. She wanted to meet the next morning at the Coliseum. Anxiety, shock and anticipation all hit me while reading the note.

I could barely sleep. I arrived thirty minutes early. Lorenza stood waiting. Her hair tinged with grey. Her shape no longer a perfect hourglass, but she stood the test of time. Words were as hard with her as they were with my songwriting. We exchanged a warm embrace without a word. She took my hand and we sat on a nearby bench.

"I never loved man," she said. "You will never know power of father over daughter in our country." She lowered her beautiful face. "I had to go. No more pretending to love this man. I move home. Si."

She told me how she now taught school. She would never marry again or have children. She had suffered enough heartaches. I could feel it all rush back to her while she slowly described all she had gone through. It tore me up inside having to listen to her story.

"I afraid my Dylan wouldn't see me," she said. "Let me see you now."

She rubbed the curve of my chin. She ran her fingers in my hair. I refused to move in fear of ruining a perfect moment.

What wrong?" she asked in broken English. "My Dylan broken. Si? Why my Dylan broken? I know accident. I know pain. Your pain not from accident. Si?"

"Si," I said.

We stood and walked holding hands. A chill came across me. One chill did more for me than all the drugs I had ingested for two years. We found a quiet spot. I held on to her assuming once I let go the world would end. As much as I loved Elise and would for life, Lorenza owned a large part of my heart. I sensed she knew it.

We let go of the embrace. The globe remained spinning its axis. We sat near a fountain.

"Tell me, my Dylan. Why sad?"

I rambled on about the drunk driver and the rehab. I told her how everyone thought I suffered from depression, and filled my mind with lies and drugs. I told her how the band no longer accepted my music. I told her I thought about killing myself or never picking up another guitar. I told her how most days I wanted everyone to go away. I told her how she was the only person who would understand.

"You have everything. Si? You have wife who loves him. I read you have children. I read you travel world with band. I read you win awards and people throw clothes at you. I read you even find sexy naked ones in your bed. You have every riches anyone have and you tell me you want to die? No. I no understand. I pity my Dylan. Now I know what wrong. You now foolish man."

My chest sunk where I sat. My heart sunk lower. Not only did the one person in the world, who I thought would understand, reject my thoughts, she pitied me. My mind searched for words. Nothing. Lorenza reacted to my stunned silence.

"I hurt my Dylan with words. Si? I know my Dylan not always fool. We will fix broken fool and find my real Dylan. Not one sitting here today."

A mild anger returned. "I'll fix myself," I said passing along a frown.

The sound check was only thirty minutes away. In all the years, never once was I late for practice, or a sound check. As upset as I was, this day wouldn't be the first. I asked Lorenza to come along and offered her and her family tickets. She declined.

"When my Dylan plays, I see him, not this man."

I planted a peck on her forehead and left. As upset as I was in that moment, I knew I could never stay mad at Lorenza. She yelled out how she wanted to spend the next day with me. I waved with my back to her.

That night will go down as the worst performance of my career. I missed my spots entering every solo and even played the wrong opening to a song. Linda slid across the stage more than once asking me if I was ok.

I had no desire to see another stage. Lorenza's words repeated themselves in my head for the remainder of the evening. Back at the hotel, I got on my knees and looked above. I searched for words for God. I wanted nothing more than to make peace with my maker. The words eluded me. I woke up on the floor the next morning to the sound of knocks at the door. I scrambled to the door. Lorenza stood there with a wide smile and tight jeans.

She did her best to remove the sting from her words. Maybe they stung so bad, because they were true. We talked about Elise and my daughters as I shaved and readied for the day. We also discussed her marriage again. She told me that she never truly loved her ex-husband even though she tried. She admitted she loved another, but knew her father would never approve the marriage.

"I hope one day to see him again," she said. "I will always love him."

Her words filled my mind like a bad riddle. We spent the day lounging around the hotel and the city. She knew good spots for photos. At the end of the day, we gave each other a gentle kiss and she handed me her current address and phone number.

"If you ever find my Dylan, and he is single man, he find me here. Go home. Find happiness and peace and always remember; our God loves you and me. We all sinners and lose our way, but the door is open to God. Find him you silly man."

I walked away in silence, feeling a sense of loss. I also felt like I had let her down once more.

As much as I wanted to quit the tour, Duke convinced me to finish it.

"You have always been a pro, don't let us down. It's your name on the bill. People come to hear you play."

The few remaining shows were a blur. I improved the second night in Rome, but my performance was still subpar. Someone must have alerted Mr. Altos about playing well below my standards. He called me in Budapest. He had never once called me in all the years while I was on tour. It was not a coincidence.

Budapest was the second to last show with Athens being the last. I walked the streets the night before the show In Budapest. I sat in the center of town all alone. The lights were on from the neighboring buildings. Most shops had closed for the evening.

I had my camera, but I hadn't taken any photographs. A red haired woman walked up to me and asked if I was a tourist. I told her I was only in town for two days, so I wasn't sure if that classified me as a tourist. Her English was quite good despite her heavy accent.

"I see you have a camera," she said. "I have lived here all my life and know where all the good places are for night time photos. I'll show you if would like."

We walked the streets for close to two hours until I offered to buy her a meal or a drink for showing me the sights. She knew of one of the few places still open and accepted my invitation.

We settled into a small restaurant owned by her uncle. She

told me about growing up in a nation formerly under Soviet rule. We discussed how she was told what color her car had to be because it was the only one made available by the government. She explained to me how they rationed heating oil. So many things I took for granted in the United States wasn't available to her as a child.

We sat until her uncle wanted to go home. As I was leaving, she turned and said, "Good luck on stage tomorrow night, Dylan."

I had only told her my first name and that I lived in America. I was too interested in learning about her country, I barely allowed her to ask me any questions.

"How do you know who I am?" I asked.

"Don't you remember? We walked right past where you are playing tomorrow night. Your picture is very large and hard to miss. When I saw you sitting alone, I thought it was you because I am a fan. However, I took you to the arena on purpose. I wanted to see if you would tell me who you were. If not, I could see your photo again.

I laughed. "Well, you obviously know how to find the arena better than me, so there will be two back stage passes for you at the window."

She happily accepted. Sometimes you don't know if people are being nice because they want something from you, or they're doing it from their heart. I would run into that problem all the time. It became hard to know your friends from the users. I counted Irene as one who wanted to show me the town because she was proud of where she resided. I suspect dinner and passes to the show were a huge bonus for her and never expected. Sometimes you can tell the difference with how they smile when offered. Irene's smile was genuine.

The tour ended in Athens, Greece. Billy and Jack never made it back on the plane with us. They had collected an entourage of beautiful Greek beauties and decided to make a vacation out of it. I had to admit Jack was good to have in the band, because Billy was going to run all over each city with or without Jack. I figured that between the two of them, one would remember to make it to the show. I could hardly blame them. They were two single men traveling all over Europe with a rock band.

I boarded the plane still carrying Lorenza in my heart and the guilt for leaving her behind. I had no choice. I had a wife and two children waiting for me back home.

CHAPTER TWENTY THREE

Returning home had a different feel. For the first time ever in my musical career, there was no future project waiting. There were however, three beauties waiting at the front door. I hadn't discussed it with anyone, including the shrink, but I was having nightmares of that car ripping into the side of me at that intersection in Washington. I had visions of Lorenza standing over me at the crash site telling me, "How much riches you have." I became sleep deprived since we left Italy. I didn't know where to turn or what to do.

Elise wanted to take a family trip before the kids started school. I had little desire to travel. She finally convinced me to head out to Disney World in Orlando. There I was, standing in a long line waiting to shoot the crap out of Buzz Lightyear. The second we piled into our seats, Diana yelped that she had to pee.

Don't get me wrong. I loved my kids more than anything during that time. However, standing in the Florida heat and humidity in August for thirty minutes so they could ride Dumbo was not my idea of what a songwriter and musician should be doing. I should have been standing on the stage at Madison Square Garden in front of twenty thousand fans, not walking amongst that same number of people to hear, 'It's a Small World' ring in my brain for hours on end. I constantly reminded myself that Dylan James the musician should be on stage, but Stu Edrich, father, was where he belonged.

The moment we arrived back from Florida, I called Carl to see how the negotiations were progressing with our next record deal. Our last contract had expired. Since our last record never reached the top 50 in the charts, the record company was putting the squeeze on us. They offered less studio time and benefits than we had with our last agreement.

They also would not commit to any more than one record at a time. Even Carl became frustrated with the lack of respect the label was showing the band. Sasha became more interested in her fashion lines than her violin strings. Billy and Jack planned a new record and a long tour with their band. Duke's passion became producing records for other bands. He wanted a break from the road.

Neither, Linda or Debby seemed inspired to do anything, but sit at home and watch Oprah. Elise looked for excuses to send me out of the house. We seemed to have needed a lot of milk all of a sudden. I swear she was pouring it down the drain, only so I had to get more.

In speaking with Carl, the record label wouldn't budge, and neither would I. Looking back, I think I used it as an excuse not to have to record with the band any more. I wanted the freedom to call my own shots again. I sensed the end for Dylan James and The Overture.

Once retirement stared me in the face, and with Elise always in my face, I decided sitting on my ass forever wasn't an option. The record company made a final offer. I turned it down. I called the other members of the band. We all agreed our home in the record business for many years now paid us little respect. I wanted to call Mr. Altos, but Carl convinced me to stay out of it. We all agreed to take a break as a band and allow Carl to find us a new home for our music. I sat deflated in North Carolina with no immediate future.

I banged around with my acoustic guitar so much even Elise and the kids were tired of hearing me play the same five songs. I tried to write new music. I wrote a few things, but nothing I thought was worthy of putting on tape.

One day while snoozing on the sofa with nothing better to do, Elise woke me and handed me the phone.

"Mr. James, big fan. The name's Ed Larson. Maybe you've heard of me? Doesn't, matter. I'm about to make you famous."

I shook my head and cleared the ears. Did he suggest I wasn't famous? He continued.

"Viet Nam, you heard of it? I'm about to produce the biggest war movie Hollywood has ever seen and you my friend are my first choice to write the soundtrack. Irving Altos and I are golfing buddies. He tells me you're stockpiling music that makes even men cry, perfect for the greatest war picture every produced. I need you here next week."

After hanging up, I couldn't believe how fast my dear wife made the plane reservations. Carl struck a deal in two days. The one stipulation I had other than a reasonable fee, was that a certain number of free tickets would be allocated for Viet Nam vets. Larson agreed.

My first stop after checking into my hotel was to see Linda. My confidence in writing songs was at an all-time low. I needed a friendly face to boost my ego. She agreed to offer whatever help needed.

I sat on the set for days getting a feel for the movie. It opened my eyes. It was one thing to donate time and money to our veterans. It was another to watch the horrors they endured through the prism a movie script. Since several veterans, who battled in the war advised the producers; I assumed much of it was true to life.

This was the perfect project for me. It called for a dark and moody sound track. I could finally expand that side of my writing and not be told my fans wouldn't accept it. Linda helped, but mostly in the form of being a cheerleader and forcing me to write.

My confidence grew with each new section of music. Mr. Larson claimed I hit the exact tone he wanted when he hired me. After I had a good feel for the tone expected from the soundtrack, I headed back to Carolina to finish my work.

My kids stopped calling me grumpy. Elise stopped making me get milk or ice cream every day. I finished the musical score a week before my deadline. I flew back to Hollywood to work in the film room to see the final version of the film without music. I worked with an orchestra and classical arranger to fill out the sound required in certain sections and later with the director and producers so the soundtrack fit it seamlessly over the film.

The experience was new to me. Elise had helped me think in terms of a bigger sound while I was at home. I worked harder on that soundtrack than I had on anything previous in my life. I think because much of the music wasn't what I had written in the past. It forced me to expand my writing style far more than I had anticipated. The musical arranger assisted in adding a part where it sounded like guns going off. I called Dad and told him I had created the modern day 1812 Overture.

"I don't think so son, but you keep telling yourself you are a real musician," he said. I knew by then he was teasing me. Sorta.

After creating the soundtrack, my mojo came back. Music flowed from my thoughts to my fingers that rose from my acoustic guitar. It became time to shed the anger. I felt blessed once more. I stopped speaking with the head doctor. My frame of mind reached levels not felt since before the accident.

I instructed Carl to call Mr. Altos to see if we could strike a deal on the next Overture album. Their offer remained the same. I called the others in the band and none really wanted to make the next album. Even Duke passed on it. He was working full time as a record producer and enjoying it.

Sasha had become a cosmetics and fashion designer. She occasionally did some studio work with her violin as a guest on other bands albums. Debby loved being mom and nothing more. She had saved enough over the years where she could take a few years off and not worry about money. Debby and I had a good job of staying in touch. She would bring the kids down to North Carolina twice a year and when I would visit Mom and Dad, I would stop by to see her.

Linda remained parked on the beach in California. Billy and Jack had mild success with their blues band. The blues genre was always a tough sell beyond its hardcore fans. Their band was never going to reach the heights of The Overture, but they didn't seem to care. They were on the road finding new women at every stop. Despite the news, I didn't want to create a new band. Deep down, I believed the stars would align and The Overture would record once more.

Elise and I made a trip out to Hollywood for the premier of the movie. Linda joined us for the premier and we ended up staying at her home for a week. While there, I convinced Linda to record another acoustic album with me. This time it would only be her voice and my guitar. She suggested adding Debby and me on vocals singing harmonies. At first, I was against the idea. My ego still wanted control, but after sleeping on the idea, I agreed.

I called Debby and she agreed to join us as long as she only had to sing her parts and leave. I convinced Linda to come to New York. We agreed to write all the music before heading into the studio to cut down on time away from home. We each wanted the studio time to be minimal. We would record the entire album in one week. I asked Duke to produce it as a favor to me. He agreed. I would pay for the studio time out of my own pocket. We would call ourselves, 'Evolution.'

Elise and I went home where I finished the concepts that Linda and I had created on our visit. I played them for her over the phone for weeks, until we were each happy with the sound. I flew to California for a week to finish them in person before heading into the studio. We wanted no surprises.

Over the course of several months, I again took myself off the meds. I ignored Dr. Summers calls. Elise let up on me going to see the doc because she noticed a marked improvement without seeing her. I think I had Elise convinced that the meds were a hindrance to me getting well. My sleeping patterns improved. The nightmares were largely gone.

I knew I still wasn't the same person I was before the accident, but I did feel I was finally releasing the anger pent up inside of me. I attended church with the family, including Elise's parents. At times, I would even listen to the sermon. My life steered back onto the right path.

Our trio hit the studio in April of 1991. We recorded twelve tracks in nine days. Partially because we had one guitar and two voices, and partially because Duke only had ten days he could offer us. Everyone was pleased with the finished work. Carl's job would now be to find a buyer to distribute it.

There was mild interest from our old label. The issue was that I took all the risk and paid to record it, yet they still wanted all the typical splits. I declined their offer. Carl's assignment was to find a home for the trio and possibly include The Overture in the deal.

We had a larger issue if we recorded a new Overture release. Duke refused to go on the road for more than two months, as did Debby. Getting Sasha to pick up the phone had become a chore, and who knew where the other two blues brothers were hiding. Linda would do about anything I wanted, although she kicked around the idea of resuming her solo career. I threatened to kick them all from the band if they refused to go into the studio with me, if Carl could negotiate a deal. Linda agreed to write a new Overture album with me over the summer.

My confidence in writing love songs returned, although not as high as when I was at my peak. I knew I could still write. The movie soundtrack proved it. However, my songs had a new feel. I still lacked the focus I had in my twenties. Linda called daily to exchange ideas.

Elise planned a family trip to Yellowstone and the Grand Tetons. I needed a break, so it came at a good time. The fresh air soothed my brain. It also offered a chance to resume my budding hobby in photography. The view behind a camera lens taught me to appreciate the smaller things in nature as well as immense things like the Rocky Mountains. I began to appreciate God again through the lens of a camera. I recalled the talk I had with Linda and realized I surely didn't create those mountains.

My daughters wanted to know if they could ride the Buffalo or run under Old Faithful. Luckily, we didn't try either. Elise didn't want to be banned for life from the National Parks for riding the buffalo. The only drawback from the trip was that Elise seemed to be lagging behind on our walks. Her lack of energy was unusual for her. We hiked near our home quite a bit. She had always outpaced me.

Spending two weeks with the glory of nature helped my creativity. My lyrics took a noticeable turn for the better. I decided to return to writing love songs, but also keep writing songs with deeper thoughts. Linda still thought they were too dark, but I saw them as exploring new territory.

Elise saw the doctor a week after we returned home. He ran a battery of tests. I assumed the aging process had caught up to her, but I still worried. Because she rarely wore anything but a smile, it wasn't easy to see when she experienced pain.

Stage Two Hodgkin's disease struck my wife. The doctors hoped they had caught it early. Radiation treatments started almost immediately. I had no time to be angry with God. My attention was squarely on the health of my wife.

My career would wait. I owed Elise everything. I drove the girls to school every day and learned how to cook. My loving wife had always been there for me. I was determined not to fail her. As hard as I tried, I did however feel like I was running in quicksand. I had no time to play the blame game or feel angry. My thoughts zeroed in on doing all I could to comfort Elise and calm our daughters.

Her mom would come over to help as much as possible. My mom came down for a few weeks to help with the girls. Despite my efforts, I wasn't the best of cooks, however the girls tired of takeout. I tried hard to be a support for Elise. It pained me after her radiation treatments. She was constantly vomiting and not from my cooking. She struggled for six months until the cancer went into remission.

While caring for Elise, Carl reached an agreement with Mountain Records, or old label to produce one more Overture album. I agreed to the deal, but everyone realized it would wait until Elise was strong enough for me to leave her. Linda worked on the music I sent her in between running the kids to and from school and caring for Elise.

Eventually, everyone's schedules aligned to enter the studio. I had second thoughts about leaving home, but the kids were home for the summer and Elise had regained her strength. She assured me she would be fine. I hired someone to clean the house, who also cooked four times a week. Her mother promised to watch over my family too. I promised not to argue with our producer or the members of the band, so we could deliver the record in a reasonable timeframe.

Linda flew to Carolina for a week before we entered the studio. We finished several songs that we had kicked around for months. Most had the old Overture sound. I was in no mood to fight.

Everyone wanted this to be a strong comeback album. We all recognized it could be our last. We made the album in seven weeks not counting over dubbing that was to be done later. Everyone had a reason to finish it quickly. Everyone focused with little drama hitting the studio.

We later played ten dates in major cities, mostly along the east coast in anticipation of the record. My thoughts were with my family the entire tour. I called home at least twice a day to check on them. I think because everyone knew the tour was limited, we put everything we had into the shows. I think they were our best shows. I still didn't have the passion as before, but with my body off of prescribed chemicals, I never missed a note.

The tour ended in time for everyone to be at home for the Christmas holidays. Elise began playing her instrument again. She told me it made her happy to play and took her mind off other things. I knew she was still concerned for her health. She was always someone in tune with her body. Even though her smile had returned, so did my nightmares.

CHAPTER TWENTY FOUR

Finding a distributor for our, "Evolution" recordings, became huge task for Carl. Mountain Records, The Overture's label thought the sound was a stripped down version of the full band and thought it was overkill. They refused to distribute the disk even though Mr. Altos did tell me the songs were some of our finest.

Billy suggested I sell either individual songs or the entire recording on the internet. He said he had someone design a web page for his blues band. I had no clue what he was talking about and dismissed his idea. He insisted most, if all music sales would be on the internet. I knew he had stayed on top of technology, but still, I thought he was crazy.

While discussing with Carl a distributor for, "Evolutions," I floated an idea. I wanted Elise to play for the New York Philharmonic Orchestra for one night or even one song. He thought that was a great idea and he thought he could make it all happen. He called a few days later and the conductor agreed to it.

When I asked how he pulled that off so fast he said, "I'm the agent for the Conductor and he owed me a favor. For another, his brother is the general that gave your band the award in Washington." Small world I thought.

I was thrilled he acted so fast. He continued, "However, there is one catch. You have to play too."

"No chance," I said. "This is for Elise. I want it be her night, not mine."

It took another few days, but we compromised. I told Elise I was taking her to New York for our anniversary.

"New York sounds fun, but can't we go back out to the mountains or something with less people?" She asked.

"We could," I said, "However the New York Philharmonic doesn't play in the mountains."

I explained to her how Carl had arranged for her to play one night with the orchestra.

Her cute cheeks turned beet red. "Are you insane?" She yelled. "I can't play at that level any longer."

"Baby, you have done so much for me over the years. You stuck by me in my darkest periods and you have practically raised our daughters alone. It has always been your dream to play with them. It's for one night, possibly only one song. Carl wanted to do this for you as much as I did. Please. Think about it. You will have plenty of time to practice and you can even pick the song."

We took a trip to New York where she met the conductor and toured the facility. She had two months to practice and then she would return to stay in New York for three weeks of rehearsals. The conductor promised one song as first chair and possibly others as second chair depending on rehearsals. I promised to stay back in North Carolina while the kids were in school and care for them. I knew her mother would also watch us like a hawk.

Elise threw me out of the room to discuss her selection with the conductor, a mild mannered chap losing his hair. When they came from the room, I asked her what she chose to play.

"There is only one song to play and you should have known from the beginning my choice."

"This about you Elise. Honestly, it has nothing to do with me. Please select any piece of music you feel you want to perform."

"Stu, honey, it has to be the 1812 Overture. We both know it. Mr. Metheny said they hadnt played it in years and would be a solid choice. It's done."

She practiced that song so many times at home, I felt like George Bailey listening to the piano in the background on New Year's Eve.

The time had come for Elise to head off to New York. The girls and I would meet Elise in New York two weeks later. My in-laws were also making the trip to see her perform. They had never been to New York, except for a two-day trip they made for her graduation from Julliard. This time I arranged for them to stay in a swanky hotel for four nights.

It took everything Elise had to convince her dad to leave the farm for the four nights in the city and two travel days. My parents were also coming to the show. We were going to have a bit of a cheering section for Elise. Sasha, Debby, Duke and even Carl were joining us for the performance. I bought an entire row of tickets.

I wanted so badly for Elise to live her dream, if only for one night. She had played with smaller orchestras in college, her Broadway Show as well as touring with The Overture, but this was always her true dream. Play with the New York Philharmonic at Lincoln Center. It thrilled me that I could assist. She had given up so much, to make sure I had achieved my goals. I couldn't think of a better professional way to pay her back.

I met with Carl, the night before the performance. He was still not getting much interest for our Evolution recordings. I told him to put them on the shelf. I would pick a better time to release them.

The performance came off very well. Elise played three songs and did a terrific job. The permanent smile across my wife's face after the show, told me she was thrilled. We were all so proud of her. I think it was good for our daughters to see Elise perform. They knew she had in the past, but had never seen her with my band or an orchestra.

My Dad waltzed over next to Elise and me after the show and announced, "You are now counted as a world class musician, Elise my dear, because you have played the 1812 Overture with one of the finest orchestras in the world. Not many can say that, including my son."

"Dad, I was invited to play as well. I turned it down because this night was all about Elise, not me. I could have played with the orchestra and your song."

He snickered. "Yeah, well, you didn't. Let me know if you ever reach the levels your wife has."

Elise and the kids returned home with her parents. I stayed in New York for rehearsals with the band. I had convinced them all to play a short tour to prop up our latest release. It was doing well, but we had only played a few shows in support of it. Elise's passion to play with the orchestra encouraged me to want to play with The Overture once more.

The band members, other than Linda and Debby still seemed more interested in other projects. Every time we joined up, I wondered if it would be the last we would work together. I wanted any time we spent as a band to be memorable.

My physical abilities had recovered quite well. All the doctors claimed my speedy recovery was nothing short of a miracle. One marveled that I could walk at all. Another told me I would never be able to stand on a stage and perform again. Yet, I did and could. Never once did I consider my recovery a miracle. I assumed it was from all the hard work I had put into my therapy.

At times however, my mental focus lagged far behind my physical recover. I had good months, then bad. My anger against the world and God had for the most part dissipated. However, small things would set me off.

Despite wanting the upcoming tour to be special, I didn't sweat the small stuff. One of the compromises I made to get them to all play again was the band could pick the set list. I had one vote, as did every other member. No longer did I carefully select each song, each night with Duke's input. To attract Billy, we added two songs from his band. We added a song that Duke had written, but we never recorded.

The tour began at the Boston Garden. Sasha appeared on stage in a skintight jump suit with a shamrock and the Boston Celtics logo on the sleeves. She had learned very well how to draw attention to herself. The band was tight. I stood off to the side much of the show and allowed Sasha and the others show case their talents. As the evening progressed, my mind wandered to the hills of Carolina and my family. I took my turn at solos, but I was happy to play the wallflower for much of the evening.

We did our usual three shows in New York City, with the last one having all the proceeds donated to various Veterans groups. Even the fee to use Madison Square Garden on the final evening was waived to add to the monies donated to a good cause.

I tried my best to focus. The crowd seemed to enjoy the show, but I knew the passion waned all night. Skunk came backstage after the show.

"I went to visit Gordy last week. We're both concerned. I listened to you play, dude. You might be able to fool those people sitting in the crowd, who have never been on this stage, but you ain't fooling me. The fire in your belly is gone. I know it and I know you do too."

I knew I couldn't argue with him. I decided to take my verbal lashing and not allow it to make me angry. It was bad enough I still had to pop the occasional pain pill for my back and lived on Aspirin during the tour, but I refused to take any more anti-depressants.

"Gordy wants you to come and see him. He thinks maybe he can help you find that fire again."

I felt my anger raise. "Never once have I stopped Gordy from seeing our shows. He knows full well, there is a pass left for him every time we are within two hours of the shop. He also has an open invitation to my home and he knows it. You tell Gordy from me that if he's that concerned, he can find me."

"Stu, I am really disappointed in you," Skunk said. "The man cares deeply about you. If you don't know by now, then you are far more miserable than you look onstage."

I did my best to convince Skunk that I was perfectly fine. However, Skunk knew me before I could find A minor in first position on the neck of a guitar. Fooling him was near impossible.

The tour moved on down to Philly, then Washington, and later to Raleigh, North Carolina. Elise showed up with the girls and her parents. Her parents had never seen the band live, nor had my daughters. I think even Elise sensed this could be the last time we would be together as a band.

Elise joined us onstage for the encore. We finished with a nugget from our first album. With my family in plain view for the concert, I focused on them and rocked the house. We added extra solos for me during the show.

The tour ended in Miami. After the show, we arranged a quiet dinner for the band at a South Beach restaurant. We said our goodbyes as if everyone knew the end was near for the current band member configuration of The Overture. It was a very odd feeling. We still enjoyed great chemistry. However, the fight in me to keep the band alive vanished.

If Sasha wanted to devote her time to her cosmetics and clothing line, so be it. If Duke wanted to live in Los Angeles and produce records and never tour any longer, good for him. If Billy and his cohort wanted to play small blues clubs and chase women, I no longer had the energy to make them see The Overture was the meal ticket that allowed them their playtime. I considered becoming a solo artist, or possibly even bringing on guest musicians with each release. Maybe the idea of going out at the top of the charts was the best option. I decided any decision could wait until I caught up with my family.

Once home, I didn't hear from anyone in the band for months. I went to my kid's school functions and played dad and husband all winter and spring. After becoming moody again, Elise insisted I see Dr. Summers once a week. I agreed, but refused to take any mind numbing drugs.

Pastor George would drop in for a free meal and asked me to look at my faith. I explained how I was secure in my thoughts and what I believed. I told him that I had largely forgiven God for my accident. At least I had convinced myself my thoughts were true. Pastor wasn't as convinced.

"You cannot make peace with yourself until you make peace with your God," he told me until I think even he tired of hearing it.

I wanted to live my life one day at a time, and be a husband, dad and musician. There was no room for anyone else in my life, including God. Forgiving was one thing, allowing God back into my life was another.

CHAPTER TWENTY FIVE

Months flew off the calendars. I became a hermit. I called Carl once a month to check on finances. I called Debby and Linda once a month just because. Duke would call and pretend as if he missed the band and wanted to head back into the studio. I knew deep down he was happy with his life and wasn't serious in revitalizing The Overture.

I couldn't sleep. My nightmares returned. Elise begged me to see our regular doctor. He prescribed valium to help me sleep. I refused to take it at first, but I took a few times and it did help me sleep better and assist with my anxiety.

We had planned a trip over summer break, but it never happened. Elise's mother became ill with pneumonia. Elise wanted to stay close to home even though the doctor told Elise her mother would recover with proper rest. Still, Elise's father relied on her mother a great deal. With Elise's mother being down for a few weeks, Elise made them dinner most nights.

My dad and brother showed up for hunting season. He saw the bottle of valium and raised hell with me. He warned me to stop taking it and live with not sleeping.

"It's the better option," he said. "I've seen two people from the office take that drug and it led to other issues. Flush it down the toilet."

Dad was the main reason why I was so against any drugs. The

man refused to take an aspirin. He swore to me he didn't even take Novocain at the dentist's office, but I wasn't buying that one. However, the time Dad caught my brother with pot, he was banned from hunting and fishing for six months and grounded for two. Drug use was the ultimate sin to my father.

Dad and I got into a big argument over the drugs and life in general. He couldn't understand how a man not quite forty could sit on the porch all day and not work.

"I've invested well, Dad. Our house didn't cost a fortune. We don't live an extravagant life style. We each have one car. Have you ever seen me waste my money on fast cars or stick my name on products that failed? Carl and his financial wizard George have looked over my money. I don't have to work if I don't want to work."

"I don't give a damn how much money you think you have in life, son. A man puts his work clothes on each day and heads to a place of business and picks up a check every other Friday. That's how life works."

My blood pressure began to rise. I popped a valium right in front of him. "Guess what, Dad. This is my office. Right here on this porch. I've produced music where four times a year my record label puts thousands of dollars in my bank account. It's called royalty checks, and I'll bet those checks are a lot more than yours. Stop telling me how my life was wasted sitting on this porch. My royalty checks not only gave me this porch, but your hunting cabin."

Dad and my brother left the next day. I didn't try to stop them. Elise made sure I kept my appointment with Dr. Summers two days later. Elise must have tipped her off about the riff I had with my dad. Summers asked me about the argument and the valium. She tried to convince me to stay off the Valium, and take what she prescribed. I didn't want to go down that path again. It took me too long to wean myself off them before. I assumed staying off the anti-depressants was better for me in the end. Dr. Summers disagreed. It was my body and my mind. I stayed on the Valium and Aspirin when my back barked. I took pain pills for the back only on rare occasions, usually if we played three nights in a row or I did too much with the kids.

After browbeating Carl for months, Mr. Altos called me directly. He asked me to reunite the band. I made the calls, but only Linda and Debby agreed to participate. I pushed the idea of Mountain releasing the Evolution tapes and then I would reform The Overture with new musicians other than Debby and Linda, who would remain in the group. I was pleased when Mountain declined. My heart wasn't totally set on tossing close friends from the band.

After Mountain again rejected the Evolution tapes, I thought harder about a solo project and finding a small indie label to produce it. I wrote new material and began started showing up in bars around my local area. I also wanted to see if I could find my passion to play live again. Elise supported the idea of going solo. I think mostly because it got me out of the house.

Dad's words stuck with me on some level. There were times I felt guilty for wasting my talents. Not because I wasn't the assistant to the assistant manager at the local department store and collecting a check every other Friday. I'm sure that way of life is good for many, just not me. No, my problem had become, I knew I had a talent few possessed. I had written as many hits in the previous decade as any songwriter. Possibly, Dad's words assisted in getting me to play outside of the back porch again. After all, it had been two years since I had played in public.

My daughters were growing up fast. You hear all the time to cherish the time with your children because if you blink, you missed it. Even being at home for two solid years, I still felt like I was missing out on something. My favorite memory was when Diana took me to her school for career day. I showed up with my guitar.

"This is my daddy," she said. "He used to play music for everybody around the world, but now he stays home and is just my daddy now."

I had written enough material that I was pleased with for a solo record. I didn't bother taking it to Mountain Records. My memory hadn't forgotten how they refused our trio with the Evolution tapes several times. I figured if they didn't want three of us, they surely didn't want just me. I called around to small labels looking for a deal. I had some interest, but nothing that thrilled me. I was committed to being a solo performer with or without a record deal.

That changed the day Elise told me that her cancer had returned. She had been doing so well. Everyone was hopeful the horrible disease had gone for good. We sent her to the finest doctors who specialized in cancer treatments. Nothing worked. It spread quickly. Her health rapidly fell apart. The next eighteen months were brutal for everyone. My nightmares increased, as did my appetite for drugs. I did what I could to comfort her. This time I sensed her slipping away. I couldn't deal with idea of losing her.

I tried every day to convince myself that my wife was the one in pain and not me. I wanted to be strong, but in the end, I was weak. I found a guy, who knew a guy, who supplied me with pills that eased my suffering. Not being stronger for my wife was a pain no pill would ever cure.

The day before she left this earth, Elise ripped my heart out, but I deserved every word. Only at the time, I didn't understand.

"Stu is the only man I ever loved," Elise said. "I wish he had been with me for the last several years. I've been living with a stranger most of the time. My dying wish is that you find Stu again and have him raise our daughters. I know Stu is still alive. I know you think you've been that man, but you haven't. Do whatever you must to find him. Please, for me and Diana and Deborah."

We buried her four days later overlooking the mountains that she loved so dearly.

Rose and George Andrews were the salt of the earth. I knew instantly the first time I met them, where Elise got her smile. They will never make finer people than Elise's parents. They worked hard all their lives to make a living for each other as well as for Elise. They gave to their community where they could and later in life being the best grandparents my daughters could ever wish to have.

They fought me when I paid off their mortgage. The gesture meant little to me in monetary terms, but it had become a debt, they struggled to pay every month. It took several months before Elise's father realized it was not Elise and me looking down on them, but a sign of respect for all the love they had given to Elise and my family. Every time my dad and brother visited for a hunting trip, Elise's mother would bring over the best homemade pies this side of the Mississippi. They truly cared for me as if I was a natural born son. There was nothing I wouldn't have done for them.

I know not only my own father, but also my father in law, lost some respect for me when I began popping pills to deaden the pain of watching my wife wither away in front of my eyes. I fully admit I was a coward. I never had words with my father in law about my drug use, as I did with my own father, but the disappointment etched across his face many times.

After the funeral, I wanted to do as Elise asked and become the old Stu and be a good father. I thought I had been a good father for years. Rose came over and cooked for us a few nights a week. My cooking skills still weren't the best. I hired someone to clean the house once a week. My cleaning skill were far worse than my cooking skills.

I was a good homework dad. Possibly, because I grew up always doing my homework, I could get my daughters to do theirs. While they were in school, most days I would sit with Elise at her gravesite. I hoped she would talk with me and help me find Stu.

Our ritual of me driving the kids to school, then heading over to sit with Elise, having dinner with my daughter, then homework, then a time to sit and watch television with them before bed, went on for many weeks.

My youngest daughter, Deborah, asked if I could teach her to play guitar. I was surprised, yet happy. Neither girl had shown any interest in playing an instrument despite being around music all their lives. We sat on the sofa. I put her fingers in position on the neck of the guitar so she could strum a simple chord. I moved her fingers to another position, then another. We repeated, only this time faster. She had played the melody to her first song. Her bright eyes stared up at me.

Her tiny hands had a difficult time managing to move around. She complained her fingers hurt. I did use heavy strings, so I had some empathy for her. She did her best. She stared up and again, this time with a wider smile, knowing she accomplished something she never had before. Her sister heard the music. Diana entered the room and applauded her younger sister.

That became the moment that would change my life going forward as a father. Elise's voice repeated itself for hours throughout my drug-numbed brain. As happy as I was my own flesh and blood wanted to learn an instrument that had made me an icon across the nation and beyond, it should have meant more to me. It meant far more to my daughter, than it did to me. Her smile, while playing, should have awoken the man who Elise begged me to find.

I called Rose the next morning and asked her and my father in law to watch over the girls while I cleaned myself up and become the father my children deserved. Elise's voice haunted me all night. Even my father's words woke me during the night in the form of a nightmare. Visiting Doc Summers or Pastor George or even trying yet another form of medication wasn't the answer. I had to rid my body of all the drugs in my system and find the root of my ills.

CHAPTER TWENTY SIX

There was only one person who could help me get clean and toss away the anger that still lingered. She resided in Italy. When you're not thinking straight, you forget things. Lorenza's plea for me was the same as Elise. However, my reasoning powers were close to zero. I realized how much the passing of my wife changed my life, but I ignored the suggestions that I needed professional help with depression. I was too proud to open myself up to think someone could help me, more than I could help myself. I compounded my bad choices by returning to Italy.

At the break of dawn, I sat several yards away from the front door of the last place I knew she had lived. I waited patiently with binoculars until Lorenza appeared. Even from a distance, I spotted more grey in her hair. Her face showed signs of age. I was scared to approach her.

I had lost forty pounds from the stress and drugs since the last I had seen her. My hair was the longest it had ever been and was void of washing for three days. My wrinkled clothes had wrapped my body for seventy-two hours. I had always prided myself on keeping my body in top form in order to handle the demands of touring. I no longer owned that body. My skin was pale and a rash covered part of my arm. I had no idea why the rash.

After seeing Lorenza, I became scared she would reject me. She walked in the opposite direction of my perch. I followed her from a distance until she vanished into a stone building with the markings of a school. I peered into a window several times over the next hour, but saw no signs of the Italian beauty.

My body began to shake. It had been days since I popped any pills. Not even an Aspirin for my back after a long flight. I realized a deeper despair would strike, if she rejected me. I couldn't take the risk. I took the next flight to London.

I decided I would spend a few days in London before heading to New York and allow Carl to put me into a drug rehab center. I didn't know which one. I knew Carl would handle it all for me. My in-laws only knew I was leaving to get better.

For months, I had only tried to speak with Carl about my finances, but I knew Elise kept him updated about my health. He mentioned it. He and the entire band came to Elise's funeral. It was the last I had seen any of them. Carl mentioned at the funeral that he was concerned about my health and would be ready to help as soon as I gave him the word.

After checking into the hotel, I took the underground train and made the walk to one of my two personal treasures for playing music, The Royal Albert Hall. There was a small line at the ticket office. I walked up the many steps and past the statue to the end of the line.

Tickets were about to go on sale for Bob Dylan. I thought that was a sign I found my way to London for a reason. I would see one of the people I was named for, at one of my favorite stops in the world before leaving the next day to get right with the world. I didn't take notice of the date, only that I knew I had to go to the show.

I stood at the back of the line and waited patiently. After a few minutes, a woman behind me tapped me on the shoulder. I turned and noticed her not so friendly stare.

"We do have soap and water here you bum," she said. "I would suggest you find some." I had been a big fan of British accents until that moment.

I ignored her. Eventually, it was my turn to purchase a ticket. I slid my credit card through the opening.

"I'm so sorry, sir," the young lady behind the glass said, "Do you have another card? This one does not seem to work."

I looked in my wallet and grabbed the only other one I had with me. I passed it along to her.

"I' deeply sorry, sir but this one has been canceled."

"There must be some kind of mistake," I said. "I have plenty of money and my bills are always paid on time. I have people who handle all that for me."

The woman, who needled me before, laughed and said, "Yeah, you have people, maybe under the bridge with the other trolls."

My blood pressure rose. My anger grew from the situation. I had money. What was happening? I pleaded with the ticket woman to try again.

"I really am terribly sorry, sir, but there is a notice that we are to collect your card. It has been cancelled."

Some jerk with the woman behind me, sneered and shoved me to the side. I took three steps from the window and fell to the ground.

I sat on the majestic stone steps leading up to the great hall feeling sorry myself. Did I not even have enough cash to go see my hero Bob Dylan in concert? The thought seemed impossible to me. What could have gone wrong with my finances? Had Carl given up being my agent and handler of all my finances? How was I going to pay the hotel and get a ticket to venture back home? I barely had enough money in my pocket to eat.

My mind raced with those thoughts and more until someone came over and sat next to me. His looks were plain. I asked him what he wanted. He didn't say much at first. I felt like he pitied me. I hated that feeling. He asked me about my life. I don't know why, but I told him about Elise and the band.

"I need my life back," I said. "I need my band. I need my music. I need to be a better father."

"What you need is a soul my friend," he said. "I can return it, but only if you are ready. Leave your anger behind. Forgive God and your soul will be restored."

I was willing to try anything, even listen to a nut case sitting next to me. "Yes, please restore my soul," I said with a snicker.

"Oh no, you don't get off that easy," the man said. "You think hard. You dig deep. Tell me. Are you ready to return to your life?"

I was. I smiled at the man. He placed his hand on my torn sleeve. I closed my eyes. I felt a warm sensation. I wasn't sure if I had peed myself or I had another withdrawal from not popping pills for several days, but it was an odd feeling.

I opened my eyes upon hearing a new voice. "Our citizens are not normally this way, Mr. James." A blonde haired woman had sat next to me. "We all have our bad apples, now don't we?"

"Wait, what happened to the man, who was just sitting next to me?" I asked.

The blonde haired woman giggled. "What man?"

I turned my neck to look closer at her face. She seemed vaguely familiar to me. "You don't remember me do you, Mr. James?" She said. Before I could utter a sound she said, "It's Feona, I took you and others on a tour here several years back. I am now the manager of the ticket office. I wanted to see why all the commotion at the window. I didn't recognize you at first, but when the agent showed me the card I wanted to see if it was really you."

Finally, a smiling face, I thought. She would make things right.

"I remember you teased me all during the tour of the building," she said. "It is still my favorite memory of taking people on tours here. Will you thank your wife for me please? A few days later, the nicest thank you card arrived in the mail for me. Rarely did anyone ever bother to thank me. Not only did you buy me dinner for my birthday, your wife sent me a beautiful card from a museum in Paris."

I didn't know if I should cry, or ask her if she knew what was going on with my credit cards. I could only say, "My wife died from cancer and yes, she was an incredible lady. Thank you."

Feona placed my hand in hers. We both sat quietly for a moment. I noticed a tear fall from her cheek.

"I am so sorry for your loss," she said.

"What happened to my cards?" I asked.

She sighed. "There was a hold put on them. Someone has cut you off from your money. Let's go inside and maybe we can find out what happened. Let's get you right with the world again."

Those words. They startled me. They were the exact words

that had been stirring in my brain right before that man sat next to me. Feona helped me to my feet. We went inside the hall.

Once inside, I scrambled for Carl's number in my wallet. His number now no longer etched on my brain. My thoughts were barely coherent. I dug around until I found his faded business card.

Feona called Carl for me. We waited patiently for him to come to the phone.

"Dylan, this is Carl. It's time for you to come home. I got a call from Lorenza. She told me that you were stalking her in Italy. I called your home. Your mother in law filled me in that you took off without saying where you were heading or when you would return. I cut off your funds figuring you had to surface."

I felt embarrassed sitting there with Feona. The last time I had seen her, my band and I were the main attraction, now I degraded into a sad site. Carl continued his rant as if I was child.

"Tell me where you're staying. I'll make sure the hotel is paid. A plane ticket will be at the front desk. Use the ticket, or you're on your own. It's time you take responsibility for your daughters and get clean."

"I'll be on the plane," I said.

I thanked Feona for her assistance. She asked if I needed a ride back to the hotel. I thanked her again, but refused. Before I could leave, she handed me a small envelope.

"Open this when you're ready to return," she said.

I looked up your bio in our records before I headed outside earlier. I wanted to see your photo to make sure it really was you trying to buy tickets. Happy Birthday!"

I was dumbfounded. I had no clue the following day would be my birthday.

It took hours to find the hotel. I was in no hurry. I did feel happier. I took in the sights along the way. Somehow, I found my way to the Abbey Road Studio. I walked across the famous crossing with several other people. A jerk in a sports car nearly ran me over. I took the tubes to Saville Road and looked up where the Beatles played on the rooftop. I walked by Jimi Hendrix's old pad. I found the pub where many famous British Bands first played. Eventually, my legs gave out and I found the hotel not far from the Thames River.

A hotel employee met me as I walked into the lobby. He informed me that his job was to make sure I cleaned up, put on fresh clothes and made it to Heathrow Airport the following morning. He refused to accept the word no from me.

I slept better than I had in many years. No nightmares. I thought about what that strange man had told me. He talked about restoring my soul. I figured he was a drunk looking for money and Feona scared him off.

The next day, I made it to the flight with no issues. Carl and Sasha met me at the gate after landing in New York. There was not time to head to my apartment, or out for a hot meal. The two of them whisked me into a private room. Carl informed me I was getting on another flight. I complained my back was sore, not one seemed to care. Sasha would be taking me out west. A huge man wearing a black suit and gold watch arrived in the room with us. Carl informed me the sharp dressed man would assure I made it to my destination.

We sat in a row of four. The burly man sat on the aisle and Sahsa next to him. I sat next to Sasha with another man, who was new to us, sitting next to the window. I was exhausted. My back was killing me. I took a couple of Aspirin. The man along the window seat kept attempting small talk.

I was ticked off we weren't in first class, where I didn't feel shoved against human flesh for four fours, but Carl told me first class was sold out. A couple people during the flight recognized Sasha, then me and asked for autographs. The big man tried to shoo them away, but I obliged, as did Sasha.

A limo met us at the airport. I instantly dozed off. I woke up as we drove past a large white gate that followed a winding road leading up to a large white building that appeared as sterile on the outside as it did once inside.

Everything inside the building seemed to be in its proper place. Several staff people with large nametags offered a faint hello as they wandered by. Sasha held my hand all the way through the check in process as our third wheel spoke with someone behind a counter. Moments later, another large fella took my suitcase and asked me to follow him. I was skeptical and more than a bit scared. However, I also wanted to change my life. Sasha kissed my forehead with the promise everyone would be in the studio when I was ready to record and feeling better. I hoped it wasn't a hollow promise.

As we headed down a wide hallway painted eggshell white, the man leading me introduced to a few others living in the building. As we walked, he informed me that I would be responsible for cleaning my own room, as well as making my bed and attending regular meetings with a counselor. It was not what I had expected, but then again, I had no real idea of what to expect. Another man came and removed my suitcase after we arrived to a small room. Two sets of white shirts and white pants hung in a small closet. Not a television or guitar in site. What kind of place did Carl send me?

When my suitcase arrived back the next morning, all my clothes were clean, even my jeans were ironed. Elise had never ironed my jeans. The pills I had hidden in the lining were gone.

Someone dared to knock on my door before the sun had risen. A skinny kid with jeans and a button down shirt entered the room. I learned later that skinny kid was only a year younger than I was. The aging process was kind to him.

"I'm Arthur," the man said. "I'll be assisting you while you live here at The Perry Drug and Alcohol Prevention Facility. My job is to make sure you do your job. Now get up and get showered. Breakfast is in thirty minutes."

After soggy oatmeal and some fruit, I met my counselor. He asked me a series of questions I didn't want to answer. I had been all through it with Dr. Summers and Pastor George. Our session ended with me counting the ceiling tiles. I wanted to change. However, change would come slowly.

I left the door to my room open. The man, who I noticed lived in the room next door, stood at my doorway.

"I've seen you on the Johnny Carson Show," he said. You a famous comedian or something?"

"Nah, my wife told me all the time, I'm not that funny. I'm not a comedian. My name is Stu."

He let out a semi-muted laugh. "Stu, now that's a funny name. You sure you aren't a comedian. I know I've seen your face."

It took several days of him pestering me at my door, before I admitted to Neil where he might have seen me.

"Holy crap, you're the guy who plays for guitar for Linda Sweet. Now I know you. Can you get me her autograph? I remember seeing her over ten years ago. Damn, she's got a sexy ass. Did you ride on her bus? I heard she became a druggie and joined up with some overrated rock band. Too bad, she had talent."

I wasn't sure exactly what he was implying about riding her bus or an overrated band, but I explained to Neil that Linda and I were still close friends.

The news that I was in the building went through the center like wild fire. Others came around asking me to recount stories from the road. They seemed disappointed when I didn't have your typical sex, drugs, and rock and roll highlights they were all expecting.

After two weeks of individual counseling and detoxing my body, they put me in a group setting. Someone asked me how I could have so much in life and throw it all way being a junkie.

I had never considered myself a junkie. I never stood on street corners looking for drugs. I wasn't into cocaine or heroin and I rarely drank. I was hooked on prescription drugs. Surely, he understood the difference. Besides, I was on heavy painkillers for years. I explained how I was not a junkie and let him know that, having it all is relative. I wanted to have my mind and body back. It did however make me think in my room, when I was alone later that night.

After three weeks, I began to adjust to my time at the center. The only drawback was when I asked if I could have a guitar. They refused. I considered it part of my therapy to play again. They did not agree. I craved my guitar.

I was now shifting from enjoying my time to wanting to do everything they asked so I could start to write and play again. They did allow me visitors during the fourth week. Linda dropped in to see how I was progressing.

I introduced Linda to Neil. The man stood frozen. She kissed his cheek and we moved to another section of the lounge. We both got a chuckle. It was nice to see someone from the outside world, but I wanted to go home and see my kids.

Linda and I discussed getting back together to write again very soon. The counselor promised if all continued smoothly, my release was within a week. When I heard that, I answered every question asked with pure honesty. I wanted out more than Cubs fans wanted to win the World Series.

The same night, I got down on my hands and knees and asked for forgiveness. Forgiveness for hanging on to the anger for too many years. Forgiveness for not having been a better father and husband. Forgiveness for thinking God was responsible for my troubles. Forgiveness for avoiding my father and friends. I cried for several hours. When the tears ended, I felt like the nerdy kid who loved to pluck his guitar again.

Carl called me the following week. Not only had my time at the center expired, my finances were made whole. Stu Edrich walked from the center a man with a soul, mind and body all working as one.

CHAPTER TWENTY SEVEN

Explaining to my daughters why I left home soon after their mother left the earth was the most difficult thing I ever had to do. I made a solemn oath with them that I would never leave them like that ever again. It took weeks before Diana would smile for me. More than once, I thought about buying pills. However, I knew if I blew it again with my kids, my days as their father would end. They would never accept me back.

We took it slow, but I began to build their trust. We did homework together. I relearned 5th grade science. Deborah asked again to teach her the guitar. I accepted the challenge with all the passion I should have borne the first time.

While they were in school, I would practice and write music. I contacted the members of the band. We discussed making another record. Everyone agreed that in the spring we would reunite. I thought by then I would have had time with my daughters before disappearing again, and it would give Linda and I time to write new music that our fans would expect.

Rose and George kept a close eye on us. Rose had moved into my home while I was away and had become even closer with my daughters. It wasn't easy to assert final decisions once I returned. The girls would always run to their grandmother if they didn't like what I had to say. It took time for me to win some respect back from Rose and in particular George. I guess I deserved what I got when I returned home.

I convinced Linda to come for the month of January so we could write. My lyrics were not nearly as dark, but something was still different. I couldn't put my finger on it, however Pastor George would stop by and remind me that his sermons held the key. I teased him that maybe the church was missing my envelopes with a nice check more than I was missing his sermons. I told him that I had made peace with God.

"You might be at peace, but your past is still your past, Stu," Pastor said. "Embrace your past with the understanding of who you are now."

Linda arrived begrudgingly after the first of the year. I reminded her that she promised at the rehab center, if I stayed clean for ninety days, she would visit me at my home to write new music. I had held up my end of the deal.

Before heading back into the studio, I wanted to play to a live audience. I started to play for patients at the local hospital. I also went back to the therapy center where I had spent many months and played in the lounge for the staff and patients. I took my daughters with me, so they knew I wasn't running away.

My mind was clear. My playing was crisp. I felt fine. My playing had improved beyond the previous two or three tours. I could play for four hours without wanting to stop. I hadn't done that since I was in my early twenties.

The time had come to leave for New York to work on the new release. My daughters threw a fit. Deborah sobbed in her bedroom for hours the night before I had to leave. I promised to bring them both to New York during spring break and let them see the studio.

After a day in the studio, it was obvious our chemistry was gone. There was no drama, but everyone had other things on their minds. Our producer remained strong willed. Duke was now a successful producer in his own right and had his opinions about shaping our sound. Billy wanted more blues added to the mix. Sasha didn't care as long she could check her email every thirty minutes.

We had grown into different factions with Linda and I wanting to go back to a more pop and rock sound with the fiddle and Billy and Jack wanted a harder edge. Duke wanted strings while Debby wanted it all done so she could get home to her kids. I fought off stress by doing every mental exercise taught to me at the clinic. Returning to numbing my mind with drugs never entered my mind.

We were crumbling as a band right in front of my now very clear eyes and mind. The worst part of it all was that we had some very good songs. My playing was the best it had been for years. We decided to break for a few days. Instead of brining my kids to the studio to watch adults bicker, I took them to Disney.

Funny thing happened this time at Disney. I saw my daughters as real people. I know that's an odd thing to say, but I had never looked at them as people with their own personalities and opinions. Maybe it was because my mind had not been clear since they were both very young, or maybe because they were not old enough to express real thoughts that seemed to matter to me. However, for the first time, I felt connected to them in a way I never had in the past. On the drive home from Orlando to home, Diana wanted me to promise that I would not leave her again. It was a very hard discussion since I was a musician. I soon discovered her words had a deeper meaning.

I teared up while driving. I'm sure Diana noticed. I suddenly realized how much they too missed their mother. I had been so self-absorbed fighting my demons; I never took the time to see their pain too. We discussed how I could balance being on the road, yet still be a single parent. Holy crap, I was single parent. We promised to talk more in the near future about my travel schedule.

Leaving to head back to New York was difficult. The girls insisted I take them with me, however they had school and I had a contractual obligation to deliver a finished product. We discussed putting them in school in New York to finish the school year. I went and sat at Elise's grave. I knew she would object. There wasn't a good option, only the best option, which was to leave them behind.

Once back in the studio, I put my foot down. It was still my band. We would create the music I wanted or they were free to leave. Billy did for a few hours. James told me that Billy had blown a lot of his money recently on buying a nightclub in Chicago and a home in the Virgin Islands. We knew he had no choice but to return. The Overture and our tours were his largest source of income.

Over the next three months, we finished the recordings. I dashed home for a few days here and there to calm the girls. After delivering the tapes and fulfilling my contractual obligations, I held a meeting with my bandmates. I refused to go on the road for long periods away from my daughters. Dylan James and The Overture would be no more. There would be no last tour, nothing. I owed it to my daughters to be their father. I finally recognized the situation Debby had been in for all those years.

CHAPTER TWENTY EIGHT

News flash. Females are odd creatures. They are emotional. They can be mean and vindictive before smiling as they rip your heart out. I think I read that in a book somewhere or saw it in a movie, but trust me; little girls aren't the easiest on the planet for a single dad. I loved them more as they grew, but it was a constant head scratcher from day to day. One day, the compliant would be that we bought the wrong style jeans. The next all I heard was that all boys are scum beings not of this earth.

Somehow, we all survived puberty. Many days I wanted to relieve my nerves with pretty-colored pills, but ultimately, I would never do that to me or my family again. I never left North Carolina expect for vacations with the girls for the next several years. I made peace with my father and my in-laws.

I built a small studio in my home. I wrote several soundtracks for low budget films from home. It was a good balance to allow me to keep working, yet stay at home with the girls. It kept my name in the industry, while providing extra income so we weren't living on my savings or dwindling royalty checks.

I never wanted to retire from the music business. I did however, want to fulfil Elise's last wish and become a good father. I'm positive I heard her voice tell me in the wind how proud she was of me while visiting her gravesite. I may have been at peace with my decision to be a stay at home dad, but I still itched to be a musician in front of a live audience. I would make a rare appearance in a local bar and play a few songs. It was never enough. I even had Debby join me one night when she and her kids were visiting. That part of my life still beat inside of me. I would pray at night that God would help me find the perfect balance of rock and roll star and single dad.

Seven years crawled by. During those years, I attended every school function possible. I cared for my children the best way I could. I attended church many Sundays with my in-laws and the girls. Sometimes I would count the tiles on the window, other times I would listen to Pastor George. I considered buying the church a stained glass window so I would have something new to look at.

I began to question my destiny. Despite having two beautiful daughters, a lovely home, a successful career from being a songwriter, musician and a busy schedule writing soundtracks, I was too young to fade away.

My girls would be ready for college soon. Then what? They would be leaving me. I knew sitting alone in a home studio wasn't the answer. I loved hearing stories about how cheerleading coaches were so unfair and boys were idiots. However, I needed to find a new path in life once my girls were gone.

I wanted to believe my writing abilities were still good. I fought many of the band to make the last Overture album my way and it paid off in a big way. It zoomed to the top of the charts faster than any of our previous releases had. Mountain called me for years to make another record. I knew how to be a successful bandleader and songwriter. I had proven it several times.

I considered trying to form the band again once the girls

settled in college. I had kept in touch with most of my old mates. Duke would show up once a year and beat me in a few games of chess. He loved producing and never missed touring. Debby would bring her kids down for a week every summer. Linda and I would talk on the phone every few months, but nothing inspiring would come from our chats. I read in a trade magazine where Billy moved to Los Angeles and worked as a studio drummer. I never heard from Jack after we disbanded. Sasha would show up every other year with a bag full of eyeliners and clothes not suitable for my girls to wear in public. I would be clicking television channels late at night and many times see her on some shopping network selling her lines of fashion.

I gave these people very good lives and never once did any of them thank me, except for Duke long ago. Was I becoming a bitter old man and angry at the world again? I had reached the pinnacle of my industry and now I was playing dad in some back woods town in North Carolina. I demanded more from music again. It was time to end my long hibernation, but to what ends?

We had a family dinner with my daughters and in-laws. I informed them it was time for me to get back to making music, other than low rent soundtracks. I told them I considered reforming The Overture, but after a few discussions with Duke and Sasha it fell apart. Debby worked part time job as a nurse. Sitting home all day drove her insane. I knew the feeling. Linda had been open to the idea, but we still had the recordings from our trio sitting on the shelf from years ago. I let them all know I had decided to fly to New York to meet with Carl and Mr. Altos to discuss my options. My daughters were upset at first, but they came around. I think they realized how much I had sacrificed for them.

I hadn't been to New York in several years. I wanted to see

my old apartment. Carl had hired a real estate agent to lease it out when I told him I would be in North Carolina for multiple years. I wanted to see the condition of it since it was again vacant. The agent told Carl the apartment would need new carpet, paint and new appliances before anyone would lease it. I figured I would stay there for a few days and see what needed doing. After a few tears and hugs, I knew the time was right to start my career moving forward again. I loved being Stu, my daughter's father, but I also loved being Dylan James. Dylan was ready to be reborn.

CHAPTER TWENTY NINE

I waited until after Labor Day in early September before heading off to New York. The girls were back in school and my in-laws were more than happy to take over again. Time had taken its toll on my in-laws. However, I knew my girls wouldn't be an issue for them. My daughters, considering everything, had grown into well-adjusted teens.

I wasn't sure what direction I would go in after meeting with Carl and Mr. Altos, but I was ready to return to recording in some fashion. I drove up stopping along the way to see Mom and Dad in New Jersey overnight, before heading off to Manhattan the next morning. I had planned to see Debby in the morning, but Mr. Altos had to catch a flight, so I had to be in New York for a lunch meeting. We met at a nice restaurant and later returned to the second floor of the north tower in the World Trade Center where Carl's office was located.

We talked about reforming The Overture, but I informed them there was little appetite from the others. Mr. Altos had a band signed to his label, who has lost their guitar player and songwriter to go solo. Unfortunately, they lived in California. I talked to him again about releasing the Evolution recordings with Linda, Debby and I, but he still wasn't hot on the idea.

I was upset, because he never listened to the work. There

was some very strong material on those tapes. I talked about doing a solo project bringing in guest performers on each song. Mr. Altos warmed to that idea. We did agree in principle to using a couple of the old Overture recordings not used from the last two releases and packaging those with another "Greatest Hits" release. I wasn't thrilled with the idea, but Mr. Altos agreed to release my solo record if I agreed to allow the "Hits" package.

I hated to take advantage of my fans that way, but I knew a percentage of fans insisted on owning every piece of material made available, and some that never was. Companies knew how to take advantage of that fact. I didn't like it, but it was the compromise I made to jump start my career. We had a nice lunch and productive meeting in Carl's office. I was pleased with the visit.

Carl updated me with my finances. I put a bug in his ear about setting up a foundation in Elise's name. I wasn't sure how or in what form it would take shape, and who would benefit, but I wanted him to start kicking around the idea. I was considering whatever the proceeds were from my next project to use it for seed money for the foundation. I was sure I could get some former band members back together for a one or two night show as well for some extra money. He thought it was a good idea and would give it some thought.

I stayed a few days at my skyline apartment. I had forgotten how beautiful the view was overlooking downtown Manhattan. The real estate people were correct in it needing some upgrades, so I delayed my trip home for a couple of days to meet with a contractor for an estimate to paint the place, refinish the floors and upgrade the kitchen. I still wasn't ready to sell the unit. I did enjoy staying there and with a tenant, it paid for itself. I was willing to treat it as an investment, rather than my home.

During the past several years, I would rise early to read the paper. I would make breakfast for the girls and get them off to school. The routine of me rising early and reading the paper would continue in the summer. I kept to the diet a health expert had offered. I would take long walks in the hills and generally was in better condition than I had been in for almost two decades.

My internal clock had me up early, even while staying in New York. One morning, I strolled down to the local coffee shop for a paper and some eggs. The contractor was expected to arrive around nine, so I hustled back to be on time. I sat on the sofa, overlooking the skyline, while waiting for him to arrive. The sun beamed through the partially drawn curtains on a beautiful Tuesday morning.

Suddenly, I noticed a huge plume of smoke near what appeared to be the World Trade Center. Sirens began to blast everywhere. I sat watching the entire scene, attempting to figure out what was going on. At first, I thought it was a big fire.

To my amazement, I watched an airplane fly directly into the other tower not already on fire. My first reaction was to wonder if Carl was ok. I sat in his office in that tower the previous day. My next thought was how could an airplane of that size be so far off course?

I moved to the window. I barely moved for over thirty minutes. I knew something was very wrong. I decided to get a closer look and made me way to the bottom floor. By the time I could make it down to ground level, people flooded the streets, each asking each other if they knew what had happened. Some of us tried to walk down the many blocks to get a closer look, but the closer we got, the more the people were running in our direction.

A plume of dark smoke and debris covered what was once a bright blue sky. Breathing became a struggle. Debris filled the twisting wind. Smoke filled my lungs. Police insisted that everyone retreat to where we had come from and get off the streets. My white shirt was now brown. I stood and cried with several others still in the streets.

People were in horror. Screams and sirens came from every direction. A few of the people I was standing near claimed to have loved ones working in the towers. I became frightened for Carl and his colleagues. I also thought about my old band mates from the blues band who last I heard were still working in those buildings as well.

So many thoughts raced through my head. I hoped my daughters were in school and didn't see any of the horror on television. I rushed back to my apartment and tried to call my in-laws. The lines were jammed. I again thought about Carl. He sat behind his desk before eight every morning. I knew he must have been inside that building when the plane hit it. I wanted to get there to see if I could find him, but the smoke and rescue people weren't allowing any ordinary citizens within blocks of the area.

I felt helpless. I called Carl's cell phone. No answer. I called his home, the line wouldn't connect. It was impossible to get any information about the towers. I stood in horror looking out my window. Eventually, I washed my face to get rid of the ash and tears. I flipped on the radio. I watched as the second tower crashed to the ground.

My body shook for hours. Tears streamed down my face until I ran out of them. I couldn't stop thinking about how I was in that building the day before watching as hundreds, if not thousands of hard working people were going up and down the elevators and bustling about with nothing like this tragedy on their minds. The radio announcers up and down the dial were now speculating this was some kind of a terrorist attack and New York was not the only area struck. I knew the world was no longer, as I had known it.

I was frantic worrying about Carl and wanting to let my daughters know I was fine. There was no way to find Carl or call my daughters. I thought about leaving the area, but I heard everywhere you turned the city was in gridlock. I also didn't want to leave until I knew about Carl. We had become close over the years, even if we didn't see each other often. I was his first client and he had done very well by me over the years with advice and finances. I had to know about his safety before I would go anywhere.

I turned on the television and watched the reports until I cried myself to sleep well past midnight. I wasn't able to reach Carl or my daughters. I woke up the next morning praying it had all be one of my nightmares. It wasn't. Eerie silence filled the streets.

I needed something for my growing anger and nerves, but I knew there was no place in the city to get drugs. Every time I felt weak, I pictured the faces of my daughters.

The entire city remained in shock. I decided to sit in the apartment for one more day. I would then try to make my way over to the Jersey side to my parent's house. I couldn't reach them either. I hoped maybe their phones would be able reach my girls.

I crept from my apartment to the ground floor. I walked the streets. The closer I got to the damaged area; the ground became darker with ash and trash. People were walking the streets putting up signs looking for loved ones. I knew I could not stay outside long because it was making me angrier and more desperate.

I was still an addict. All the memories of my daughters would eventually fade if I kept looking at the disaster in the streets. I would eventually seek something to remove the pain. I forced myself back into my apartment and watched the news. I was fixated to the television.

It had become apparent terrorists attacked American soil. This fueled an anger that had remained hidden for many years. I fell asleep with more tears streaming down my face. For the first time, I wanted to kill another human being. I would have been happy to pull the trigger against anyone who was responsible for this senseless attack.

The next day I made it to Debby's house. I was able to reach my daughters. They were relieved to hear from me. I also contacted my parents. I think it helped to be with another person that I had a connection with, as opposed to sitting in my apartment alone. There was a huge sadness sagging over the city. I hoped that if I stayed with Debby for a few days, my nerves and anger would calm down. I sat with Debby for two days watching the news reports with the rest of the world. However, my anger of what had happened continued to build.

Debby did her best, but she didn't know how to react when I started to yell at the television. I tried to be respectful of her children in the house. When I felt I was about to lose it, I would walk around her yard. I knew as gracious as she was being, it wasn't good for her or her children to have me stay any longer.

I went into her bathroom to wash up and get ready for my ride to North Carolina. I opened up her medicine closet. There was a bottle of pills with some unknown name on the bottle. I didn't care. I opened up the bottle and poured a few into the palm of my hand, hiding them in my pants pocket. I went out and gave Debby and her kids a kiss on the cheek. I drove off into the darkness.

CHAPTER THIRTY

My emotions were as tattered as the rubble strewn across the streets around the site of the World Trade Center. Only forty-five minutes from Debby's home, I realized how drained I had become in so many ways. Life had been great one day, and the next the day the world entered a new era. It would have been be impossible to drive another twelve hours to North Carolina without rest. I didn't dare wake my parents near midnight. They were usually in bed before ten.

I could have found a local hotel, but the nervous energy kept my car in gear. I figured once the energy dissolved, I would pull over somewhere. The pills in my pocket were yelling at me to pop them in my mouth. I had no clue why they were prescribed and to who. They could have been anything from stomach medicine to blood pressure medicines. I didn't know.

It was more a need to take something, as opposed to any rational thinking. My car drove itself. My mind wandered. I tried to find anything on the radio, other than the constant news stories of misery and destruction. At one point during the night, it seemed I passed the same building multiple times. I drove past my parent's home. The lights were out. I refused to wake them. I was exhausted, the nervous energy gone. I knew I had to rest my eyes, so I pulled into the next parking lot I could find, and turned off the engine.

The next few hours I pounded my brain with an endless cycle of how could all this happen and was life now worth living with such despair and destruction everywhere. I thought about turning the engine back on and driving to places in town where I thought I could find some harder drugs. I was again so angry at life and God.

Why could I not just be happy playing guitar and doing what I could to make the world a better place through music? Why were people in the world so determined to destroy others? How could a merciful God allow such a thing to happen in this world? My mind replayed many thoughts. I considered ramming my car into a tree and ending it all. I fought the demons reminding me that I was still a junkie in need of a fix.

I thought about my daughters. I knew George and Rose would take good care of them. Then the next moment I would recall Diana begging me to never leave her. Engrained in my head since a child was the premise that suicide was still taking a life and I would never get into heaven. Was there a heaven? What did it all matter any longer?

I drove my car around town not sure what I was looking for, but I ended the night in what was a familiar shopping center. I closed my eyes as the sun began to peek over the horizon. I pulled the pills from my pocket and held them firmly in the palm of my hand, squeezing them so tight that I could feel them leave a mark.

I woke hours later with the sound of cars driving by and voices of shoppers tending to their needs in the center. My blurry eyes spied my watch to see it was past ten in the morning. My right hand remained closed with the pills intact. I was hungry and needed a restroom.

I recognized a coffee shop in the corner of the shopping center. I wandered in and washed up before grabbing a table and ordering breakfast. I sat alone eating and listening to the news and the locals muttering amongst themselves.

The server came over after I had been sitting for maybe thirty minutes and asked, "Sorry, sir, I don't mean to disturb you, but you look familiar to me. Did we go to high school together?"

She went on and on about her high school and questioned where all her classmates were now. I was barely paying her attention when she blurted out, "I do know you. You're Stu. Oh don't tell me your last name, I'll remember. I saw you play guitar at a dance one time in high school. Do you still play?"

I looked directly into her eyes. She seemed sincere.

"I haven't played in days, but yes I still play guitar from time to time," I said.

She smiled. "Oh Stu, I knew it was you. We were biology partners for an entire year, don't you remember? We dissected a frog together. Those were some of the best times in my life."

I looked closer at the faint lines on her face. Her blue eyes weren't striking a chord. I listened as she continued.

"Oh, we sat joking around looking at that tiny little heart inside that poor dead frog. I'll never forget the day we opened it up and you told me that one day you would give your heart to anyone who would listen to your music. Wow, that was such a cool thing for someone to think their life could touch others like that. Then I saw you play at the dance two years later and you were right. I wish I could have done that for another person in my life. You did touch me with your music way back then."

I asked her to sit.

"The boss will fire me if I sit," she said. "He's already giving me the stink eye for standing here this long."

Only two tables still had patrons. I asked who her boss was and paid my tab by adding a two hundred dollar tip asking if his employee could sit for ten minutes. He scooped up the crisp bills and nodded.

He came over and told her it was ok to sit until the lunch crowd arrived. We sat for over twenty minutes, while I listened to her ramble on about high school and how her life was nothing like she had planned, but was happy and content. She was divorced and had two daughters, who were about to start college. My old lab partner wasn't sure how she would pay for it all. She said she went to the last reunion from school and had hoped to see more people like me, but not many showed.

I remembered getting my invitation to the reunion, but it was during the period I stayed planted in Carolina.

She gently smiled. "So tell me, Stu. Did life turn out the way you expected it?"

I sat stone faced. I had no instant response. My pent up anger was gone. Here was a woman, who was working in the same coffee shop for years, after being laid off from her job, only so she could make it all work for her daughters. She was as content and happy as I had seen a person in years. I still could barely remember her, but she was telling me about how much of an impact I had made on her life over thirty years ago by one school dance and a few comments about a dead frog.

I felt like such a fool. I desperately tried to remember my sophomore year in high school cutting open a frog in biology, if only so that I could tell her one thing I remembered about our time together. I wanted to make her day. She had made mine. I was failing miserably. After some thought, I asked her if she remembered Debby.

"Uhm, was she the red head in the band that you hung out with in the cafeteria?"

"Yes she was," I said. "Debby and I played in a band for many years, but now I'm looking for something else to do."

She fixed the clip in her hair and scratched her head. "The guitar store at the end of the center has a sign out looking for help. Maybe you can get a job in there," she said. "I don't know anything about music, but my kids buy their sheet music in there."

I busted out laughing. I was sure she didn't understand why I thought that was so amusing to me.

"So tell me, Stu. If you and Debby played in a band around here, how come I never knew about it? I don't get out too much now, but years ago, I was into clubbing. "

I was having such a hard time holding back from kissing her right on the lips. "After your shift is over, go to the music store next to Gordy's and if they have anything still in there that Debby and I recorded, it will be waiting for you all paid with your name on it."

She squinted her eyes and looked closer at me. I should have come clean about the band, but I thought it was best to leave her with thoughts about me just being Stu. I went back over to the counter and had him ring me up for another eight hundred dollars with the promise she would get the entire thousand. The shop owner looked closer at my credit card. I begged him not to tell. I only told him that she was the best server I had ever had the pleasure of speaking with and asked the manager to tell Sue that she affected my life more than I ever had hers.

I marched down to the music store and bought every Linda Sweet and Overture compact disk I could find and signed them all for Sue. I paid for them and decided then to deliver them personally. I walked back to the coffee shop and handed her the bag. Her boss had told her about the tip and that I was Dylan James.

We laughed about it. She wanted to return the tip, but I felt guilty it wasn't more. She had taken me from being miserable, to making me realize a few things about my life. I assured her it was my way of thanking her for being so kind to me.

In many ways, my life had turned out, as I had wanted and better. It took a waitress in a coffee shop to allow me to see it. I walked back down to where 'Gordy's Guitars' was still in business. I entered the place as if I owned the joint. I walked up to Gordy gave him a huge bear hug. I told him I was now ready to listen and make peace. His return hug was limp.

Gordy walked back into the main section of the store and glared at me long enough to make his point. "What really brings you here, Stu? It's been over ten years and you have not bothered to come, but today you come here? I'll admit I'm happy to see you, but why today?"

I didn't have a good answer, other than the truth. "I wish I knew why today, Gordy. Can't we both accept that it is today? You told me once I lost all my anger and found my soul, I could return. Here I am."

He invited me to sit while he gave his scheduled lesson. I did. While sitting there my cell phone rang. It was the credit card company wanting to know if I really had paid one thousand dollars at a coffee shop, then another three hundred dollars in a store in the same shopping plaza. I thanked them and assured them it was all ok. It made me think about Carl again. I walked outside to make another call to his cell phone and home. Still no response at either number. I called my daughters and in-laws to let them know I would be another day or so in the area and not to worry. I also called my mother and told her I would be over for dinner.

After listening to a horrid lesson of some poor child struggling to play, 'Twinkle Twinkle Little Star' and Gordy berate the kid for not practicing, I experienced a throwback memory long forgotten. Gordy told kid that if he didn't start to take his instrument seriously, he wouldn't allow him to take lessons any longer. The words and tone had not changed in over thirty years.

Gordy then asked me to come closer and tell the kid what I had to do the first two months of taking lessons. Again, the memories I had long forgotten started to rush back and I quietly stated, "Scales, Gordy. Scales and more scales until my fingertips were so sore I had to stop practicing."

Gordy turned to the far wall and pointed to a poster on the wall. It was an image of The Overture taken from behind the stage overlooking a huge crowd with a spotlight on me wailing on a solo. Gordy looked at the young boy and told him, "That guy on the wall is a pretty good player. I taught him in that exact same spot you're now sitting. I'm willing to bet he's playing a scale in front of twenty thousand people that I taught him. Is that not right, Stu?"

I chuckled and agreed. I'm sure the frazzled kid had no idea that was me on the wall or even realized how close to the truth it was that my solo was mostly a scale I had learned from Gordy long ago. I think those comments were directed at me as much as they were at the young lad.

Gordy then scolded the boy and told him to go home and practice his lessons or don't bother to return for his next one. I remembered the look on that boys face as if it were yesterday. I had a sneaky feeling I was about the hear more of that tone from Gordy.

"Tell me again why you're here, Stu?"

I wanted to get upset, but it was Gordy's way. He was never going to change. "Look, I'm not sure why all the anger I carried around, maybe I never will, but it's time to let it go and in truth I have nowhere else to go. So many have tried to get me to understand what my real issue is and I don't know, so maybe I'm coming home to see if I can find the answers. If you want me to leave I will, but I don't have any more of an answer for ya."

I felt my anger start to return when Gordy walked over and put his thumb and finger on my chin. He stared in my eyes. "Maybe you have found your soul. But, there's so much more for you to discover about your life. We're going back the basics, like your scales. If you gripe one time, I want you to get back in your fancy sports car and don't ever enter my doorway again. Is that understood?"

That same exact feeling I had as a thirteen-year old boy came rushing back. All I could do was stand there and say, "Yes, I understand."

"It's lunch time," Gordy said. That little coffee shop at the other end of the plaza has some good homemade soup. I'm buying."

As I opened my mouth to tell him the story about my morning, he said, "Not another word."

I chuckled and followed him down to the coffee shop. When

we walked through the door, both waitresses started to fight over where we would sit as if they were about to strike gold.

"You must eat here a lot," I said with a smirk. "They're fighting over where to seat you."

"They take good care of me here," Gordy said.

I laughed. We had great service for only ordering a bowl of soup. Gordy refused to let me leave the tip or pay the bill. Our new server looked as if we took away her last meal when Gordy left a fifteen percent tip. He had no clue what was going on and I refused to tell him.

After lunch, he sent me away and told me to come back the next day. I would get a history lesson. I wasn't really sure what he meant, but I drove over to my parent's house so Mom and Dad could remind me that I didn't come home nearly enough.

CHAPTER THIRTY ONE

My back ached from sleeping in my car one night then, the on my parents couch the next. I was cranky, but drove over to see Gordy. I wanted to erase fixing my relationship with him off my bucket list. I mulled around the store waiting for Gordy to give another lesson before he turned his attention to me. We sat on the same stool where he once gave me regular guitar lessons.

"Have I ever told you my background?" Gordy asked. "I think not. Well let me tell you a bit about me and why I love sitting on this stool day after day."

Before he could say more, I interrupted him with yet another brilliant comment or so I thought. "You know, I always did feel sorry for you stuck inside this store when I knew you are capable of doing so much more with your abilities."

I soon found out my observation and comments weren't so brilliant after all.

"Is that what you really think of me, Stu? You feel sorry for me?"

I don't think I had ever seen Gordy laugh like that before. It was a genuine belly laugh. Customers in the shop took notice. "Sit back, my friend, let me tell you my history."

Gordy Davis was born in Tupelo, Mississippi in 1942. His

mother was a piano teacher and his dad an insurance agent, who played guitar. Gordy was raised a strict Southern Baptist. Gordy did well in school, but he shared his father's passion for the guitar and his mother's passion for studying music.

He would sit as his mother gave lesson after lesson in their small home and looked at the expression on the student's faces after they either succeeded or failed with each sitting. They were scolded for not trying hard enough, and praised for extra effort by his mother.

His father would invite over kids from the neighborhood on weekends. They would all sit on the front porch and strum guitars. Years later, Gordy's dad would tell the story about how a young Elvis Presley would sit on that same porch with the other kids. As a kid, Gordy didn't profess that to be accurate, though Gordy never really knew for sure if one was Elvis or not.

His dad would give Gordy guitar lessons, however his mother made him sit and do scales on the piano.

"Learn the disciplines first, songs later," Gordy said as he showed me a photo of his mother he pulled from his wallet.

He continued his story. Gordy gave up the piano. He wanted hide in his room with his dad's guitar and write music. Gordy told me that he wrote his first song before the age of ten and still wrote on an almost daily basis.

After high school, he packed his bags and headed to Nashville, Tennessee to audition for the Grand Ole Opry. Gordy played the Opry many times and wrote songs for some of the biggest country stars of the time.

"Who did you write music for?" I asked. "Have I played any of your songs?"

"Possibly," Gordy said after a smile. "Just as I was getting known in Nashville, Uncle Sam came calling. Before I knew it, I went from being the next Hank Williams or Bill Monroe to lugging my rifle through rice fields in Viet Nam.

I never knew Gordy to be a liar. If he believed he was about to be a country star, I believed him. He continued his story about the horrors of war and seeing his mates shot and killed before his very eyes. He would patrol swamps and fields never knowing if his next step would be his last.

"Them sons a bitches' shot me, Stu. They hit me three times in the back. The platoon leader had to carry me out. By the time they got me proper treatment, it was too late to save my kidney. I got sent back stateside and they gave me the Purple Heart, but my fighting days were done. I was honorably discharged."

Even though he lost a kidney, I assumed it was a good thing, because he could go back to his music career. Then I heard more of the story.

"I guess the doctors didn't have the time to care for us vets like they do now," Gordy said. "They saved my life, but I hit a rough patch. They stuffed me so with much pain medications, I didn't know who I was most days. I started to have nightmares about seeing members of my platoon losing body parts. Once, a fella next to me had his brains splattered across my uniform from a sniper. I spent years fighting my fears. That's why I saw it in you, and why I still think it remains. I guess it always will."

I nodded and said, "I struggle every day to be at peace. I know I've had a great life, even with the pain in my back that reminds me of the accident every day. I guess it could have been worse."

Gordy rubbed his chin. "Yeah, like pushing up daisies. I

begged the doc for help. I knew my mind wasn't right. On the day I was being released from the hospital, I figured they were sending me to another facility to detox me from all the pain meds. A big ole' fella came to the desk and grabbed my duffle bag. He stuffed me, and my bag, into the back of a black Cadillac. Who knew the army sent us round in Caddy's?"

I laughed. "Our tax dollars well spent, eh?"

Gordy smiled and hollered at the man behind the counter to help a customer wandering in the shop.

"It weren't no army fella or a government car picking me up. This is where my story seems unbelievable, but every word is true. Next then I knew; I had my own room at Graceland. The king himself, Elvis Presley came to the room and told me anything I needed, just ask. I had a nurse check on me twice a day. They tended to my every need. I had one last problem to deal with before I was allowed to leave."

"What was that?" I asked.

"My body was healed, my faith in God wasn't. I had lost my soul on that battlefield. Everyone knew it but me. The staff at Graceland and Elvis himself worked with me until I found peace. I carried around an anger so deep, because I knew I was a rising star in the country charts. They dun took it from me. It took months of fighting my demons until my soul was restored."

It all made sense now. Why Gordy treated me the way he did after my accident. In a way, we had shared similar lives. Only, I had already been a star before they took it from me.

Gordy continued. "I did play the Grand Ole Opry again in a band one night, but I felt like that was no longer what I was put on this earth to do. I can't explain it to you. It was just a feeling I had that my time with being a stage performer was over. I was still living at Graceland, but I knew I had overstayed my welcome."

"Where were you going to go?" I asked.

"I had no idea. I only knew I had to git from Graceland and find something to do with my life. Then Elvis popped his head into my room and asked me to give my regards to my daddy. Elvis told me that my daddy inspired him to be who he was and never knew of a way of paying him back."

"Come on, Gordy, is this all true?"

Gordy pointed to the front door of the store at a young girl walking in her with her instrument.

"I packed my belongings and called a cab for where I wasn't sure," Gordy said. "I was intercepted at the front of the mansion and told to jump in the car. I was handed an envelope. The driver was a former bodyguard for Elvis. He lived here in Princeton until he passed away a few years back. He drove me to his home. Inside the envelope was a key and note from Elvis. The note read, 'Bring peace to others as we have to you.' The key was to this shop."

Everything came into view. Why Gordy dragged me to see Elvis perform and why cried so hard when Elvis died. It also made sense why Gordy was so protective of the store.

I sat in the chair taking it all in when Gordy asked me a question.

"Do you still think I've wasted my life here in this shop? How many lives have you touched with your music, Stu? Remind me again, who taught you how to play? Does that mean I touched them too? Do you know Father Joe, the new priest who took over for Father Daniel? Well, when he was a young boy his parents died in a car accident. His grandmother was left to raise him. Joe was a lost soul. He never could forgive God for the horror of losing both parents at once. I gave him free lessons for years and eventually he found his soul through the music. How many lives does he now touch as a priest? Did I help touch those lives too?"

I had to admit I had never thought about it in those terms.

"I've taught hundreds, not only music, but about how to be a happy person and enjoy their time on earth. How many lives did they touch, Stu? Now tell me again how my life was wasted by not playing a few extra nights on a stage in Tennessee."

I felt incredibly stupid and humbled at that moment.

"I want to tell you one more thing before I kick your sorry ass out of my shop for the day. I was in the coffee shop this morning and Sue told me what you did for her yesterday. She now wants to take guitar lessons. She wants to feel what it's like to have a heart like yours. I've known her for almost ten years, and not once did she ever ask me about music. Go back and have dinner with your folks and have your sorry ass back here tomorrow at six pm sharp."

My legs could not move fast enough to get out since I felt so terribly embarrassed by my years of misjudging my friend and mentor. When I got to my parents, they could tell I was upset and we didn't talk too much that evening. I called my daughters and told them how much I loved them and would be home soon. I tried contacting Carl again, but still no response. I thought about going back to New York to look for him, but I could see on the reports it was next to impossible to find others in the area.

I went back to see Gordy the next evening a little more subdued and with my tail between my legs. I had never thought about just how many people Gordy had touched over the years, let alone how many I had with my music. I know that sounds crazy, but I was so busy grinding out songs and tours that I had never really taken a step back to look at it all in that light. I realized that Gordy had not wasted his life sitting in that tiny shop for over thirty years.

"Does that fancy car drive slow enough not to give me a heart attack or shall we take my car?" Gordy yelled at me from in front of his store.

We got in my car and proceeded to drive to a meeting room in the back of a local church. We met with a group of Viet Nam veterans, who Gordy met with once a week for many years. He had kept that private all these years.

"I wanted you to meet some of the fellas, Stu. Well, meet some for the second time or so I have been told."

I didn't recognize any of the men already sitting there. There were seven older men, who all introduced themselves. They explained how they had all served in Viet Nam and lived in the area.

After all the introductions, and a few dirty jokes, one of the men asked, "So, Dylan when are you planning on coming back to Fort Dix to play again?"

I remembered playing there many years ago with Debby during one of my private shows for the staff and a few who were there for medical issues.

"You and some good looking red head came and played for us for hours. I never had a chance to let you know how much we enjoyed it. Not many would take the time like you did for guys like us. Thanks."

Before I could say much, Gordy asked me, "Do you have any

idea where some of the money went when your band played all the charity events?"

I had to admit, "No, I guess I don't."

"Well maybe you don't, but I do. I checked on it through Carl and the General, who arranged it all. I want you to know that Bob Moore, who you just met, had his house paid off with some of the money. He sustained injuries in Nam and had to retire from his job earlier than expected because of the lingering health issues. His wife and three kids didn't have to move from their home thanks to you and the band. I also want you to know that Nate, who is sitting next to you, went back to college and learned bookkeeping from tuition that was paid for with a fund established after the first event you did. He now owns his own business and employs ten people in the area. I'll bet you never gave it a second thought about what happened after you did the show."

Gordy was correct. I had never given it a second thought.

"Explain to me, Stu why all these fine men were being punished by their God?"

Gordy jolted me with his question. I didn't have time to think about it before he smirked and continued.

"Every man here was drafted to support our nation and all are fine men. Each one injured in the line of duty. Yet, somehow, each has a smile on their face. You have enough money to support you and your family. You've traveled the world doing what you enjoy most, have two beautiful daughters and because a drunk driver whacked your car, you were convinced you were being punished? Ask these men why they were punished."

Gordy had made his point loud and clear two days in a row. I decided that I had heard enough and offered to buy drinks at the bar down the street.

The next day I got in my car and drove back to North Carolina. It gave me time to reflect on my life. It all seemed too simple to think the way Gordy had presented his thoughts to me. Could I really have missed the obvious after all these years?

Gordy had slapped me into a reality that had been long lost on me. I guess the larger question now was; what would I do with this new reality?

CHAPTER THIRTY TWO

"**I**'m sorry I couldn't reach you sooner, but my cell phone was lost in the rubble," Carl said from a phone call I received while driving back to Carolina. "I've barely been home since the attack. In all the shock, I left my phone in the building. I just now got a new one."

"I understand, Carl. Man, have I been worried about you though."

"We lost one of our staff in the bombing. Reports are he was inside helping others get out, when part of a wall fell on him and trapped him in a fire. I was there for days helping others and accounting for our staff. We've lost all of our paper files and are trying to get back online using all the backup systems. It will be a few more weeks until we can find office space. We're doing the best we can to get back in business."

I was sad to hear about the loss of one of his co-workers, but thrilled to know Carl was alive and well. We spoke for a few moments, but he had to get off the phone and continue to put his life back together. It made me think of Phil, our old drummer, after hanging up with Carl.

When I arrived home, Rose had just finished dinner with the girls. George and I snacked on a few leftovers. I gave them all big hugs and felt some security in being home. I dug out Phil's number and got him on the phone. He and Matt had been out of the state at a seminar the day of the attack and were fine. He thanked me for thinking about him. We chatted for over an hour before I headed to bed.

The next morning the girls were returning to school. Most schools had closed after the attacks. This was my girls first day back since the closure. I visited Elise at her gravesite. We sat together for more than an hour. I asked for her forgiveness for not being there when she needed me. I still couldn't shed the guilt of not being of proper mind and spirit when she was dying. I assumed I would never lose the guilt. I sat there quietly and thought about all the good times her and I had over the years.

I always knew she was a better wife to me than I was a husband to her. The time had passed for me to fix it. All I could do, would be to keep living her our last wish and be a good father to our children.

I left and drove along the back roads until I came across the spot where I asked Elise to marry me. I pulled over and sat thinking about what Gordy and the other men had told me the past few days. I thought about how I had made my choices in life and that God was not responsible for my car accident. That man who hit us made the choice to get drunk, get in his car and do damage to others. Maybe the others were right years ago when I was told, "You were lucky you survived." I shed a tear for Elise and thanked God my life could continue.

The skies opened up. Rain pelted me. One tiny cloud hovered directly over me. I'll never be sure if that was God's way of crying with me or we shared the same sense of humor. It also could have been Elise's way of cleansing my guilt. I chalked it to one of life's mysteries.

I spent the next few weeks at home. The world geared up for war and people were afraid to get on airplanes. The economy halted. This was no time to run around the country attempting to find others to record a solo record with yours truly. I wrote most of the material at home and recorded my parts on my home recording studio. I used a local drummer and bass player for a few songs and used a Gospel singer from the local church as backup on a few songs.

After a few months, I drove back to New York and had Debby record lead and backup vocals on two songs. Once all the commotion died down and the airlines started to fly again, I went out to California where I had Billy play drums on some of the songs and Linda sang lead and back up as well.

I used a few studio musicians from California as well as some friends from other bands, who lived in that area. People were afraid to fly, so I had to do most of the traveling to finish the project. I refused to allow the terrorists to alter my life. I had let forces change me for too many years and I refused to play the victim any longer. I knew my time was limited on this earth and I was determined to make the best of it.

I did get in trouble with Diana once back home. It was not my fault. One night she asked if she could invite over her new boyfriend to the house. I was excited to meet him. It wasn't often she brought them around, and this time she actually seemed excited by the prospect of me meeting him.

It didn't take me too long to figure out what was happening. It didn't take her long either. The boy only wanted to meet me because he was an aspiring guitarist and he wanted to spend the entire evening with me and not with Diana. I did my best to be polite, but eventually, I excused myself to the bedroom.

I got cold stares the next day. They stopped when I announced we would be taking a trip to Europe in the summer. It was time to cash in my gift from Feona. The envelope she had given me sat in my bags for many months. Long after the rehab stint, I opened it. Inside was a birthday card. There was also a note that promised a tour of Albert Hall for me and the girls and front row seats to a show. I contacted Feona. She was still willing to make good on her promise.

Diana was entering Duke University in the fall. Our trip was her high school graduation gift. Others told me that once they left for college, it would never be the same. However, Diana had grown into a beautiful woman and I'm sure Elise was smiling down on her. I wanted to believe that Elise was proud of what I had done with the girls too.

Deborah on the other hand was a mischievous one. She was pretty much the exact opposite of Diana, but never got into any real trouble. Her grades in school were still above average, but she was way ahead of the curve. She didn't work nearly as hard as Diana did in school. It came to her naturally. I loved them both the same, even if each assumed I loved the other more.

We vacationed through much of Europe in July. First stop was London, where we hit many of the historic landmarks. Feona gave us a wonderful tour and we heard an amazing orchestra perform later that evening. Feona was doing very well for herself. She was a big shot with a nice office. She really didn't have to go out of her way like she did, but the girls were impressed that I knew connections across the ocean.

We left England for Holland, then to Germany, down to Paris and over to Italy. During the second day in Rome, I wandered near the old school where Lorenza had taught. I stood near the entrance to the school on the old stone street daydreaming for several minutes. A young man came up from behind and tapped me on the shoulder.

"Come. Si?"

The boy reached for my hand and tried to pull me to the school building. I followed with some hesitation. He led me into the school, where I had been gazing into a window.

"Ciao, Dylan. Come here. Let me see you now."

Lorenza had a few new wrinkles. However, her eyes still displayed the same radiant beauty they had in the past.

"I knew it was you peeking in my window," she said. "Let me see face. I know you were here years ago and would not see me. Now you don't look the same. You grow in the belly, my friend. Let me see eyes."

I let her touch my face. She stared into my eyes for thirty seconds before wrapping her arms around me with a huge hug.

"My Dylan has returned." I could her sniffle as she rested her face on the top of my shoulder. She then ran her hand along the back of my head. We talked for several minutes until she told me that she was now in charge of the school, but was growing tired. I could see the weariness in her face. Even though she was rarely without a smile, I could see the sadness in her eyes.

My daughters joined Lorenz and me for dinner. I told my daughters that Loranza was an old friend from many years ago, when right on cue, my dear Deborah blurted out, "Did mom know?"

We got a chuckle, but the girls weren't willing to let it go. They peppered me with questions. I told them that I had met

Lorenza before I married their mother and never once did I break my vows. I'm not sure they believed me. Lorenza and I barely stopped looking at each other the entire evening. My daughters were smart enough to realize our dinner date wasn't a random chance meeting with a school teacher from my past. I didn't care. I knew Lorenza and I never broke our vows with either spouse.

Lorenza gave the three of us a grand tour of Rome on Saturday. It became incredibly difficult to leave her, but we had tickets to move on to Greece for our last stop in Europe. I promised the Italian beauty that I would be back very soon to see her. She gave me that same frown I always got in disbelief, only this time, we each knew I meant it.

When we got home from Europe, the girls again asked about Lorenza. I guess it wasn't for them to think there was anyone but their mother in my past. I knew it was a subject that had to be explored, since it was very likely they would see Lorenza again.

Enough time had passed since we had lost Elise. I dedicated many years to my daughters. I couldn't feel guilty about feelings for another woman, even though I did. However, everyone needed to understand that it was time I moved on professionally and possibly, romantically. My girls broached the subject of my friend at dinner with Rose and George in our company. I told my in-laws the story of Lorenza. I ended with the fact that I had married Elise, loved her dearly and that was the end of the discussion.

Mountain released my solo effort in time for holiday shoppers. We called it, 'Dylan James Alone with Friends.' The reviews were excellent. The sales were slow. A casino in Las Vegas approached me about playing solo. At first, I refused. After another offer and more consideration, I agreed to play ten shows and did so the following spring.

It felt great to be on stage again, but I felt naked without a band. The girls were busy with school and had grown sufficient over the years. It became easier to leave them behind. Diana was only an hour from home, living in the dorms, and rarely came home. If she missed me that much, she knew where we lived.

More offers filtered into Carl's office to play solo on the east coast, but it wasn't something I wanted to do. Linda had played one of the shows with me in Las Vegas. I performed better knowing someone else shared the stage with me. I convinced myself I needed a band to play live in groups larger than Veterans hospitals.

The world had changed. In my down time at home, I would sit and think about all the men and woman oversees fighting a war that seemed so senseless, yet unavoidable. It had changed most people's lives in the United States. Security increased around airports. One time, I had to remove my belt and shoes. Yikes. Carrying instruments on flights became harder than before. Articles surfaced in news reports about envelopes filled with chemicals and mailed to important people across our land.

I would sit and question why a merciful God would make such a world. I was at peace in my heart, but still wanted to know more. I tried talking with Pastor George about, but we never could agree on much. My belief system was still shaken, but I couldn't allow myself to ever return to where anger could drive me back to drug addiction. Overall, I was pleased with my life.

It took years before Carl and his firm returned to normalcy in New York. Office space became a premium since the Towers housed so many of the area offices. I tried not to bother him with my ramblings and issues, but I called him one day and asked him about my thoughts on a trust for Elise.

We both decided that having a building named after her or possibly a musical scholarship in her honor would be a good way to proceed. It would be dependent on how much money we could generate in the beginning and what the plan would be to raise money in the future to keep the fund sustained. I was willing to offer my royalties from the recordings still in the vault from the music I made with Debby and Linda as well as some other cash from my recent release. We needed a bigger plan to get the idea off the ground. I wanted something that could continue long after my ability to play guitar or raise money.

After many phone calls, it was decided we would take a huge risk, but one that seemed to make sense. We would get the Overture back together with some guests and record the 1812 Overture as well as other songs that Elise enjoyed. Duke and Tim were always pressing me to add an orchestral sound to our music. Here would be their chance to go crazy and I wouldn't object.

We wouldn't make the recording with a pure classical sound, but there would be strings added and in some of the songs we would add vocals. Some of the musicians from the New York area orchestra volunteered to join us as well as a few members from other bands who Elise and I had met over the years. All the proceeds would go to a trust set up for Elise.

Mountain agreed to distribute it at their cost. That agreement came with a catch. Mr. Altos and I came to a gentleman's agreement that if The Overture ever recorded with your usual sound, Mountain would get first shot at the deal. Second, the band had to all agree to play at his upcoming retirement dinner. I called in a ton of favors with the band to make it all happen.

The project was in the can within six months. It was a mixture of classical, pop and rock and roll. Different producers, including Duke and Tim each produced different numbers on the disk.

I personally delivered the first disk off the press to my father. I showed him that I joined the ranks of professional musicians who played The 1812 Overture. He had a way of masking his appreciation for my music, even though I knew he had a copy of every recording I was ever on, including the movie soundtracks I had written sitting in his private office. Some never made it out of the wrappers, but he displayed them in his home office.

Sales were better than expected. To assist with the sales, there were five hundred disks autographed by several members, who played on the recordings, including yours truly. You had to purchase and open the disk to see if you were one of the lucky winners. A sales gimmick thought of by Carl. I'm sure that idea boosted sales.

In the first month, we raised over three hundred thousand dollars from the disk sales. The other positive development from getting together was that the old members of the Overture were all hungry to play a few shows as a band again. Other than Billy, I don't think anyone really was doing it for the money. I think everyone missed playing with the band in front of an audience.

We decided to play ten shows, mostly along the east coast with one show's proceeds all going towards the trust. For the first show, the band would play The 1812 Overture at Radio City Music Hall in New York City with an orchestra. We would compensate the members of the orchestra and the venue, but any of the remaining proceeds would go to the trust fund.

The next performance would be at Madison Square Garden the following night with the proceeds going for the veteran's charities. I was really going to be playing The 1812 Overture in a live performance with my father sitting in the front row.

We had three weeks to practice as a band and had to remember how to play some of our older songs. We also had scheduled two practices with the members of the orchestra. The orchestra also played on some of the songs from our bands catalog to make the night unique for the fans.

When opening night arrived, there were a few surprises in the audience. Besides my parents, front and center, Gordy and Sue the woman, who I had met at the coffee shop, joined my parents. Gordy rarely saw us play and hadn't for many years.

The bigger shock came when I noticed Lorenza standing offstage moments after the show started. My sneaky daughters had arranged for her to come for the opening night. They hid here away for two days in New York without my knowledge. I almost messed up the opening number, as I stood stunned not believing it was really her standing next to my girls.

Her silky black hair matched beautifully with the radiant red dress draped across her body. Her curvy shape nestled perfectly in the attire. I noticed even Sasha gave Lorenza a second peek. Lorenza's eyes were burning into my brain as I tried to concentrate on my duties as lead guitarist and bandleader. It took several minutes before my hands would stop shaking. Her smile originating from mere feet away made my heart pound like it hadn't for years. I had to keep in mind this was an evening for Elise. However, I couldn't turn my back to what my heart desired.

The night opened with the regular band playing three of our biggest hits to get the crowd in a good mood. I then introduced the orchestra during the fourth song. We played three more of our hits with the orchestra. After six hits, the stage went dark. A single spotlight hit me after I had positioned myself on stage directly in front of Dad.

"Thank you everyone for joining us this evening for a wonderful cause that we trust will help so many in the future. Because of your donations, students across the country will have instruments if they can't afford one. Also, one worthy student a year, who majors in music, will have their college tuition covered by the trust. We have other plans in the future as well with your kind generosity."

I stopped for a moment as the audience offered a polite applause.

"Also this evening, I will officially be graduating to the ranks of a world class musician by my father's standards. Without further delays, I give you, 'The 1812 Overture.'"

The lights hit the stage as the orchestra played the first notes. We played a fifteen-minute version before allowing the orchestra to play a selection from Beethoven. We took a break before coming back and playing Linda's hits, cover songs from the 50's and 60's releases and finished with a few more of our songs.

As I walked back on stage for an encore, I realized that a large part of my life was staring back at me. The two men who shaped my life were sitting next to each other. For the most part strangers to each other, yet neither knew how close they were in so many ways. The woman who taught me how to smile again sat next to Gordy. The only other woman, who I loved the way a man loves a woman, other than my wife, stood close by next to my children. My agent Carl sat in the row with my family. My band stood with me on stage. They were the people that I spent the majority of my life from birth to that moment. I loved my bandmates as much as anyone in the house.

I thought again how we were doing a concert in tribute to the only woman, who saw me at my best and my worst on a regular basis. I loved and appreciated Elise far more than I ever told her. Everyone who really meant anything, including our ardent fans, were onstage, looking back at me, or smiling down from heaven.

The show ended up being a huge success. I think because we hadn't performed together for many years the entire band was happy to be as a unit, even if for a short time. There was a live recording made of the evening, but it was never released to the public due to difficulties with royalties. Shame. It was one hellava performance.

After the show ended, I ran off stage to embrace Lorenza. My daughters stood there beaming as if they had just cured cancer. I gave them each a hug and quizzed them about how they got Lorenza to come to town. Diana had secretly asked for Lorenza's email and contact info when we were in Italy. She had been updating her over time about how I was doing. When it was obvious, we would be performing a special show, Diana arranged for Lorenza to make the journey. I begged the woman who made my heart beat to stay longer, but she had to return to Italy for school. She stayed for the next show at Madison Square and in Boston, but flew home from there. I was heartbroken. We both promised to join up again as soon as her school year ended.

The tour ended in Los Angeles with the band playing at the retirement party for Mr. Altos as promised. It was a grand evening with many celebrities in the crowd as well as a few bands that were on the Mountain label, each performing a few songs. It was a good night to catch up with some old friends as well as join in with performers I had never played with onstage.

As most filed out of the building, a young punk looking kid

dressed in an Armani suit, asked to have a few words with me. I stopped out of courtesy. He introduced himself as Mr. Altos' replacement, as if anyone could replace the man, but I listened with half an ear.

I'm sure he told me his name, but after the first few utterances I could only remember his name as Mr. Idiot and that was being kind.

"Dylan, I hear you have a new disk almost completed with your band? I'd like to hear it and make some suggestions and offer you my ideas before it's a wrap."

I stopped him in his tracks to inform him that no such disk or recording was in existence.

"I was informed by Mr. Altos that you both had an agreement to continue on with our label. Is that not true?"

"Like I said, we haven't begun recording any new music and none is planned. Our handshake was an agreement that if ever did want to enter the studio; Mountain would be the first label we contacted. Nothing more.

Mr. Idiot made a few remarks that changed my entire line of thinking about the music business, as well as signing with a company where he ran things.

"Well, Dylan, as you are aware, hip hop and rap are very popular genres of music now. I would like you to record a song or two that would remind our listeners of Snoop Dog. I find the seventies and eighties, well just so dated."

Did Mountain Records really turn over the daily operations to this knucklehead, I thought. He kept right on jabbering.

"Guitar dominated music with a rock edge died decades ago.

It's time you realize that and show us what you can do now. I've been told you've written several soundtracks, so I know you can adapt."

I stood there not knowing if I should punch the smarmy little ass in the mouth, or walk away. Duke, who had been nearby and must have seen me clench my fist. I do believe I started to rock my arm back when Duke grabbed my hand long enough to slow it down and direct me to shake the idiot's hand.

A wise man once said, "Clothes do not make the man." Never was that more true than at that very moment. The idiot piled on when to told me that Jay Z would be calling me to offer his advice on how to write current hit songs. I knew instantly that my time with Mountain Records was over. I didn't care what handshake deal I had made. The end of an era had arrived.

CHAPTER THIRTY THREE

An old teacher once told me, "Chose a job you love and you will never work a day in your life." I find that rings only somewhat true. Yes, no question, I loved what I had done over my career, but to think I didn't work to earn what I had enjoyed would be silly. Only a few saw the hours I would spend on a daily basis practicing my craft of mastering the guitar as well as creating music. I knew what the quote was intended to mean.

I was much happier with my life than I would have been in a retail management position somewhere. I needed and thrived with an audience. It was something I wasn't sure would continue. Linda was so terrified to fly after the attacks, she wasn't willing to make long tours a reality unless we traveled mostly by bus. Duke was semi-retired, however, still produced for a band here or there. He no longer actively pursued new bands to use his services.

Duke was willing to record, but he too no longer wanted long tours to promote a new recording. Debby was working as a nurse raising her kids and had a new boyfriend. Sasha had expanded her fashion lines back home in Russia and had employed her sister. Sasha would record, but a tour was out of the question for more than a few weeks at a time.

Billy was willing to record, tour and do just about anything.

He had wasted most of his money on two ex-wives, as well as ruining his relationships with his old band mates from the now defunct blues band. He had never eliminated his wild streak, but Billy still loved life and playing drums. If I wanted to start a new band I think he would be the only one really up for playing with me again long term. James found a wife, quit the music business, and bought a farm in Iowa.

On the home front, both daughters were in college. I spent many days home alone. My life had evolved from playing for thousands of adoring fans to a few deer feeding in my back yard. The girls would come home occasionally to appease dear old dad, but they had moved on with their lives. Diana would soon graduate with a degree in physical therapy and Deborah was limping along as a business major, not sure of her future.

Deborah had grown into a respectable guitarist. She started a band with college friends. She wanted to have a future in music, but the industry had changed so much since I started. No matter how hard I tried to convince her of those facts, she was not going to listen.

I begged her to complete her studies in business until I realized that I had become my father with my sermons. Who was I to tell her not to reach for her own goals? I was her father, who knew it was going to be very difficult to make a dent in the music business that's who, but it really didn't matter. She was always the stubborn one in the family and in the end, all I could do was be there for support and help should she fall.

The more the years passed, the more it was evident that my girls were very different people, but I was proud of both. It was never more evident when they would come home on breaks with one being a student at Duke University and one attending the

University of North Carolina. For anyone who doesn't understand the consternation of having that mix in the household, just have mercy on me. It didn't help that my father in law was a diehard Carolina fan, who chided Diana about her choice of schools at every turn. I did my best to stay out of it and keep the peace.

I think deep down part of the reason I had done all the work starting the trust in Elise's name was to attempt to remove the guilt for not being stronger when Elise needed me. I sat at her grave. We prayed together that the answer would come. I was never a perfect person. Time had come to accept that fact and forgive my shortcomings. I knew for years, I had been trying to do just that, but I had to learn not to constantly rip myself at every turn when I did fail.

Failure is a part of life. I needed to accept that concept. The Bible taught me that I was made in God's image, but I'm not sure it ever read where I was intended to perfect. I had to stop assuming I had all the answers and that I could control all aspects in life. I could only do my best to control me and be thankful for all I had in my life.

I woke up one morning with a bug up my butt and asked Carl to sell my apartment in New York. The market for real estate had rebounded after the terror attacks. Carl planned to invest the profits from the sale into commercial real estate. I didn't have a good reason to sell it other than I got tired of paying the bills when it sat vacant, which was a lot after the attacks.

There was a huge hole in my heart. Deep down the reason I never ran to Lorenza was my guilt over Elise. I had to release it and move on with my life. I was scared my guilt would worsen if I allowed my heart to be with another. I had to take solace that Elise was with God in heaven and it was ok for me to make a new life here on earth.

I never knew for sure if Lorenza would ever start a life with me, but I had to ask. People around the world hung photos and posters of me on their walls. I felt as alone as those images. I needed to fill a void in my heart. Maybe the only time in life when you are totally at peace is when your heart and soul join you in that peace.

I threw a couple pair of jeans and a few shirts into a travel bag and headed for the airport. A sudden sense of urgency came with every step. During the long achy flight, I arranged and rearranged more times than I could count. I needed to find out if my love for her was genuine or a dream I always wanted to keep at a short distance. Could she fill what was missing in my life?

I became giddy with anticipation for the moment we would lock eyes. Perspiration formed on my forehead, as I rewrote words several times on paper napkins. This time, we would either never leave or leave forever.

I reached Rome in the dark of night and checked into a hotel until daybreak. Despite my exhaustion, my eyes had barely closed all night. The anticipation of seeing Lorenza filled my senses like a water balloon ready to explode from reaching its intended target.

I went into the hotel bathroom and made myself look as proper as possible. My teeth brushed extra careful, my hair combed several times. I acted like my daughters did on prom night. I even ironed my jeans and shirt.

I walked the several blocks to her home, becoming even more anxious as her home came into view. I knocked. No response. It was still early, maybe she was sleeping late I thought. I knocked again. Nothing. I peeked into a window. Only two small chairs against a far wall came into view. I knocked again. No response.

A neighbor came out of her home and towards me from across the stone walkway. She spoke in Italian. I didn't understand a word. Through hand gestures and each of us giving an effort, she convinced me that no one was home. Gee thanks.

I wandered down the street to the school where Lorenza worked. It was summertime. I assumed the school would be closed, but I thought I would look anyway. I pulled on the front door. Locked. There were no signs of children or teachers. I walked around the area of the school hoping someone who could tell me where I might find the most beautiful schoolteacher in the world. There was no one.

I sat on the stone steps leading up to the main entrance of the school when an older woman appeared.

"Ciao," she said.

"Do you speak English?" I asked.

"Very small, sir."

"Do you know Lorenza and where I can find her?" I asked.

"Lorenza. She not here. School close. She move to America."

The blood rushed from my head. I thought I would pass out.

The woman pointed to the sky as an airplane flew above. "School over. Lorenza go."

I wasn't sure how much the woman understood, but I rattled off thoughts and questions faster than a machine gun in gangster movies. I asked where she might have gone to, would she be returning to the school. How could she do such a thing to me?

The woman smiled. "Her mamma and papa go to new town.

Lorenza go to, err, how you say, uhm, boyfriend."

I went from pure peace to total devastation. For a moment, it almost seemed worse to me than watching the plane hit the World Trade Center in my gut. What was I going to do now? I walked back to her parent's home to confirm what I had heard. No one was around who could speak English. I thought about buying a book to translate my words, but I was too down to want to try. I headed back to the airport and took the first available flight home.

When I landed in New York, I had a few hours to make my connection back to North Carolina. I called Carl to get an update on my apartment. He informed me that he had been trying to reach me, but since my cell phone didn't have service in Europe, I wasn't getting my messages.

The real estate agent had a buyer with a near full price offer. I told him to call the agent and make the deal. I was in no mood to haggle over a few thousand bucks. He made the call and within an hour, we had reached an agreement. I decided to stay in town over night to sign the papers. I would fly home the next morning. I was no longer sure of my future and for a brief moment thought about selling my home in North Carolina and keeping the one in New York. I guess they call it seller's remorse.

Diana called frantically, letting me know that she had been trying to reach me. In my haste, I forgot to call the girls to let them know I was heading to Europe. I had told Rose I was going on a business trip for a few days.

School was on summer break, but the girls had gone to an outdoor festival with friends when I left. "Dad, where are you?" She asked. "When will you be home? We need you to come home right away."

I knew they didn't need me home for my cooking. When I was home, they were glued to their laptops or televisions. Deborah had gotten a lot like me and would spend hours with her guitar on the porch, or in her room. Diana would spend most nights out with friends. I couldn't imagine why they needed me. Rose and George always watched over the hours when I was away.

"I'm in New York," I said. "I sold the apartment and have to sign some papers at Carl's office in the morning. After that, I'll be home. What's the big emergency that can't wait?"

She stammered. Diana was never a good liar. "We came home from the music festival and were worried when you weren't home. We bought you a gift and wanted to give it to you."

"I'll be home tomorrow. You can give it to me then. I was still in shock over Lorenza. I didn't even want to see my kids. I needed a day to sulk.

The entire flight home, I crucified myself for allowing Lorenza to slip away. I couldn't blame her. I moved in and out of her life like a hurricane leaving nothing but pain and destruction in its wake. It was wrong of me to expect her to keep waiting for me, and I knew it.

On the other side, for years, I wasn't healed enough to offer her what she needed and deserved from me. I had to accept the thought that I wasn't ready for another relationship until the moment I packed my bags two days earlier. Both sides of the equation fought in my brain during the plane ride home.

I drove myself home from the airport to an empty house. How excited could the girls have been to see me when they knew I would be home and they couldn't bother to greet me? I threw my travel gear on my bed when the phone rang. Rose was calling to let me know she cooked a large dinner and everyone was there waiting on me. I declined the offer. I wanted to beat myself up without company.

"Look you stubborn man, get in your car and come to dinner and not another word," Rose yelled over the phone. Rose never yelled at me.

I was no mood for a big family dinner, but if I didn't go, I knew I would only be in bad straits with Rose. I washed up and drove over.

CHAPTER THIRTY FOUR

My girls met me outside when I pulled up to the front of my in-laws farm. We exchanged hugs.

"Dad, we were looking for you for a couple of days. Where were you off to this time? Diana asked. "It's not like you to take off and not tell us. We had a deal. Remember?"

I told them both I made a quick trip to Europe to finish some business, but I was home now. I made a stop in New York to sign the sales contract on the apartment.

"What business did you have in Europe? You getting the band together and touring again?" Deborah asked.

"I really don't want to talk about it," I said. "I'm home now, that's all that matters."

Deborah giggled. "Dang. I was hoping you would get the band going again, so I could play on stage with you, like Mom."

"Sorry," I grumbled. The last thing I wanted to think about was touring Europe. I didn't want any reminders of Italy.

"Let's have some dinner and you can tell us all about why you would go to Europe for two days, and be so secretive about it," Deborah said.

She never was good at letting topics die. I recalled a time

when she asked me why centipedes had so many legs and wouldn't let it drop until I read all about insects and did my best to answer her questions.

We walked inside the front door, where I greeted Rose. I wandered into the back room where George was watching a baseball game on television. I sat down on the tired sofa with one daughter on each side of me, leaning into me with affection.

Rose popped her head into the room, "Dinner will be ready shortly."

George gave me a smirk. "What the hell were you doing in Europe for two days? No one but a crazy fool goes to Europe for two days. I would think if you were playing for the Pope or the Queen it woulda been on the news. Why else would you go there and turn right back?"

I'd had enough of the questions with the insulting tones. "I went to Italy to find Lorenza. I failed. Is everyone happy now? She ran off with some jerk. So here I am. I hope everyone can have a good laugh about it so can we just eat and let me forget about her."

Deborah let out a large laugh. "That's going to be hard, Dad. She's having dinner with us."

"I'm really not in the mood for your jokes, Deb," I said.

"Dad, you told us after the show for mom that you wanted Lorenza to come and visit once school let out," Diana said. "We made the reservations for you. We knew you would be too stubborn to do it, so we did it. We didn't go to any festival. We went to the airport to pick her up. We've all been sitting at the house looking for you. You could have at least told Grandma where you were heading."

"I taught her how to milk cows while we were looking for you," George said. "I could use a spare hand round here and I know you won't git dirt under your nails from some real work. I like this girl."

It had been an emotional roller coaster. I took in a big gulp of air and knew they were telling me the truth. Lorenza always wore a unique perfume. I jumped up from the sofa with a pounding heart and rushed around the corner of the room to the other side of the wall only two feet away. We fell into each other's arms. I will admit it felt odd kissing her in my in-laws house, but they seemed very happy for me. Since they had always been very gracious to me, maybe it shouldn't felt so odd, but it did.

We had a wonderful home cooked meal. Lorenza told me about her journey. Her parents had sold their house to her cousin, but he had not moved in yet. They had waited until the end of her school year so not to interrupt her life too much. Lorenza informed me that she didn't want to buy her parent's home because she wasn't sure if she would living in her hometown in the future.

"Where you planning to move somewhere else and quit your job?" I asked.

She gave me a smile that made my heart pound even harder. "It not so close between ocean," she said. "Long plane ride to sleep at night."

After a few days of enjoying each other's company, it was time to get serious about our future. I could sense she wasn't ready to make a move to the hills of North Carolina full time and leave her elderly parents.

"What about your father," I asked. "He never approved of

me."

She giggled. "Silly man. Papa knows now you make me happy. He sees me sad. He will give blessing, if not I milk cows for George and live here with my Dylan."

I decided that we'd find a small villa near where her parents were moving. They were both moving into a retirement community where they no longer had the upkeep of a home. After I closed on the sale of my New York apartment, I would take some of the proceeds to buy a comfortable place in Italy. It seemed like a fair compromise. I wasn't used to having to make big compromises other than with band mates.

Lorenza and I took a trip to New Jersey to see my parents, then up to New York to sign the papers to close on my apartment. Signing in person wasn't something I had to do, but Lorenza was in awe of New York. I wanted to propose to her at the top of the Empire State building. We talked about getting married the next day, but she wanted to have her parents at the wedding. We decided to get married in Italy.

We quickly made plans. I flew my girls and parents to Italy for a small ceremony in an ancient Roman church. My mother had never been outside of the United States. I made me happy to give her a nice vacation in another country. I had never considered that she had never been to Europe. My dad had been oversees serving in the army, but never as a civilian.

Lorenza became a gracious host, showing my family around Italy. Mom had a difficult time walking long distances, especially in the heat, so we made short day trips. I hadn't spent much time with my parents for years, other than when they would visit for hunting season. It was nice to spend time with them and my new wife.

Lorenza and I found a beautiful home near her parents. We packed up many of her belongings while in town and had them shipped to North Carolina and left some behind in storage until we closed on our new home in Italy. It took a couple of weeks before it sank in that I was married for a second time.

I was at peace with the entire arrangement. I had wasted too many years being angry at the world, God and myself. I wanted the next stanza of my life to be slower than it had been in the past. We all flew home after three weeks in Italy. A few weeks later Lorenza and I had a real honeymoon with two weeks in Hawaii. We decided to leave the girls and parents home this time.

After our honeymoon, the girls were ready to return to school. Deborah tried to let her rebellious side come out when she informed me that school is no longer for her. I let her know that wasn't a problem. However, she no longer had access to my credit card or checkbook. School became a better option within seconds.

After both girls returned to classes, it was time for me to get my career back on track. I called Linda to see if she had any ideas. She told me that she was considering making a recording made up of Broadway show tunes. I thought that idea had some merit and after speaking with Duke, he agreed to produce it. I would play guitar.

The issue became, who would release it? Carl told me that the little smarmy man in the Armani suit kept calling his office wanting to know when our next record would be finished. Carl was under orders to inform him that The Overture was no longer making new music. However, after being home with Lorenza for a short time, I knew sitting home watching the deer feed in the back yard was not a viable option. How many board games can one play with a new wife and mother-in-law?

Lorenza and I flew to New York to meet with a few retired record executives, including Carl's dad. We decided that I would create my own independent record label. The old tapes from the trio with Linda, Debby and me would be the initial release. I offered Linda an opportunity to release her project on our new label. She respectfully asked to think on it.

I sat with Carl and we created EA records. Carl and Duke both became minority shareholders in the company. I tried to entice Linda and Debby to join, but both passed on the offer. Billy was broke. Sasha was interested, but by the time she could make up her mind, we had created the company.

I made Billy an offer to start up a blues band and I would add him to our catalogue, but he wanted no part of leading another band. I spent the next several months getting the label organized, as well as scouting bands to add to the label. I did add Deborah's band to our label, but only if I approved of the final songs and she graduated on time from college. She agreed despite her initial grumbles.

The new venture put my mind back into overdrive. It also gave me an excuse to get out of the house with and at time without my new wife. We were getting along great, but it had been years since I had to think about anyone except my girls.

When I was at home, Lorenza loved hearing me play and sing. That gave me an excuse to keep up my skills, as well as continue to write songs. My last solo disk received several good reviews and sold enough units to encourage me to make another. I was proud of the effort. I decided to record another solo disk. It would truly be an individual effort. I created the sound with me, and my Martin guitar. I named it Dylan James, 'Alone with One.' I recorded the entire disk in my home studio over the course of the next several months, while also getting the new company up and running.

After many attempts, we finally released the, 'Evolution' tapes that I had recorded several years earlier with Linda and Debby on the new label. I hired a first class web designer, since our business plan used the internet extensively. I didn't know the power of the internet until it all came to light that my girls and Lorenza had become close via the internet, before they invited her back to the Unites States and we had married.

It seems they spoke to her far more via emails than I ever did over the telephone. It was a big reason why they never asked about her after her visit to New York. I knew it was time for me to understand the power of the internet and computers. EA records would take advantage of a new way to market products.

Linda ran into trouble selling her show tunes idea. I was surprised. I had heard a few of the demos and they sounded great. Since Duke was associated with our new label, he agreed to produce it for a smaller fee, if she signed with EA records. She reluctantly agreed.

She still refused to fly, so we recorded it in California. Lorenza went back to see her parents for a couple of months, while I went to the west coast to record Linda's disk. We used Billy on drums along with mostly studio musicians. Duke played bass on four of the tracks and I played guitar on all but one.

Duke and I believed in the project from the start. I think that relived some of Linda's trepidation of releasing it with a new label, even if she did have a long history of success with her working partners.

We released it in big cities as test markets. We were working with a limited budget as well as limited distribution channels. We made it available on our web site as well as online companies who specialized in internet sales. The future seemed to be in internet sales, as opposed to old style record stores. It was all a big learning curve for me, but one I was willing to accept.

CHAPTER THIRTY FIVE

Diana graduated from Duke University in May of 2005. She wanted to tour Europe for a month before looking for work. I paid for her trip as a graduation gift. She had graduated with honors and had worked very hard in school. I felt she deserved the trip. Deborah wanted to join her, but after seeing her grades she was lucky I let her return home to eat and sleep.

Deborah's effort in school fell far short of my expectations. She allowed her band to consume too much of her study time. I was not pleased. She was constantly asking me to hear her band play live. I finally agreed once I returned from California. I was impressed with some of the musical abilities of the band members, but the songwriting needed work.

My daughter had improved as a player, but they didn't have good enough material to make a record. I told the band to get better songs. Then we would talk again and after Deb graduated. It made for a very cold summer at home. Deborah wasn't mature enough yet for an honest critique. It too me years before I could handle a poor review of my work. I'm not sure anyone can ever ignore a bad review, but you have to be happy that you tried your best and leave at that. The other way to look at was, how many of those same people offering critiques ever stood on a stage or wrote anything beyond yellow journalism?

After some internal debate with myself, I offered Deb two of my songs I never recorded for my last solo project. She tossed it back in my face telling me that her band didn't play old people's music. I told her to look around. Her home, clothes and instrument were benefits from people buying old people's music. It was a low point in our relationship.

The next year, I focused on the new label. I ran around the country looking for bands to sign. I worked much harder than I had anticipated when the idea of starting a label began. Linda's show tunes disk received a fair amount of radio play and turned gold a year after the release. A second one was scheduled.

She called me one day and thanked me for pushing her to our startup company. We did very well by her. Linda admitted that I had never failed her professionally in the past. She wouldn't doubt me again. It helped that I remembered what Billy had told me years before that about how the internet would be the place for sales. He was right. We sold over half of Linda's disks and my solo project online. The 'Evolution' songs were sold as individual songs as well as the entire disk online. Duke and my web guru gave me a lesson in mp3 downloading. I was good in a studio, but a computer, I had a large learning curve ahead of me.

Our independent label began to turn a profit. Duke signed up one of the bands he had been producing to our company, as well as a band I had discovered from some demos sent to me by Debby. My own daughter was still grumbling about recording her band, but I still felt the songs were weak. I asked Duke for his opinion about Deb's band, thinking possibly, I was being too rough on my kid.

"They have talent, but lousy songs," Duke said after hearing a demo they had made.

Diana was hired by the physical therapy rehab center where I had been many years earlier. She was doing very well and seemed content. She had moved home to save money for her own home. She was always the one with a business sense and knew the value of money. She had a boyfriend with whom she was serious with, however they focused on getting their careers going before getting married. Diana seemed to be on the right track with her life. I was very pleased with how she had matured.

One night at dinner she told me about how her building needed some upgrades, but her company wasn't willing to do what she thought necessary. I questioned if maybe it was more about funding and not they didn't want to upgrade. Since I knew the owner from my time there, and I knew, it was a small independently owned business, I called the next day to see if I could help in some way.

Christina, the owner, told me that she had considered selling the business since she was growing tired and wanted to retire. That's all I had to hear. I called Carl and within a few weeks, the Elise Andrews Rehabilitation Center became a reality. I sold some stock for a down payment to buy into the business, while keeping Christina in charge for another three years. She would train Diana to take over the business. Carl worked the finances so that all the profit went towards paying off the debt to Christina, and she would make a good salary. It was a win-win for everyone.

My youngest daughter became a larger headache. She had so much ability, but could never seem to focus. She was obsessed with her band. Her class work still suffered. She was doing ok in school with average grades, but I knew she was capable of much better. I made her an offer one day while she was home visiting. If she got straight A's for one full year, I would record her band before she graduated, if I approved of the songs. If she made the honor roll, she could either play guitar with me on my next disk or I would find her studio work with another band. She accepted the offer. I also told her that I really didn't want to run the label forever, but I would not turn it over to someone with average grades in school. Problem solved.

Carl called one day and asked what I knew about Afghanistan. There was a request for The Overture to play for the troops overseas. I was willing to do it as were a few others, but Linda wanted no part of flying that far, even if it was on military planes.

Debby, Duke and I went for several days to a base in Sharana, then later to Bagram. Lorenza was not happy that I had agreed to go. Not because she didn't see a need, but she feared for my safety. I will admit it scared me as well, but it was something I felt I had to do. It also fed my desire to stop running the company for a few weeks and allow me to play music with some old friends again.

I had never played for troops overseas, only within the cozy confines or our nation. For the three of us, it was about putting on a good show, but for the troops, it was about seeing someone from home. I'm not sure how much they paid attention to the music versus watching Debby strut across the stage like she had not done in many years.

Towards the end of the show in Sharana, we had to end it prematurely. A suicide bomber blew up a truck near the facilities main gate. It was a quick reminder we were playing in a war zone. It also made me question how so many people could use religion as an excuse for devastation. It was something I don't think I would ever come to understand. We made two other trips over the coming years.

Deborah as expected, raised her grades to straight A's her

first semester of her senior year at University of North Carolina. When I asked how she could do that so easily during her last year and not the three previous ones her only remark was, "The classes are easier in your senior year, Dad."

I didn't remember that being true, but if she wanted to use that as a reason I really didn't care.

Linda's second release of show tunes went gold as well. In fact, the record label was doing so well that Carl called one day to let me know that my old record label was interested in purchasing our company. Carl of course only saw it as in investment and tried to get me to sell it, but I knew I could not let all I had built end up in the hands of that idiot who wanted The Overture to be a hip hop band.

I declined the offer much to Carl's objections. Duke and I bought out Carl's share. Lorenza wanted me to focus more on her and spending time in Italy, but I was driven to make this company a success. I would visit our home in Italy with her from time to time, but I wanted to prove I could run a successful business.

Deborah came home in the second semester with all A's except for one B. She had carried all A's during the entire semester, then didn't do well on her final exam, which brought her last grade down to a B. Of all the subjects to get a B in, she failed her music theory exam. When I asked her how this could possibly happen, she laughed it off and said, "Does it really matter? I hit my goals and now you're stuck making a record with me."

We not only recorded my third solo release later that fall entitled, 'Dylan James Lost A Bet,' but the following year the label released, 'Carolina Sky featuring Deborah James.'

Over the next few years the record label flourished. Duke and I built a successful company we were both proud to call our own. We filled out a roster with fifteen bands recording on our label. We again received offers from larger labels to buy our catalogue.

Duke and I had nothing left to prove as being able to deliver quality music to the market, via songwriting, touring, producing or as musicians. I had nothing left to prove to myself. I realized that after all those years; I had in fact been in management, like Dad wanted. I had managed a band and all the personalities involved in it. I managed my daughters and my personal demons. I managed my relationships with my wives and families. I managed my friendship with Gordy. I manage my relationship with my maker.

Running a company wore me out. I thought running a band was hard, the record label was more difficult. I wanted to go back to only being Dylan James in the public eye, and Dad and husband at home. I was a songwriter and a musician, not a suit.

Carl arranged to take our record company public, but I sold most of my shares. I kept enough to stay on as a Board of Director, but the daily operations were turned over someone with more experience to take the company to an even higher level. Duke kept many of his shares, but he only wanted to produce when he wanted and live part time on the big island of Hawaii the other times.

Carl and I took some of the capital gains from the sale of my stock and we invested heavily into real estate. The first property we purchased was the shopping plaza where Gordy Guitars was still in business. I reduced Gordy's rent to one dollar a year. The first thing Gordy did after hearing I bought the place was to call me and remind me he needed a new storefront window. He also wanted his bathrooms upgraded. Some things never changed.

CHAPTER THIRTY SIX

Diana got married last year. I'm gonna be a grandpa soon. Go figure. She is doing well with the rehabilitation center. She revitalized the center and paid down the loans. Christina is staying on until after Diana comes back from maternity leave. After that, I intend to sign over my percentage of ownership to Diana. She has worked hard, and deserves it. I have no doubt that Elise is smiling from heaven as she watches her name being used for such a good cause with her daughter in charge. Diana and her husband come over for dinner most Sundays to visit with me, Lorenza, George and Rose.

My dear Deborah is struggling along in the music business. I tried to get her involved a few times with the record label before I sold it, but she wants to make it on her own. Her band, Carolina Sky, is still suffering from poor songwriting. They still refuse my help with hints on songwriting, or in finding them a songwriter, who fits their musical style. Deb always was the stubborn one. Her songwriting boyfriend, who doubles as the lead guitarist, apparently is more stubborn.

It pains me to see her struggle, but I've done all I can to help. I also tried to get her involved in the property management company that Carl and I formed. She only wants to make music. She has moved in with her boyfriend, which annoys me, since he is the reason they won't accept my help. She's a big girl now and I have to let her live her life. It's a very tough way to make a living playing small clubs, like they do, but I've learned to keep my mouth shut. She drops in occasionally, especially when she's low on funds.

Linda Sweet has become a recluse. I begged her to make a third release of show tunes or play live with me, but she refuses every attempt. It's a shame, since I think her voice has improved over the years. She no longer wants anything to do with the music business. Lorenza and I stop by to see her when we're in California, but she's a shell of her former self. I suspect she has other issues at play, but she swears she's fine. She sits overlooking the Pacific Ocean from her patio. Who knows? Maybe she's outsmarted us all.

Debby remarried. Her two kids have moved out west. She still lives in northern New Jersey and remains good friends with Kevin, who we went to high school with years ago. Debby and I sneak into veteran's hospitals and play music from time to time. We also are known to show up at open mic nights in Jersey bars, when I'm visiting her or my parents. This time I like her husband, and I'm very pleased she's happy. She too is going to be a grandparent in the coming months. She swears she doesn't color her hair and it's still the same shade of red from when we were teens.

Duke comes around to beat me in chess when we can get him off the island. He is still in big demand as a producer, though only works a few months a year. He will occasionally play bass as a special guest on recordings. He invests with Carl and me in real estate. Together we own several shopping centers and a few office buildings. Duke is still an incredibly talented musician and producer. He has always been an even better friend.

If you stay up late, you might catch Billy playing drums for a late night television host. He still works as a studio musician and calls me about making one last Overture recording. I don't see that ever happening. He still chases women and drinks too much. He's never going to change and that makes me smile. Maybe Billy was always my alter ego.

Sasha, well, she has certainly lived the American dream. Not bad for someone who defected to this country decades ago with less than one hundred dollars in her pocket. She has fashion lines here in the United States as well as Russia. Her company is expanding into other parts of Europe. She is Chairman of the Board. She too invests in our real estate deals, but honestly, I think she does it too keep in touch. I see her about once a year somewhere, and we speak occasionally over the phone. I have to go through her personal assistant to talk with her, but it's the price you pay I guess.

Carl has become the managing partner of his firm. He is a brilliant man. I'm lucky to have met him years ago. I know I get some special attention for being his first client and that's fine with me. We stuck with each other when neither of us had anything. We have invested wisely over the years, though he still regrets not listening to me when I told him not to sell his shares of the record label to me. It was maybe the only time he guessed wrong with an investment. Overall, we've done well individually and collectively with our investments and careers.

George and Rose still live on the farm. However, they now have people caring for the property. They're looking forward to being great-grandparents. Rose spends time at Diana's home picking paint colors and buying baby furniture. Rose and George have accepted Lorenza as another daughter. They spend many hours together and even traveled to Italy for a few weeks to see our home and meet Lorenza's parents. I could not have asked for better people to have as my in-laws.

My own mom and dad are doing fine. Dad and my brother still show up for hunting season, even if I don't trust Dad with a gun in his hand. I won't go near him when his gun is loaded. His reflexes stink and his eyesight isn't so hot either. Mom will be showing up more often as the baby's birth nears. My parents have both long retired and moved into an adult community. They now have nothing better to do than harass me about whatever is on their minds that day. They complain, but I know they're proud of me.

My stubborn wife doesn't let me far from her sight. I've been so blessed to not have one, but two women, who have loved me with no reservations. Lorenza has stuffed me with so much homemade pasta; I have to buy larger jeans this week. She gets more beautiful every day. I sit on the back porch at least once a week and give her a private concert. She takes such great joy in hearing me play. It's the least I can do to pay her back for all the love she offers me on a daily basis.

Gordy Davis still offers guitar lessons in that old shop. I visit every now and again and harass him and his students. When he threatens to toss me out, I tell him I'll raise his rent. We did replace his storefront window. When I last visited, he surprised me with the old Martin D-45 that once sat in his window back in 1969. The man, who received it as a Christmas gift, had it sitting in his closet for years. He sold it back to Gordy. It sits in my home in North Carolina. Gordy is now grey and frail, but still has that biting tone when you don't practice your scales. I owe him so much. The best I can do is offer him free rent and one day some new bathrooms. He refuses to accept anything else from me and still bitches when I refuse the checks he sends for his rent at the old rental rates. He's a very proud man and I love him dearly.

For me, I'm simply a kid from Jersey who made a good living in the music business. Rumor has it that Linda and I will be inducted into the Songwriters Hall of Fame, but they haven't finished building it yet. Fans have called for Dylan James and The Overture to be inducted into the Rock and Roll Hall of Fame in Cleveland, but we've not received the call. None of that concerns me. I would hope that others have enjoyed our collection of works over the years. I realize now, I can't control who likes our music and who doesn't.

Our music plays around the world. When I know someone appreciates it, I smile. I still think I have one or two great recordings left in me, and I'll do my best to deliver them. After all, it's what I do. However, in recent times, my mind is starting to fail me.

After years of doctors telling me I suffered from depression, they are now telling me that I have early stages of Alzheimer's disease. I know that can't be possible. I'm far too young for such a disease, but even Diana claims it's possible. They ran more tests last week. I still hate going to doctors. We're waiting on the results. I want to think it's more me getting older, than to think there is something more wrong. If it's true, then I'll accept it and live my life as best I can until my time on earth has expired.

I bought the local church a new sound system and a new stained glass window. I needed a new window, so I can count tiles. I do listen to the sermons, mostly because Lorenza now knows when I'm counting the tiles in the window and not listening to the sermon. She gives me a good pinch.

I do believe in God. However, I also question many things about my faith. I no longer think God was punishing me when I failed. I don't have all the answers as to why I am here on earth, nor do I punish myself for not knowing. Every time I think I know what the plan is for my life, it changes. I have to now accept that today is a new day and maybe another phase in my life is about to begin.

I am so blessed. I have lived a life few ever can. I have met people from around the world and been adored by people I will never be able to meet individually. I have done my best never to take advantage of others. I am a human being like anyone else, only maybe God's plan for me has always been simply to entertain.

God bestowed upon me a great gift. I do my best to use that gift. I still struggle to be a good father and husband, but I give it my best effort. If my mind does eventually fail me, don't feel sorry for me. As I sit here, I hear a song on the radio reminding me about how memories may fade over time, but dreams they never do. I have lived my dream. I am at peace with my life and the man I am today. Looking at the clock, I see it's the time of day that I like to write music. As I end my journal, I wish you all the best and hope you find the happiness in your heart and the peace in your soul that I now have in mine.

THOUGHTS

If you ever get a chance to visit Ireland, I suggest you go. It's a beautiful country. While I vacationed there with my wife, I decided to tweak this story. Why would I bother to do it? I guess a few reasons. For one, while writing, A Beautiful Song, I had no future plan to continue a writing career. I wrote the original version as a bet I couldn't do it.

Once it was finished, I had the desire to write another, then another and even more. For readers of my other stories, you know that Dylan likes to poke his nose into my other novels. I decided to change a paragraph here and there to reflect the fact that not only Dylan, but other characters have found their way into future projects.

For example, Dylan's financial advisor was in the original story, but never named. I didn't realize at the time, but George McAdams was born. He is the main character in, Three Long Days, the book that succeeded this one. Caeles Novo is the man who Dylan met on the steps at Royal Albert Hall, however he wasn't fully formed in my thoughts until a year after this book was originally released. His story is told starting with Soul Intentions.

I have not altered Dylan's story from the original and I fought my intentions of completely rewriting this closer to the style of a later release such as, Presidential Shadows. I think my writing style has changed over time. So my intention wasn't make this story closer to my more recent releases, but to tweak it. Oh, I enlarged the font for this version too, since a few griped the last one was too small.

Since I have released more titles now, I wanted to make it known to readers of this story that there are new titles at michaelcantwellbooks.com. I do tend to offer freebies on the site, so please pay it a visit.

As I write this, I am undecided if the next release will be the fourth in the Presidents series, or a completely new series. Alex and the Presidents will return eventually, but there is always something else rattling around in my head. I also have a sneaky feeling that Dylan will return beyond the Soul Series.

As always, I appreciate all of my readers. I hope you enjoy reading about my characters as much as I love creating them. I like hearing from you all. I am always curious as to what you like or didn't like about each story and character.

One last thought, if I may. Reviews are hard to come by these days. You, my reader, have the power to make or break my stories. If you have the time, please leave a review on Amazon or wherever you purchased this book or any of my others you have read in the past or future. Thank you in advance and again thanks for taking the time to read my story.

Michael Cantwell, CCTM